MW01138224

Madness Heart Press
2006 Idlewilde Run Dr.
Austin, Texas 78744

This is a work of fiction. Names, characters, places, and incidents either are the product of the author's imagination or are used fictitiously. Any resemblance to actual persons, living or dead, events, or locales is entirely coincidental.

First Edition
ISBN: 978-1-955745-85-7
www.madnessheart.press

THE HOME

JUDITH SONNET

A Madness Heart Press Publication

FOREWORD

Horror authors often get asked if they believe in ghosts, and I hate the disappointment I see in a reader's face when I tell them I don't. But I'm going to let you in on a secret; I actually do, just not as the spectral remnants of our dearly departed. I do not believe in the ghosts of people. Instead, I think ghosts are the lifeforces of the intangible. Dreams. Ideas. And yes, stories.

Those ghosts? Well, they feed, and they grow.

I first met Judith through social media and was quickly astonished by her passionate knowledge of horror history. I'd imagine most authors love the genre in which they write, but Judith seemed to care about horror as more than just a collection of books. To her, it was the story of the genre itself that she understood on a fundamental level. Pick a subgenre of horror and ask Judith for some suggestions, and she'll have a list for you, rated and ready to go. And you can get as niche with it as you want. She'll have an answer. 1970s horror with villainous crustaceans? Why, Night of Crabs by Guy N. Smith of course. More than that, she'll be able to tell you why that book was written at that time.

See, horror has a ghost, and Judith knows it well. In modern horror, you'd be hard-pressed to find an author who won't reference Stephen King's On Writing as an influence. It's the bible of modern-age storytelling for a lot of fresh-faced authors. And yet, it's a wisp in the ghost of horror. Or, if you want to get Lovecraftian, a tentacle of the genre's old gods.

Stephen King was influenced by Matheson, who was influenced by Henry James. Grab your flashlight and head through the catacombs of the genre, and you'll find branches for days. You'll never reach the end. Shirley Jackson. Edgar Allen Poe. Lovecraft. They all influenced a generation who influenced another, and after a while, you'll realize that the ghost who's lurking the corridors and feeding on the stories got too large for horror and started consuming the rest of the literary world. Anne Rice turned the ghost on the romance genre. You'll find it gnawing on YA books and historical fiction. It's bloody teeth have chewed through fantasy and science fiction. Horror's ghost feeds!

In Judith's short time as an author, she's already made her own corridor in the genre. She's the queen of extreme. Her name became synonymous with both extreme horror and splatterpunk, and holy smokes, are her stories beloved. In fact, her books are so popular, I once told my audiobook publisher I hoped to someday be his best-seller, and he responded, "Shoot for second place. You'll never surpass No One Rides for Free."

But the book you're about to read proves Judith can write in a multitude of horror's many subgenres. The Home contains the ghosts of all of Judith's influences, and there are many on display here. I think after you read it, you'll agree with me that Judith's niche isn't splatterpunk or extreme horror, nor is it Lovecraftian, psychological, slasher, folk, or gothic. It's none of those, and it's all of those. Judith's subgenre is Judith.

If you felt like it, you could pick pages of The Home and find the influence of horror's many greats, but you wouldn't stay there long, and your answer on which great most influenced it would change by the page. Because Judith spent a lot of time wandering those corridors, studying the branches, and like horror's ghosts, she's been feeding.

I have another confession to make. This book scared the shit out of me. There were moments so intense, I found myself digging my claws into the couch arm. Judith's writing is so visceral and real, I felt trapped, confined to The Home.

When I finished, I'd become close to Orville, Griffin, and Eunice, and I didn't want to let go of them just yet. When I went outside to have a cigarette and think about the shocking direction the book went, I found myself alone in the thick darkness of night, and I felt a little close to Mr. Friendlyman too. In fact, I felt too close to him. I may never finish a cigarette again.

So, do I believe in ghosts?

Yes.

I have to. Because I read The Home. I saw the ghosts of horror. I witnessed how Judith ate them, grew more powerful, and spun them into something that will one day influence a new generation of writers.

This isn't just a book. It's a corridor in the catacombs of fiction. A fresh path filled with old gods.

Welcome to my new favorite subgenre of horror: Judith Sonnet.

Gage Greenwood
11.14.24

PART ONE
I AM THE EATER OF GHOSTS

CHAPTER ONE

Griffin Chalks had been told that he would hate retirement. That he wasn't independent enough for such a venture. "Give it a week," they—the eponymous "they"—said, "and ol' Grif'll have a part-time job." He'd seen it before. Deacon Royce, who'd once been a star quarterback, then worked insurance, had gotten a job tearing tickets at the local cinema, just like a teenager. He sat at the box office, a single senior citizen amongst a nest of chatty high schoolers.

Not me, Griffin thought. *I'd sooner die than work part-time at some entry-level kiddie job! No, I reckon retirement will suit me fine. Yessir.*

Unfortunately, some cliches hold truths.

It had been seven years—take that, naysayers—since Griffin had retired on his seventieth birthday. And now, for the first time in those seven years, Griffin Chalks was finally awake at night, feeling lonely and pointless.

Seventy-seven was a strange age, he mused. Some aged hard, like him. Others were still bouncy and active, as if they could fight off the horrors of eighty and the hard-to-reach ninety.

He sat on his porch. The sun had just slipped behind the Ozark Hills that rumpled the landscape across from his house. Tilting back in his rocking chair, he tried to remember the last bit of fun he'd had.

Eloise had brought the grandkids around for Christmas. That had been nice. He'd been overjoyed to see Mary's face spark up when she opened her presents.

But it was April now. He realized, with trembling terror, that he hadn't seen his daughter or grandchildren in—he did a quick count—*three and a half months.*

If Prudence was still alive, the children would visit more often, he thought.

A gloomy sadness curled over him. He sank back in his rocking chair and looked toward the stars, as he often did when thoughts of Prudence Haymore struck him—and no matter how many years they'd been married, he always thought of her with her maiden name. He couldn't explain it, but he'd always known her to be Prudence Haymore before they'd wed. And he didn't mind that Eloise had kept her maiden name— hyphenated—when she married Boris Norton.

He may have been an old man, but Griffin wasn't tied to the old ways. He'd seen numerous geezers get frustrated with the ever-changing world, but Griffin had been observant in his youth. He recognized that change was constant, even if it was different. And Griffin didn't *need* to understand everything to accept it. In fact, he'd been alive during the Civil Rights Movement and the Vietnam War. He'd seen radicalism shift and morph and replace itself. The ideals his generation had fought for were now outdated. So what? He was simply lucky to have been aware of it all.

His thoughts had strayed.

They so often did.

What had he been thinking of?

Maybe a beer would help. He reached over and pulled a can from his six-pack. Popping the tab and taking his first sip, he watched the net of stars above his home.

Oh, yes. Prudence.

If his wife was still alive, he was sure Eloise would be visiting more often.

But isn't that unfair?

How so?

She's a busy girl, Griffin. She's got three kids and a husband to tend to. And with the economy as it is, she also *has to work a job! Women can't afford to stay home anymore. That's another thing that's changed.*

Don't say that out loud.

It was true. Eloise was working multiple jobs between her home and her career. More than Griffin could ever imagine. All his life, he'd only worked at one place, and that was Dick's Auto Shop. Hell, it'd been Dick Duffin himself—the man, the myth—who had hired Griffin back when he was just a sprout.

"You ever worked on cars before?" With his thick Maine accent, it sounded like "ca-ahs."

"No, but I'm a quick learner."

"Learn this. You break it, you bought it. You don't fix it, you don't get paid, yeah?"

"Sure."

"I ain't got time ta babysit. Fincher will show ya the ropes. Though I reckon you'll mostly stay behind the *reg*. You can count, right?"

Griffin's head swirled. It took a second to translate "reg" as register.

"Yes, sir. I can count. I'm good at math." It was the one thing Griffin was good at. He was failing English and history and skating by on loose C's with the rest. Numbers always made sense to him. They were tangible and applicable, unlike similes and metaphors, which evaded him.

"You know who Fincher is?"

"Black guy, right?"

"Yeah. We give him a hard time, but he's one of the good 'uns."

It was a different time, Griffin thought with flinching shame.

Griffin stayed out of Dick's hair. He stood behind the register and filled out receipts for oil changes, engine repairs, and tire swaps. Sometimes, Fincher stood by him just to ensure he was doing it right. When the two had downtime, Fincher took Griffin into the shop and showed him how things were done.

"Someday, this'll be easy as breathing," the old man claimed. "But you just stand by and watch now, you hear? Don't fiddle with nothin' because nuthin' needs fiddlin' with."

It was strange, thinking back, which parts of his memories Griffin could hold on to with crystal clarity. Like how Fincher had pronounced nothing two different ways in one sentence. One snappy and the other drawly. The differences between "nothin'" and "nuthin'" were vast and slight all at once.

"Do I gotta go to school for any of this?"

"More formal places might tell ya to, but not Dick's. I ain't had a lick of school my whole life, and I'm doing just fine here."

"Good."

"Don't like school?"

"Not much." Griffin had shrugged his shoulders.

"What do you not like about it?"

"I mean, it's okay. I struggle with classes. I don't like waking up early. I liked math until they started puttin' letters in it."

"They put letters in math? Like what? A plus B equals C?"

"That's it."

"Ridiculous."

"Besides, I don't have many friends there." Griffin was fifteen, scrawny, and his face was quilted with acne. He wasn't nerdy enough to be bullied, but he certainly wasn't a popular teenager.

"Is that why you tried getting a job? So you could

socialize?" Fincher asked in a way that confused Griffin. He couldn't tell if the old man was sympathetic or was chiding him.

"No. I got the job because Dad said I needed to work," Griffin said. He flushed red, realizing he sounded like a little kid instead of a man. Although he was fifteen, he felt he should be *grown* by now.

"You oughta have friends. Hell, I 'member having a whole group of guys I hung out with when I was yer age. We'd hit the town and raise so much hell . . . Ah, but those times were more dangerous for kids like me. Raising hell is a little different nowadays, I'm sure. You ever go cruising?"

"Cruising?"

"Kids do it all the time. They just drive up and down the town and all around it. Playin' their music loud enough to wake the dead." Fincher winked. "I'd be mad if I hadn't gotten up to worse shit in my youth."

"I don't have a car yet." He didn't have a license either, but he didn't bring that up to Fincher.

"That what yer first paycheck is goin' toward?"

"And every paycheck after." Griffin smiled bashfully. "Dad said if I wanna drive, I oughta earn it."

"But you do have a license, right?"

"Right."

Fincher fished his keys out of his coveralls and tossed them. Griffin fought to catch the jangling keys. When he had them looped around his finger, his face was painted with shock.

"You don't mean—"

"This is a loaner. You go out tonight and make some friends, and bring the car back without a scratch, and thank me later, yeah?"

"What if—"

"If you ding it up, then you *know* who to hand yer first paycheck to." Fincher smiled.

So, thought Griffin as his rocking chair squeaked him back into the present. *It was Ol' Man Fincher who was to blame for everything that happened in the summer of nineteen sixty-one. It was his fault I met Orville and Eunice . . .*

Everything bad and beautiful about that year began . . . because I wanted to go cruising, and an old man trusted me with his car. He didn't even ask to ride with me for a trip around the block, just to make sure I could actually drive. I was lucky my dad gave me lessons.

From inside his house, Griffin heard the telephone ring.

Despite the advancements in technology, he still had a landline. Eloise had bought him an "old person cell phone" for his birthday one year. Some shrimpy piece of plastic with buttons that were too small and an assortment of annoying sounds it liked to make at odd times. Eventually, he'd gotten so angry at the thing that he threw it across his lawn. When it struck the trunk of a cedar tree, it detonated like a landmine. He'd had to pick the bits of plastic out of the lawn before running his mower again, or else he worried that the chips would shoot out like bullets! So, with apologies to Eloise, he'd stuck by his tried-and-true landline telephone.

Slowly and grumpily, wondering who would dare call at whatever time of night it was—it was really only nine, but it felt so much later—Griffin hoisted himself out of his rocking hair. On plodding feet, he went to the door and nudged it open with his shoulder, carrying his half-full beer in one hand and letting the other dangle.

"I'm comin'!" he shouted, as if the person on the other end of the line could hear him. "Hold yer horses!"

The phone rang blaringly. He scooped it up and looked at the caller ID. It read *Caller Unknown* in blocky text. Frowning, Griffin considered declining the call. It was probably just a robot anyway, looking to phish him out of what little he owned.

Despite this, his finger hovered over the TALK button. He was pressing it before he'd even realized what he'd done, and then he was holding the phone up to his ear, which was crosshatched with wiry, white hair. Slowly, he licked his dry lips. His spare hand gripped the aluminum beer can tightly.

"Hello?" he answered with a whimper.

No response. The other line was silent.

"Who is this?" he asked.

"*It's Mr. Friendlyman,*" a strange, high-pitched voice whined. "*I'm on my way, Griffin. I'll be there in no time at all!*"

Griffin dropped the phone and the beer. It was as if someone had stuck a cattle prod to his lower back. His fingers seized into fists, and his eyes rolled into his skull. In a jabbering voice, Griffin repeated the word "No," over and over. He tried to walk backward, to put as much distance between himself and the fallen phone as he could.

Mr. Friendlyman . . .
He's not dead . . .
He was never real . . .
Mr. Friendlyman . . .
Gonna getcha . . .
Mr. Friendlyman . . .

If his thoughts were confused before, they were jumbled now. As if a child had taken his head from his shoulders and shook it with all his youthful might. Griffin had gone blind and deaf. All he could see was the darkness behind his skull, and all he heard was a high-pitched droning note. One which bore down upon him with the weight of a cinder block.

I'm dying . . .
Mr. Friendlyman . . .
Come and get me . . .

Mr. Friendlyman's killed me . . .

Griffin fell to the ground. His knees cracked against the hardwood, deafeningly loud and jarring. On his hands, he crawled back across the floor, knowing he needed the phone even though he was terrified of it. A slushy foam fell from his lips, staining the floor.

Hearing his voice did this to me.

Imagine if he'd touched *me!*

Mr. Friendlyman could kill with his fingers. That had been part of the legend, he remembered. One touch . . . and yer gonzo. He'd laid Mrs. Platter down flat. They said she was stiff as a board, all dried up inside, her face frozen in an unending yet silent scream.

Yer jokin'. Yer jus' tryna scare me. Ain't no such thing as Mr. Friendlyman!

But there's the rub: Mr. Friendlyman doesn't target those who believe.

He sets out to get the kids that don't!

Sylvia Platter hadn't been killed by Mr. Friendlyman. That was ridiculous. It was just a rumor, made up by a bunch of bored kids who had nothing better to do than speculate over the fate that had befallen the old neighborhood hag.

Mr. Friendlyman's been around since even I was a boy, Fincher had said. *Our version of it, he was a white man who stole Black babies from their cribs and ate them. Same name, different monster. Maybe we thought of it first and y'all took it. You have a tendency to do that, you know?*

She'd had a stroke. That's what had happened to Mrs. Platter. She'd had a stroke and died, and then all the neighborhood kids had decided to attribute it to an urban legend. The monster under the bed. The slimy boogeyman who lurked in the darker corners of the closet. They did this because they were too young to grasp this simple concept. Bad things . . . happen. To anyone. Even people you know.

But being children, they needed something to fear. A sociological monster which went by the name Mr. Friendlyman.

If a kid went missing . . . it was because Mr. Friendlyman got him.

If a house caught fire . . . it was because Mr. Friendlyman was bored.

If you saw a shadow in the woods while you were playing freeze tag, then chances were it was Mr. Friendlyman watching you . . . trying to deduce whether you believed in him or not.

His hands scrabbled over the ground. His knuckles knocked the beer can and sent it rolling away, a slug's trail of beer behind it. When his hand landed on the phone, Griffin released an exasperated sigh. He held the device up to his ear. The ringing persisted, but he could also hear a muffled dead tone.

He forced his eyes open. They hadn't rolled back as he'd envisioned. Instead, they'd been sealed tight behind his frightened lids.

Color burst across his field of vision, vibrant and blurry. He struggled to make sense of the phone while he dialed nine-one-one.

Impatiently, he began to speak over the woman on the other end of the phone.

"You have to help me! Please! He's found me! He's found me!" Griffin shouted. "You must help me, please! His fingers kill!" He didn't care that he'd never be able to explain to these strangers what he meant.

He lay flat on the ground, breathing huskily, spewing foam from his aching mouth. His heart hammered against his rib cage like a prisoner in a dank cell searching for light. His face felt fuzzy, and his stomach ached. He realized he'd wet himself, but he was too panicked to be ashamed.

I'm dying.

19

I'm dying . . . because Mr. Friendlyman found me . . .

Later, he'd realize that Mr. Friendlyman didn't have to look far.

Griffin had never left his hometown.

Starch, Missouri, was the only place on Earth he knew well enough to love.

CHAPTER TWO

Worst of all, Orville North hated the smell of The Old Folks' Home—he thought of it like that, all capitalized. It was like stale cat piss left to ferment in a neglected carpet. That was bad enough, but there was another smell. A smell *under* the smell. A moldy scent that encompassed many meanings and names. Putrefaction, rot, decay . . . but, chief of all, Death. Another word he always thought of with a capital letter.

Orville sighed greatly. He was in another of his "moods," it would seem. No capital letters, but liberal quotation marks. His "moods" struck him at odd hours. This time, it was twelve at night, and despite his regimen of medications, he was struggling to sleep.

"Blast it," he muttered to his empty room. "Blast it to Hell. Straight there and back." Sometimes, he spoke to himself. It was an old habit he'd had all his life. The doctors said it was because his father had never been around, but that was a load of crap. What did doctors know? Sure, Dad couldn't spend every second at home, but that didn't mean Orville was attempting to "supplement a guiding, nurturing voice with his own."

"What do they know?" he snapped aloud. "Nothing. That's what!"

It wouldn't be a problem if his hearing was better. He needed to speak loudly so he could hear himself, which meant that sometimes when he spoke to himself, he shouted. He'd had more than his share of complaints.

Back in his youth, he'd even had the police called to his apartment after neighbors reported they'd heard him getting into a screaming match! They'd assumed he was battering some poor, defenseless woman! In reality, he'd been writing a short story and had been struggling to make the dialogue sound realistic, so he'd decided to "talk it out."

"Writers are odd folks, Orry. Don't turn odd on me," his mother had told him after discovering the journal stowed beneath his bed, which had been filled with story ideas, characters' notes, scraps of descriptions, and bits of strange dialogue. To an outsider looking in, that first journal had been madness. But a few years later, before he'd even graduated high school, those notes had become the first draft of what would eventually become a national best seller. *The Moon Rings of Ernth.*

His mother's voice returned to him. Well-meaning but insidious nonetheless. *You aren't only going to write silly-fantasy, are you? You'll write something real someday, won't you?*

Maybe if he had, he would have made more money. Though he couldn't complain too much. Not many writers had even *one* best seller, and thankfully, *The Moon Rings of Ernth* was still in circulation. He'd even once been invited to a college campus, where an extracurricular class on the book had garnered a strong audience and a resurgence of sales. He'd been surprised to find his book appealed to modern youths, but then he considered the fact that he'd written it throughout his childhood and young adult years. It came to him in parts and pieces. Sometimes, it came to him as other stories which didn't feel right until they'd been chopped up and added to the *Moon Rings* stew. And that was legacy enough for him, even if he had put his heart into *Soul Sortum* and *Fern Forest*—both of which were reviewed harshly. "Derivative of better writings," some asshat had said. "We all know Orville North to be capable of more, unless, of course, *The Moon Rings of Ernth* was a fluke."

Well, the difference between *Moon Rings* and his other works was time. There'd been a pressure crunch from the publishers to repeat his success immediately after *Moon Rings* had taken off. He'd received too many advances and perks to say no, even when he had no new ideas to offer. *The Moon Rings of Ernth* had been created over an entire life, from age six to age twenty-six, when the final draft was passed from his hands to his publisher's. Being young, being stupid, he figured that it'd be easy to just . . . write a new book. One that made *Moon Rings* look like hog slop in comparison. One that stretched the boundaries of his and his readers' imaginations.

No such book had come to be.

He'd come close with *Paraflex*, he felt. The story was strong, the characters realistic, the twists subversive without being gimmicky, and the monsters were so well described he could see them lurking outside his window above his writing desk. But that book dropped the same week a writer named George R.R. Martin seemed to take the world by storm. Now, nobody wanted science-fantasy blends. They wanted realistic, historical-sounding epics with sprawling, bloody battles, dragon maidens, and lengthy prose that felt like homework. In comparison, Orville's books were simply too short to demand attention from booksellers. Most of his books barely reached two hundred pages, with *Moon Rings* being the longest at two hundred and ten.

With his advances becoming smaller, his workload becoming more stressful, and the market simply being a burden to keep up with, Orville North had retired from science-fantasy and began writing romance books under the pen name Janice Glick. He wasn't the *only* writer working under the Glick name, but his books were the best sellers of the bunch. They never made *Moon Rings* money, but they made life cozy. If only his mother had lived long enough to see it.

He looked toward his bookshelf, where the first edition printing of *Moon Rings* sat discreetly nestled between *The Return of the King* and the first book in *The Wheel of Time* series. He'd memorized the cover art. Every brush stroke, every blot, and even the artist's scribbly signature on the bottom left-hand corner, nearly cropped off by the trim. On the cover, there was a depiction of a flourishing mountain topped with unearthly sprouting plants. In a meadow stood a young boy, his arms tattooed and his head shaved bald. Next to him stood a creature like a caterpillar with a frog's face. Above them, a bright moon bloomed in the dark sky. Wrapped around the moon were three rings, but the fourth was shattered, and out of its fragments emerged a massive dragon with white flesh and wide, bat-like wings. Its mouth was a toothless vacuum the size of the mountain the boy stood upon. The image was complicated and multilayered and was painted by hand, commissioned by the publisher—Bardock Books. In every way, it was patently unlike the recent reprint, which was so minimalistic that you couldn't tell what genre the book was in. The new cover was all black except for a smooth moon. That was it. According to browsers, the book would probably have sat better next to Arthur C. Clarke's *2001: A Space Odyssey* instead of near the works of Piers Anthony and Frank Herbert.

Sure, there were moons, and aliens, and the dragon *did* come from outer space, but *The Moon Rings of Ernth* was not a science fiction book. There, in fact, little science to be found in it! Most of the book was concerned with its young lead harnessing sorcery to protect his planet from the terrible dragon, which had broken free from its prison.

Silly-fantasy. Mom always said it like it was one word. Like, some writers write "fantasy," Orville, but you? You write "silly-fantasy."

His mood wasn't getting any better, and the smell persisted underneath it all. The terrible smell of the nursing home, where old folks like Orville were shipped off to when they'd become a hassle. Or, if they had no one left to hassle.

Orville had never married, and he didn't have any kids—none he knew of, at least. No one had been around to care for him when old age settled in. When he'd gotten confused and driven into the wrong side of traffic, no one had been there to help him at the hospital. He'd been all alone.

He didn't know whose idea it was to stick him in The Old Folks' Home back in his hometown of Starch, Missouri—who names a town S*tarch?*

Maybe the idea was his own. Maybe a publisher had stepped in. Either way, his books afforded him some pleasant care, and he didn't even mind seeing his house get sold off. At least someone else was going to enjoy it. And he was kept well-stocked with books. Whatever he couldn't find during their excursions into town, he'd have ordered in. He wasn't a hoarder, or even a collector, so whatever he'd already read tended to get loaned out, either to other elderly folks, visiting families, or nurses who struck up conversations with him. The only book he told himself he'd never relinquish was his original print version of his own debut.

But even then . . . now that he was older and slower, he thought he ought to choose someone to take it off his hands. Someone young and in need of inspiration. When he passed, of course, and not a second before. It would have to be inherited.

Orville stumbled up to his feet and padded across the room. He pulled the book from the shelf and turned it over in his shaky hands. If he was still writing, he figured the arthritis would have caused quite a few problems. Thankfully, he'd given up the game a long while back. The ideas had simply stopped flowing shortly after he fulfilled his Janice Glick contract. At first, there'd been fear. As a young man who'd been a robust writer bursting with concepts, he'd simply assumed that would last him until the day he died. But, alas, he was a different person now than he'd been as a young man. As soon as he'd reckoned with the fact that artistry didn't equal identity, he was a lot happier about fading into normalcy.

None of the nurses who worked at Everly had read his books, even though they were all aware that he was something of a minor celebrity. And he was okay with that. He didn't need doting fans to be present during the more embarrassing parts of aging. The days when he got confused. The days when he went into crying jags for no discernible reason. The days when his bowels were temperamental and gusty.

Christ, but we are shells, aren't we? Crumbling shells, designed for vigor, with a short shelf life!

Observing the book and its crinkled spine, he wondered if *Moon Rings* would ever be made into a movie. It happened frequently that certain books didn't receive that treatment until after the author's death. Poor Frank Herbert never got to see the recent *Dune* films, and J.R.R. Tolkien hadn't been around for Peter Jackson's *The Lord of the Rings* features. When he'd written *Moon Rings*—and it'd been published in the early '70s, when he was twenty-six and still felt like he'd never grow up—he'd had a childish dream of seeing it adapted for the big screen. Of course, back then, *Star Wars* was only just around the corner, and science-fantasy films were looked down upon. Now, they seemed to be all that populated the box office . . . and yet his phone never rang with news from Hollywood.

I'd have liked it to happen before I died. But the book was published nearly fifty years ago. If it hasn't happened yet . . . I doubt it'll happen any day soon.

He was suddenly seized with confusion. Swaying on his feet, Orville wondered why he'd left his bed. He'd almost forgotten he was holding his book, and he had to catch himself before he dropped it. Wiping the cover, he returned it to its spot.

You need to try and sleep, Orry, his mother's voice came to him once again. *Poor Mom*, he thought. She'd died in a car accident shortly after *Paraflex* had been published in 1981. She'd been driving without her glasses and had swept through a red light. A Ford truck T-boned her on the driver's side, crushing her little body. Orville had always thought that old age would claim his mother, just as it was claiming him. Besides, she was a smoker, a drinker, and she'd lived a hard life before a sailor got her pregnant.

He hadn't expected her to die suddenly in a car accident, and it had shocked him so badly that the book following *Paraflex* was a cynical, nihilistic horror novel. What he considered to be his worst book and one he wished he could simply scrub from existence. It was his only foray into the darker side of literature. Typically, Orville's novels were about hope, friendship, and overcoming adversity. His horror novel, *Ghost Chain*, was a somber, saddening book about hopelessness, with a narrative that followed a junkie who gets lost in a mazelike crack house filled with slavering ghouls, demonic spirits, and an evil killer who took great joy in carving up his naked victims with a butcher's knife.

It was tasteless, trashy, edgy, and angry. It was unlike him. He'd actually gone to therapy after writing it. Reviewers seemed to feel the same. They bemoaned Orville's sudden divergence from his norm, even though they'd *also* complained about those books being too safe and tame.

Oh well, Orville thought. *Can't win 'em all.*

Another wave of hot confusion swept over him. His face felt fuzzy and warm. He waddled back to his bed and sat down with a grumpy groan. He felt something burble deep inside him, like the noxious brew in a witch's cauldron. He held his stomach and winced. He'd been having a lot of tummy troubles lately, which was concerning. He worried sometimes that cancer could be developing inside of him, but he was too frightened to get it checked out.

It's my diet. The food at Everly is fine, but it isn't always balanced. Lots of hamburgers and carbs. Bet that's all it is.

Abruptly, Orville's attention was drawn toward his door. Outside, he could hear footsteps. Someone was stalking down the hallways of Everly.

Probably a staff member checking to make sure all us geezers are still on this side of existence.

The footsteps froze outside his room. A strange chill conflicted with the heat in his stomach. Orville pursed his lips and squinted his eyes, trying to see in the dark.

The door creaked slowly open, whispering against the carpeted floor as it moved.

"Hello?" Orville asked, suddenly feeling vulnerable and weak.

Orville North was a stout, short man with a thick chest, a full, white beard, and a bald scalp. His nose was crooked from when it had been broken in a barroom brawl when he was thirty—he couldn't even remember what caused the fight; all he knew was he'd gone out drinking with a few other fantasy authors and had woken up with a broken snout, a black eye, and a terrible ache in his balls.

In a scrap, Orville used to be a safe bet. Now, his bones seemed to be rotting in his cumbersome flesh. Even walking up the two steps into a gazebo winded him. If someone was coming into his room to torment him, Orville knew that he stood little chance of defending himself.

"Who is it?" he demanded, trying his best to sound brave. "C'mon! Speak up!"

He heard a tittering giggle. High-pitched, airy, and crude. The sort of laugh one expected to hear from a bothersome child sitting in the back of a classroom. Not the typical noise created in an old folks' home.

Orville squinted so hard his vision blurred. He wanted to reach over and turn on the light on his nightstand, but he also didn't want to see the laugher. He had a feeling that seeing him would give him a heart attack.

"Who is that? Answer me!" Orville snarled.

"Don't you recognize me?" The voice broke through the darkness, and with it came a musty gust of wind. A smell that was worse than the death smell that permeated through the Everly Retirement Home. The odor was as sharp as it was brief. It vanished the way noise does, dissipating and becoming a memory.

Oh God . . . he knew that voice better than his own. It haunted him like a ghost, hovering over his worst nightmares and slinking around in his darkest thoughts.

"Mr. Friendlyman?" he asked.

In the darkness, white teeth flashed in a gruesome smile. It was there and gone before he'd even had a chance to grapple with the reality of what he'd seen. Then, the door swung shut, banging loudly.

Orville didn't have a heart attack, but he had wet himself. A pool of urine soaked the edge of his bed where he sat and felt tacky on the insides of his pajama bottoms.

Oh, God. Dear God.

It was HIM.

He's back . . .

Orville heard screaming. Long, high-pitched, wailing agony . . . coming from inside The Old Folks' Home.

CHAPTER THREE

Typically, when Ocean Pertwee's parents were out, she'd invite over her boyfriend—a senior named Marcus Ferran. They'd been dating for a year now and had begun to inch past heavy petting, although both of them were skittish about going all the way. That was, she'd decided, something she liked about Marcus. Normally, the boys at her school were hound dogs, energized by the very notion of sex. Marcus treated it seriously. He was excited about it—probably even more than she was, judging by the way he flushed whenever she touched him—but he wasn't going to pressure her to do any more than she wanted until she wanted to. He was also a handsome boy, with blond hair, thick muscles, and a sharp jawline that reminded her of a movie star. He listened to cool music—music she liked, such as The Cure and Depeche Mode—and he'd promised to take her to a concert that summer.

"Not one of those shitty barroom concerts they've got in town. Not a local band. No. I'm gonna take you to the city. We'll see something cool," he'd said.

Summer couldn't come fast enough. It would be the season before she became a senior herself, and it would mark the end of the last year that she and her boyfriend attended the same school. He had already applied to St. John's in Annapolis, and her parents had informed her that she'd be attending College of the Ozarks—a Christian school in Missouri that offered free tuition in exchange for student labor. She'd looked up the school and it seemed fine, although her parents said she would have to act a lot more Christian than she was if she wanted to fit in.

"Why can't I go to a real school?" Ocean had whined.

"It is a real school!" her mother said. "It just also happens to be free!"

"We can afford college, can't we?"

Her mother shook her head sadly. The stock market crash of 2008 had depleted the middle class, Ocean knew. Their parents were hanging on by a thread just to keep the house they'd raised their daughter in. Her father may have just gotten a hard-fought promotion, but it wasn't enough to afford anything fancy.

The facts of the matter dismayed her, but Marcus had promised that they would make a long-distance relationship work.

"I'm serious about you," he said, holding her sweaty hands in his.

"You say that now . . ." Her voice trailed off tearfully.

He lifted her chin, holding her eyes with his own. Then he kissed her.

In all of Ocean's short life, she'd never been kissed so truly and kindly.

It was, she realized, more than a teenaged smooch.

It was the sort of kiss adults shared. Adults who'd already lived a full life together and knew love inside and out. How could it be, she wondered, that someone as young as Marcus and as silly a girl as her had already familiarized themselves with love?

Sighing wistfully, her eyes darted away from the television and toward the landline, which sat like a plastic gargoyle in its cradle. She knew she couldn't bother Marcus Ferran. His grandmother was in town for the weekend, and he'd told her he wouldn't be around much due to the visit. He didn't sound ungrateful, which earned him another point in his favor. She *hated it* when boys acted like their relatives were a burden. But still, she couldn't deny that there was a Marcus-shaped ache in her chest.

Ocean—her parents were ex-hippies, so thank God they hadn't named her Moon Flower or something even more absurd—wished she could call him. Wished he could pull himself away from his family and come over just to lather her in kisses and feel her breasts and—

And she was getting too far ahead of herself. She looked back at the screen with a groan. She'd missed something important. She really wanted to see this movie, but now it was about over, and she couldn't even tell the good guys from the bad guys. The screen was a chaotic cluster of noise, gunfire, and explosions.

What a waste, she thought ruefully.

Her parents had left her home alone after they'd been invited out to dinner at the last minute by one of her father's coworkers. They'd dressed up for the occasion and left the house in a rush, barely pausing at the door to assure Ocean they'd be back before midnight. She'd waved them away, standing alone on the porch.

When they were gone, she tried to call up some friends to see if anyone wanted to come over. Lucy was swamped with homework. Hilda had the flu. Gretchen was going out with Todd.

Ocean decided that with all her friends occupied, she had nothing better to do than watch a movie. There was one video store left in town, an obstinate relic of a bygone era. While streaming had devoured the market, The Video Vault remained. And it seemed to be doing just fine—but only ever "just fine." It appealed to cult movie fans, teenagers, and the town's elderly folk who didn't care about new movies and just wanted to rewatch the classics.

Ocean considered getting dressed in "real clothes" before going out, then decided it wasn't worth the effort. It was April, and the air was drizzly, so she put on her favorite neon-pink hoodie and a pair of sleek sweats. Nothing too heavy. She rolled her brown hair into a bun with a purple scrunchie.

Ocean loped out of the house and picked up her bike from its place beside the garage. The bike—which didn't get used as often anymore—was a little rusty and unwieldy. She struggled to catch her balance on it, but as the old adage stated: "Once you learn to ride a bike, you never forget." Before long, she was sweeping through the suburban streets, heading quickly toward town.

The chilly wind burned her face as she went.

It wasn't too far of a trip from the end of Sycamore to town.

The suburbs were wrapped tightly around the small town of Starch, Missouri. For Marcus, it was an excursion. He lived in The Heights—an outcropping of McMansions built into the hills that overlooked Starch's downtown district. It took Marcus about twenty minutes to get to school every day because the roads from the Heights to the tri-county school district wound languidly through the hills.

Ocean pedaled rapidly, swaying over the seat and leaning toward the handlebars. She could never relax while she rode. It was a bad habit she'd picked up as a child and had never thought to correct. Even tonight, on her way to the store, she rode as if she was being pursued.

Breathlessly, she steered herself up to the door of The Video Vault. The store was crammed between a yoga studio and a miniature health food shop. She knew Rufus Steward, the manager of the Vault, hated both his neighbors.

"Acrobatics on one side, health nuts on the other. I'm in hell, man. I'm in hell. This country is going to shit."

That had made her chuckle, and he did have a point that things were changing. The flea market had been replaced with a Swedish furniture store, the graphic tees shop was now a Hollister, and there had been chatter about tearing down the motel and turning it into condos. Starch was becoming less small-town and more corporate. Even a seventeen-year-old like Ocean could see it, and even she was scared of it. So renting DVDs at The Video Vault felt less like a luxury and more like a civic duty. She was also always sure to pick up a bag of microwavable popcorn and a soda pop as well, just to help Rufus out.

When she walked into the Vault, she was immediately assaulted with the scent of pungent incense. She'd heard that Rufus lit the terrible stuff to mask the smell of the marijuana he smoked.

The old man was sitting behind the counter reading a horror magazine. She flinched at the cover, which showed a gory decapitated head, its hair bundled in the pudgy hands of a maniac, smiling, his mouth filled with razor-sharp teeth.

Ocean couldn't do horror flicks. Marcus had taken her to one, and she'd hidden her face against his chest until the credits rolled. That said, she *loved* action movies. She wasn't against violence in cinema, she just preferred seeing it directed toward bad guys instead of innocent, screaming women.

Rufus was an obese man with wiry hair who smelled like body spray and coconut oil. His arms were carpeted in fur. He caught her eye and beamed.

"Movie night tonight, huh?"

"Bit last minute," Ocean said, looking up at the wall clock. It was already eight thirty. The store would close at nine.

"Most of the action flicks have been pilfered," Rufus said. He always remembered exactly what kinds of

35

movies his customers preferred. "Bunch of skater punks came in. Figured they'd appreciate some Michael Dudikoff flicks, even if no one else does. We'll see if they bring 'em back in time."

"I'm sure I'll find something," Ocean said.

"And return it?" Rufus chided.

"And return it." She rolled her eyes.

Rufus snapped his magazine like a newspaper. "That's what I like to hear. Well, happy hunting!"

Ocean went to the action section. An older man was in the aisle, standing at its end and scrutinizing a tape. He looked up and smiled at Ocean before waddling toward the register.

Browsing quickly, Ocean settled on *Gamer*, which she'd seen trailers of but had somehow never watched. It had Gerard Butler in it, so there was a high chance she'd enjoy it.

"Hey." A slimy voice crept up behind her.

She turned and froze.

An adult male was standing on the other side of the aisle, smiling at her widely. She shrank under his leering gaze. He looked like someone she'd seen before, but she couldn't place his face to a name. He was pudgy around the middle, with a thick mustache and Coke-bottle glasses. His hands were in his pockets, and he was leaning on the balls of his feet.

"That's a good one," he said.

"Yeah," she muttered.

"You watchin' it alone?"

His bluntness scared her. So did his eyes, which seemed to be peeling her modest outfit apart in strips.

He'd be looking at me like that even if I told him I was a minor, she thought with sickening clarity.

The man licked his lips. "Movies are never as fun when yer watchin' 'em alone, right?"

"I— My boyfriend is coming over tonight. We're

watching this together," she fibbed.

The man's smile wavered. "Your boyfriend, huh?"

Swallowing a lump, she spun on her heels and marched toward the register, deciding that the man's non-question didn't deserve a response.

She must have looked tense because Rufus set his magazine down and stood. Usually, he could complete transactions with his eyes closed, but he appeared alert now.

"You find everything okay?" he asked, taking the DVD case from Ocean and fiddling with it.

"Yeah, I—"

She heard footsteps behind her. Her heart swelled, then turned hard. She realized she was holding her breath, as if she didn't want to breathe in the same air as the stranger.

He walked past and out the door. A bell chimed loudly when he left.

Ocean released a gust of breath and leaned against the counter, relieved the creep had disappeared.

"That guy bothering you, hon?" Rufus asked.

She paused. Technically, the guy hadn't done anything illegal. It wasn't like he'd flashed her or— God forbid—touched her. But he'd given her the willies nonetheless. *Maybe he was just an awkward conversationalist,* she thought.

"I'm okay," she said. "Just got a *super* weird vibe from him."

Rufus snorted. "He was in here a while. I don't think he was here for movies, you know?"

She must have looked perplexed because Rufus elaborated.

"Some guys just go trollin' for girls wherever they can. Bet he's not welcome at many bars or clubs, so I guess he figured he'd try his luck here."

Ocean grimaced.

"Hey, if anyone is givin' you a hard time here, you lemme know, yeah?" Rufus crossed his arms over his chest and spoke in a stern tone: "That shit don't fly at The Video Vault!"

Ocean couldn't help it. She giggled, then laughed.

Rufus flushed red. "Hey, I'm a badass, ya know? I've been in my fair share of scraps!"

"I believe you!" Ocean chortled.

"Two hits. I hit him . . . he hits the road!"

She laughed helplessly. Rufus joined her, rubbing the back of his head self-consciously.

"Thanks," she said when their laughter had run its course. "Seriously, that guy really creeped me out but . . . I'm all right now."

"Well, good. Glad I could help. You want some popcorn to go with this?" He held up the DVD, which she'd forgotten about in all the commotion. He seemed eager to change the subject, and that was a relief to Ocean.

Like all teenaged girls, she'd had many encounters with creepy older men. She was even aware of their leering, lusting eyes back when she was in middle school! Her mother had been forthright with her, explaining the danger of strangers when Ocean was as young as five. Now that she was older, she understood that strangers were more than just "bad men." They were perverts, degenerates, and, sometimes . . . murderers.

Ocean never accepted rides or invitations from people she didn't know. She didn't go to parties at houses she didn't recognize. She especially didn't hang out with Cal Moodey, even though the rest of her classmates thought he was *so* cool. Cal was a thirty-year-old burnout who allowed teens to use his farmhouse for drinking and partying. There was even a rumor that he gave free weed to teenaged girls who allowed him to cop a feel.

Cal and Mister Creep-O would definitely get along, she thought, recalling the salacious way the stranger had scrutinized her figure. *Maybe they could exchange notes! They could even write a book together!* How to Freak Girls Out 101! *It'd be a hit with scumbags!*

She realized that she'd dissociated. Returning to the present, she nodded.

"Okay! Well, one movie . . . one popcorn . . . one soda . . . that'll be nine bucks, fifty!" Rufus declared.

Jesus. Everything is so expensive now!

Ocean reached for her purse.

Her hands met empty air.

She tilted her head down, looking toward her hip, where her purse usually rested when it was slung over her shoulder.

It wasn't there.

"Oh!" Ocean whined. "Nuts!"

"What's up?" Rufus asked.

"I'm an idiot, Rufus," Ocean said.

"Join the club," he scoffed.

"I left my house without my purse!"

"Really?"

"Yes! Shoot! I didn't even realize it until just now! God! What a dolt!"

Rufus cackled. "Listen, hon . . . you don't even gotta worry about it."

"Huh?"

"Take the movie. Take the popcorn. Take the drink. Bring it back on Monday after school with nine-fifty. We'll be square."

"Are you sure?"

"What are you gonna do? Skip town?"

Ocean grinned at this absurdity.

"Besides, if you forget, I'll just talk to yer folks. Tell them their delinquent daughter owes me money and if she doesn't pay up . . . I'll bust her kneecaps!"

His kindness brightened what had become a dour and uncomfortable day. On her way back home—with her movie and snacks in a plastic bag dangling from her wrist—she didn't even think about the creep in The Video Vault, or Marcus's absence, or her friends being unavailable to keep her company. She thought instead, and rather blithely, that there were good people in the world. People like Rufus who didn't mind helping someone out in a pinch or cheering them up when things were gloomy.

She decided it would be a good idea to get him something to brighten his own day. One good turn deserved another, after all. But what did Rufus like? Aside from movies—and he had plenty of those—Ocean couldn't even guess.

The quickest way to a man's heart is through his stomach, right? Maybe I could make him some cookies or something. I'll bet he wouldn't say no to a bag of snickerdoodles!

Most of the ride home was uphill. Ocean pushed herself, straining forward and pedaling harshly. She panted and heaved, swaying on the bike as she ascended. By the time she was riding into her driveway, she'd run out of breath.

Overhead, lightning crackled through the sky. The drizzle was going to become a downpour.

She walked her bike up to the garage and left it leaning against the side wall. Then she marched up the porch and pushed her way through the door.

Later, she'd realize the door had been left unlocked the entire time she'd been gone, but she was too lost in her own thoughts to notice it at that moment.

An hour later, her cogs were spinning again. She was struggling to pay attention to the movie because all she wanted to do was call Marcus. She licked her lips and refocused on Gerard Butler.

He's handsome, sure . . . but unobtainable. Marcus is just thirty minutes away, up in the Heights with his grandma and the rest of his family.

Ocean wondered why she hadn't been invited to dinner. She'd have made a good impression with Marcus's grandmother.

What if he's planning on dumping you? Yeah. I wouldn't introduce him *to my grandparents if I was planning on dropping him.*

Ocean huffed and crossed her arms. She hated the way her brain ran down its own rabbit holes. It was ridiculous to construe tragedy out of something as innocuous as a night apart.

Besides, you like him because he isn't *clingy. And you don't want to be a nagging girlfriend, do you? You don't want to follow him around everywhere he goes, right? Space is important! Space is healthy!*

Calm the hell down, Ocean.

Reason had prevailed, and she'd missed a few more minutes of the movie.

Ocean scooped up the remote and paused the TV. She'd have to give the flick another try tomorrow when her head was clear and focused.

Rain ran wet fingers down the windows. The roof was tapped percussively. Ocean could hear thunder rumble.

Hefting herself off the sofa, she stamped around the house to make sure it looked clean before she went to bed. There was no point in staying up and waiting for her parents to come home, and going to sleep would prevent her from calling Marcus and bothering him.

I could send him a text, she thought.

Unlike most kids, Ocean didn't glue herself to her phone. During the weekends, it tended to rest on her nightstand. If she needed to contact her friends, she conserved her minutes by calling them on the landline.

Padding up the stairs to her bedroom, Ocean realized that a small fire had started to burn in her chest. It was a familiar feeling—the sensation she experienced when Marcus touched her. She hoped it never went away and this spark would shimmer brightly until the day she died.

Will absence keep our hearts fond? Or are we doomed to grow apart?

This thought was a blade to her heart. She wanted to ignore it, but the notion persisted. It was bad enough that she realized she was about to consider calling him. Grandma be damned!

You're just feelin' punchy tonight, Ocean. You need to chill out. Let things unfold however they may. Send him a quick text, then try your best to sleep!

Ocean stepped into her room.

She flicked on the wall light.

She expected to see her room as she'd left it. Her pink bed sheets a mess, her closet door propped open by a pile of discarded clothing that hadn't yet made the pilgrimage to the hamper.

She expected to see her vanity mirror, which was bordered with pictures of herself and her friends. Her lacy curtains, which she'd picked out herself during a thrift shop excursion.

These weren't the things she saw. They were there— all of them—but they were overshadowed by the intruder.

The man posed by the foot of her bed was wearing gloves.

One hand held a gun, and the other a bundle of rope.

The weapon was already pointed at her.

It seemed to gleam in his hand as if it had been recently cleaned.

The gun was a revolver, which looked heavy and dark. The hammer was already cocked back—she had seen enough action movies to know what that meant.

The rope was tangled up in his fist like a ball of Christmas lights. White, slender, and reptilian, it seemed to *hiss* when he loosened his grip on it.

Ocean took a jangling step back.

The man stepped forward. His arm was steady.

There was something *wrong* with his face, Ocean observed. It wasn't normal. It seemed as if it was—

No. But that couldn't be.

Human faces didn't *shift*. That only happened in movies.

The man had red hair, greased back. His eyes were blurry with tears, and his smile was ghoulish. His cheeks were narrow, and his chin was sharp. But the flesh was rumpled, then smooth, then rumpled again, like his face was a mask and something was *breathing* underneath it. His teeth, as well, were morphing from shattered nubs to long fangs to almond-shaped blocks. His voice was in a constant state of change. Sometimes it was high-pitched, and then it dipped down into a gut-rumbling baritone.

"You see me, don't you, little girl? God . . . how I've missed . . . my little girls . . ."

There was something else in the room with them. It was both a part of the intruder and something different. A huge column of black, buzzing flies that swirled behind him like a living shadow. Then it, too, was taking a new shape. One that was grinning and horrible, with long fingers and bright red eyes that glowed like moonbeams.

Frozen with fear, unable to comprehend both what she could see and what she couldn't, Ocean felt her throat tighten. A fist held her heart, threatening to crush it.

"You . . ." the man said.

"Are . . ." the darkness behind him said.

"Going . . ." The man.
"To . . ." The darkness.
"Hurt . . ."
"So . . ."
"Beautifully!"

He was sobbing. He was laughing. He was here, and he was somewhere else. And as he walked toward her, the gun became a knife, and then a gun, and then a hatchet, and then a knife, and then it was something slimy and wriggling like a fat worm, and then it was a hissing snake, and then he was laughing, and his laughter was shrieking, it was the sound of suffering girls, oh God, and she could hear herself joining the choir, wanting to scream but laughing instead, and the hurt was there . . . it was there inside her . . . the hurting was present and past and future, and the hurting was God Himself.

CHAPTER FOUR

While Griffin was transported via ambulance to the hospital, he relived the night he'd met Mr. Friendlyman . . . the same night he'd also become best friends with an odd kid named Orville North, and the night they'd saved young Eunice Lee from a terrible fate.

He'd taken Fincher's car, driving cautiously at first because he knew that if he did put any damage on the vehicle, he'd never lose that shame. It'd be tattooed upon him like the day he'd broken the family TV while roughhousing with his visiting cousins, or the time he'd wet his pants at church camp. *Things that may have seemed inconsequential in the grand scope of the cosmos could weigh heavy on a young heart*, Griffin thought. Even one chip on the already scruffy paint job would torment Griffin's soul for eternity.

He hadn't told his parents what he was doing that night, only that he was going out. They presumed he'd probably be nestled in the back seat of a friend's car. They didn't know how joyless and empty his teenage years were, assuming that he was simply having the time of his life and living every day like it was his last, the same as they had done in their youth.

Maybe, Griffin thought after walking over to Dick's and climbing into Fincher's car, *that'll be the truth after tonight.*

Beggars couldn't be choosers, Griffin rationalized when he hit the road. Fincher's car was . . . shabby. It smelled like smoke and stale peaches inside, and there were greasy stains across the dashboard. It was a red Austin Mini. A cheap car, cheaply constructed and cheaply painted, and yet Griffin drove like he was in the Taj Mahal on wheels. As if the car had never weathered any abuse before his scrawny butt occupied the creaky, springy driver's seat.

Into town Griffin went, steadily and slowly. Thankfully, the cruising teens he found himself surrounded by were driving similarly. They revved their engines, but nobody was looking to hassle anyone, it seemed. Also, you couldn't talk to people if you were speeding.

Griffin saw two drivers having a conversation through open windows, so he cranked his down. At the first stoplight, he tried to initiate a chat with the jock in the convertible next to him. The driver—and his gal— ignored him.

No worries. On to the next one.

A few girls walked along the streets, chatting it up with anyone who slowed down beside them. Wearing A-line skirts—miniskirts were all the rage in the big cities, but they were considered scandalous in a small town like Starch, so the girls made do. They wore their waists high so they could easily pull down and lengthen their skirts whenever adults were around.

Griffin gripped the wheel and turned Fincher's car around, strolling back up the center of town.

The girls were all beauties. He wondered why they all looked like strangers. Surely, they were from the same school he went to.

He was a ghost in the halls, he noted. Nobody talked to him, and he didn't talk to anyone. The girls at his school intimidated him, and he often tried his best to avoid eye contact.

Well . . . not anymore! I've got a car now! I'm a man about town!

Trying to work up some nerve, he slowed down by the curb where a gaggle of teens were hanging out. He honked his horn, goosing them upright, then shouted out the window, "Hey! Anyone need a ride?"

There were three of them. Two girls and a scrawny-looking boy with bright red hair and glasses. He looked really young, like someone's kid brother who'd whined enough to be brought along. The girls were statuesque blondes. One had a red sweater and the other wore sunglasses, even though the sun had set.

"Sure!" the sweatered girl said in a chatty tone. She hopped in the passenger seat. "I know you! Aren't you the kid that did that *Hamlet* speech in English?"

Griffin blushed. "Yeah. Embarrassing, right?"

"Nah! I thought it was cool!"

He'd rushed through that assignment, hating having the spotlight put on him. Rarely did Griffin Chalks answer questions or engage in English, so performing a speech he hadn't understood from a play he'd barely read had been a living nightmare.

"I doubt you remember, but I had to do *Antigone*. I wanted Shakespeare instead. Shakespeare is romantic. *Antigone* is just . . . gruesome. Where you headed?"

Her sister and (assumed) brother got into the back seat. The little boy squirmed around uncomfortably. "Geez! This car's a mess!" he whined.

"Yech!" the more stoic sister said.

"It's a loaner. Friend gave it to me," Griffin said, deciding the truth would be less humiliating. "I was gonna clean it out but . . . I forgot." This line, on the other hand, was a lie. He hadn't thought at all about cleaning up Fincher's messes.

"What's yer name again?" the chattier girl asked.

"Griffin Chalks."

"I'm Eunice Lee. That's my sister, Catherine, and our little brother, Ed. He's a pain."

47

"Am not!" Ed kicked the back of Eunice's seat, which made Griffin flinch.

Little shit better not break nuthin'.

"Hey! You heard Scott Malcom and Teddy Walsh are gonna race out on Ponder's Point, right?" Eunice asked.

"Hadn't heard that!" Griffin pulled away from the curb and started down the strip. He didn't actually know who Scott Malcom or Teddy Walsh were, but he knew all about Ponder's Point—a lonesome stretch of road where kids drag raced.

"We should go ta the drive-in!" Ed shouted. "They're playin' scary movies tonight!"

"Yer too chicken for scary movies!" Eunice laughed.

"Am not!"

"Shut up, you two! God!" Catherine moaned.

Griffin couldn't help it. He started laughing.

"What's so funny?" Ed demanded.

"Sorry. Y'all just crack me up." He turned the car and went back down the strip.

"Hey. A movie might not be a bad idea. What are they playin'?"

"There's somethin' called *The Creature from The Haunted Sea* playin' at The Moonlight!" Ed declared. Obviously, he'd hoped the night would end at the theater and had come prepared. "C'mon! It'd be fun! I heard it's about a monster that sucks brains outta people's ears!"

"Yuck!" Catherine looked pale.

"We're not goin' to the drive-in. We're *always* seein' movies," Eunice said.

"Aw, that's just a rerun. They showed that movie in June. It's not too scary, and no brains get sucked out of anyone's head."

Ed frowned. He looked as if Griffin had just told him Santa wasn't real.

"How about dinner, huh?" Griffin suggested.

"We already ate at home." Ed sighed.

"Are you sayin' no to hamburgers and French fries?" Ed perked up.

Griffin turned at the next light and drove toward Quakes Shakes.

The little burger stand was the local hangout for the teenage populace of Starch. They only had five items on their menu. The hamburger, the cheeseburger, a bag of fries, and chocolate or vanilla shakes. A while back, they'd added a chicken sandwich to the menu, but it'd turned out soggy and unpopular, so they gave up on it. There was a patch of black tape over the placard where the sandwich had once been displayed.

Quakes was a circular building, like an oversized hockey puck. There was a window where you could place your order, and if you wanted, you could take a peek inside. The interior was cramped, with an overstuffed grill, a boiling fryer, and a milkshake machine that looked like a hunk of farming equipment. Typically, Quakes was run by teenagers, but sometimes the old man who owned it stepped in to make sure things were being done right. If he hadn't gotten the job at Dick's, Griffin would have brought his ass to Quakes.

As he drove into the crowded parking lot, Griffin decided he was lucky Dick's had hired him on. Even when the auto shop got busy, it was never *this* bad.

"Whoa," Griffin muttered.

The parking lot was clogged with cars. Teens hung from windows or simply kicked their feet out of open doors. Some even sat on the hoods and roofs of their cars. A jock necked with his gal in his convertible, right in the open for all to see. As they drove by that car, Ed planted his face against the Mini's window, fogging it with his breath.

"Yowzah! He's got a handful of tit!"

"Eddie!" Catherine scolded.

"What? It's true! See for yerself!"

Slightly embarrassed, Griffin decided not to take the kid up on that offer. He searched for a parking spot, eventually finding one to the side of the lot, where Quakes' property was cut through by a high wooden fence.

Griffin realized that he'd put himself in a strange position. He'd promised these two beautiful women and their bratty brother hamburgers and shakes, and now he had to deliver . . . even though he only had a few coins in his pocket.

"I'll see what I can rustle up," Griffin said.

"Wait. I'll go with ya!" Eunice said.

"I don't want cheese on mine!" Ed cried.

"Just meat and ketchup? Gross," Catherine scoffed.

"What about tomatoes?" Griffin asked.

"Yech!" Ed said.

Smirking, Griffin climbed out of the driver's seat. He circled the car and opened the door for Eunice.

"Thanks for taking us out!" Eunice had to shout. Someone had propped their door open and cranked the radio up. Some rockabilly music was droning from the car, polluting the air. Together, Eunice and Griffin walked up to the small line for the order window.

"Really nice of you to pick us up the way you did," Eunice said.

"Thanks. Wasn't a problem."

"I don't see you much at school. Why is that?"

She cut right to the bone, didn't she? Griffin considered things before answering, "I'm kinda shy, I guess." He put his hands in his pockets and kicked the concrete. "I dunno. I'm trying to be more outgoin'."

"Well, you have nothing to be shy about," Eunice said. "Yer very handsome."

He smiled. "And you're pretty."

Blushing, Eunice shrugged her shoulders. "My

sister's the pretty one."

"Nah. I mean, she ain't bad or nuthin'. But yer prettier."

In the ambulance, Griffin wondered if conversation was ever that easy after the early '60s. The hippies may have ruined it for everyone. And they were just around the corner, weren't they? In 1961, it was still malt shops and soda fountains. Still teenyboppers and sock hops. In only a few short years, everything would shift, and then the Vietnam War would no longer be so easy to ignore. It would be as if a madman had buried a knife deep into the spine of America.

He couldn't think about the future. Couldn't think about the culture. He was in his memories now. Deep in them. He was standing beside Eunice, waiting in line for burgers he might not have been able to afford. He was thinking about sex . . . about getting Eunice alone and putting his thing in hers. About how sweet her lips looked and how he wanted to kiss them, how he wished he had—as Ed put it—a handful of tit. But her sister and brother were in the car.

Maybe he could shake them.

How?

He could decide later. The line was thinning. The rockabilly was still loudly blaring, filling the air like a dust storm. He wished someone would play something different. Something romantic. It'd give him an excuse to dance with Eunice.

At the window, a bedraggled teenaged boy asked what Griffin wanted.

"Four cheeseburgers. Sorry. Three cheeseburgers, one hamburger. And four shakes." He hoped no one would notice the missing fries.

The teen gave him his total. Griffin dug his coins out and looked glumly at them.

"We could share a shake," Eunice offered. "I don't

mind."

Suppressing a joyful smile, Griffin told the boy to change it to three shakes. He had enough money, but just barely.

"What flavors?"

"Two vanilla—"

"I want chocolate," Eunice interjected.

"One chocolate."

"Okey-dokey." The boy shouted Griffin's order over his shoulder.

Griffin and Eunice stepped aside. Their meal was ready in no time. Griffin carried it all while Eunice walked beside him.

"You wanna see that movie Ed was talkin' about?"

"The one about the brain slurper?" Griffin beamed. "Can you imagine?"

"I swear, movies are getting dumber an' dumber," Griffin griped. "But yeah, I wouldn't mind rewatching it. Even if the monster does look kind of stupid."

Eunice laughed. "What are you doing tomorrow?"

"Maybe going to the drive-in. You wanna join me?" Griffin asked.

"I'd like that."

They arrived at the car. Catherine and Ed were in the midst of a heated argument. Griffin couldn't tell what it was they were scrapping over, and he didn't actually care. He had a date with Eunice, and this fact alone made his heart feel like it was the first day of summer.

After slipping into their seats and pushing a straw into their chocolate shake, Griffin realized that they'd only given them three straws. He was about to leave to get a fourth when Eunice said, "I don't mind." She took a long sip, then passed the drink over to Griffin. The straw was marked with her lipstick. He cherished his turn before passing the drink back to her.

"We oughta see the drag race," Ed said. "That'd be

cool."

"You're too young for that. Besides, it could be dangerous."

"I'm not too young for nuthin'," Ed whined as he munched on his cheese-less burger.

Griffin rolled his window down. It was getting warm inside Fincher's car. He wondered if the old man would let him borrow it again for his date to the drive-in.

What if he doesn't?

Dad won't let you borrow his car if he knows yer goin' on a date.

Is it even a date? She didn't say it was. What if she just wants to see the movie?

No way a girl as good-lookin' as Eunice wants to see a movie like The Brainiac. *She wants to see* you, *Griffin. She said it herself. She thinks yer handsome.*

His mind felt like a beehive. He hoped the night air would clear things up.

"Hey! How about we go out to The Home?" Ed asked, his mouth stuffed with a mixture of hamburger and milkshake.

"Don't talk with your mouth full," Catherine stated.

"I mean it!" Ed shouted. "You've been to The Home 'fore, right?"

Griffin shook his head. "What are you talkin' about, squirt?"

Ed huffed. "Don't you guys know *anything*? That's what they call the haunted place out on Sycamore. The Home! It's where those kids went missing—"

"You're morbid."

"—back a few years ago. You oughta 'member *that*!"

Griffin did, only because his mother had warned him about it back when it happened. Two years ago, three young boys had broken into the abandoned house at the end of Sycamore Lane. They'd left a pile of comic books and toys behind . . . as well as blood. Their mutilated corpses had been found in the attic, strung up by their ankles and drained like hogs. And they hadn't been the last. A few weeks later, two teenage girls were found in The Home. They'd been tied together by their hands and ankles, and their throats had been cut wide open. It was theorized that the killer had used a meat cleaver to hack through their slender throats. Since they had been a few years older than Griffin, he hadn't known them . . . but school felt surreal the week they'd been found. Lots of upperclassmen had broken into tears, and there was an assembly hosted by the chief of police, who told the kids to avoid the house at the end of Sycamore Lane. He'd also told them to hang out in groups at night and warned them that if there were any more deaths, then a curfew would be instated.

Thankfully, no more children had been killed.

But the house on Sycamore—which was apparently being called The Home—was still vacant. Who would move into a place where such horrible things happened anyway?

"They say that place *still* smells like blood!" Ed sneered.

"Gross. Why would you even want to go there?" Catherine moaned. "Yer sick!"

"Am not!" Ed countered.

Before they could run a marathon of "Am not!" and "Are so!" Griffin made a suggestion.

"We could swing by and look at the place, but I don't think we should go in."

"Why not? You chicken?" Ed asked.

"No. But breaking and entering is a crime," Griffin defended. "I'm not gonna contribute to juvenile delinquency."

Eunice snorted.

"What's delink-kin-see?" Ed asked.

More laughter filled the cab. Even Catherine, who'd been putting on a stern and motherly performance, cracked a smile.

"You serious, though? We can go to The Home?" Ed asked, his eyes big, wet, and pleading.

"We'll drive by it," Griffin said. "But that's it. Sycamore ain't far from here, is it?"

"I think it's just down the road and around the corner," Eunice said.

"Okay." Griffin took another bite from his burger. "This place is too crowded anyways. We can head over."

Ed whooped loudly.

"I can't believe you're encouraging this," Catherine muttered.

"We'll just drive by and take a peek. Hey, maybe we'll see some"—Griffin waggled four of his fingers— "ghosts!"

Eunice giggled. It sounded like water from a babbling brook. Clear and refreshing. Griffin pressed his tongue against his cheek and wondered if he'd lose his virginity with Eunice. He knew he was jumping the gun, but it was hard not to consider what a night like this could lead to.

CHAPTER FIVE

Mr. Friendlyman stepped back. There was nothing left of Ocean Pertwee to kill. Her corpse lay on the bed, her arms and legs tied to the posts. Her middle had been sawed open, her organs towed out from her inner chambers and now steaming on the floor. Her blood fanned around her, staining the headboard and the wall with crimson spiderwebs. Her face was broken apart like moldy fruit. He'd used a hammer to separate her jaw from her head. He'd shoved so many pins into her eyes.

Oh God. Is this really happening?

Mr. Friendlyman—who thought his name had once been Robbie Miller, yes, he was sure of it—looked down at his gore-greased hands. His fingers were tentacles for one second, then chicken heads the next. His flesh warped as if he were looking at it through a funhouse mirror. Now his fingers were gleaming blades . . . now running water . . . now skeletal—

Change is part of it.

His image became solid. It was like he'd been hit with a lightning bolt. Stumbling drunkenly, he whirled away from the girl he'd butchered and slithered toward her vanity mirror.

Yes.

It was Robbie Miller's face, after all. Just as it looked all those years ago . . . back in the "good ol' days."

Mr. Friendlyman/Robbie Miller smiled at his

56

reflection. He was a stern-looking man with high cheekbones and a small, gray mouth. His teeth were crooked and yellow, as were his eyes. His stringy red hair was greased back over his crinkled scalp.

He looked down at his hands. They were human, with knobby fingers and jagged nails. Their backs were coarse with fur, and his palms looked like used napkins. It was because, when he was human—only human—he'd smoked with his fingers curled over his cigarettes. He had no idea why he smoked this way. It was how his father did it, he assumed, although he barely remembered that old man. Anyway, the nicotine had stained his flesh, leaving it blotched and filthy-looking.

Hands—

Reaching out—

He could reach out, but he couldn't touch. He was only tangible so long as he was in The Home . . . where he and Mr. Friendlyman had become *one*. So his psychic threats to Griffin were empty. He could not leave The Home and go after the old man . . . but he knew there would be no way the codger could resist Mr. Friendlyman's call. He'd be here soon . . . and they would finish what they had started.

So long ago . . .

Griffin . . . Orville . . . Eunice . . .

His brain felt like a jigsaw puzzle. Putting thoughts together was a task, and it was hard to parse which thoughts belonged to Robbie Miller and which ones belonged to Mr. Friendlyman. Sometimes, they fell into synch and the thoughts were unified, but there were times when they felt fractured. Like two souls in one body—only the body kept changing shape.

Outside, thunder rumbled.

He tried walking toward the window, but his feet floated two inches above the ground. Still, his legs pedaled beneath him, and he moved his arms, which stretched and shrank in rhythmic waves.

He could hear a car rumbling up the short driveway. *The parents.*

He'd watched them closely while they were living in this place—a place they thought they owned. No, this was not their house. It belonged to Robbie Miller/Mr. Friendlyman. It wasn't their home . . . it was *his*!

It was where he kept his collection.

He looked back toward the bed where Ocean's corpse lay. She'd been ruined beyond repair, and now her soul screamed with the others, with every boy and girl that he'd killed, and the ones they'd killed when they were two separate entities—before they'd become conjoined spiritual twins.

Struggling to organize his thoughts, Robbie Miller/ Mr. Friendlyman decided that Ocean's parents needed to die.

***

Anne Pertwee looked at the dashboard. She couldn't explain it, but *something* had told her to insist upon leaving the party early and coming home. Colm had appeared disappointed at first, but halfway home, he seemed to fall under the same spell. She was glad he said it first, breaking the ice.

"Something's wrong, isn't it?"

Anne shivered. "Yes."

"How do we know?"

"Parental intuition?"

"You think Ocean is in trouble?" Colm scratched at his neck as if his collar had shrunk.

"I don't know," Anne lied.

Something bad happened. These three words rotated around Anne's head like a halo.

When they'd met, Colm Pertwee and Anne Jessica Blanks were both hippies stuck in the nineties.

Now that they'd grown up—although both of them still felt like kids in adult costumes—they'd shed their rebellious skin and replaced it with sheep's wool.

Anne didn't miss the old days like she thought she would. Her idealism had been swapped for creature comforts. Once, she'd been shouting into a bullhorn on campus, hoping the march would turn into a good old-fashioned riot—they never did, no matter how often she reread *The Strawberry Statement* or admired documentaries about activism from the '60s and '70s.

Now, she watched daytime soaps and fretted over her lawn.

She'd once scoffed at the idea of marriage, believing it to be nothing more than a social construct. Then she'd become pregnant when she didn't expect to, and the notion of having a child out of wedlock had been too frightening for her. So, she'd pressured Colm into a fast marriage, and now here they were . . . in their thirties and living in suburbia.

What she missed was Colm's beard. It used to fall from his face like a beehive from a branch, all wispy and scratchy. He used to wear circular sunglasses—like John Lennon—and he'd rub his beard contemplatively while he read Marx on their waterbed.

Once Ocean was born, things changed.

He shaved his face, set aside his staunch politics, and accepted a job at his brother's law office. Eventually, he moved over to an accounting firm, where he put his latent math skills to good use.

"If I didn't smoke so much pot, maybe I'd have a degree from MIT hangin' in my office," he'd once half-joked.

He was a workhorse, putting in as many hours as he could. Despite this, Colm wasn't an absent father or a neglectful husband. When he was home, he made certain that his presence and love were known.

One gift they both shared was parental intuition. The last vestige of their hippie days was their belief in the metaphysical and the psychic, and that such phenomena were as integral to Earth's makeup as dirt and water. When their daughter was hurting, they felt it. When she cried, they heard it. When her heart was deflated, they could sense it like a bad smell. And now, on their way home from the party, driving through the rain, it was as if a Klaxon alarm was blaring ahead of them.

Get home, it cried. *Get home because your daughter needs you!*

Anne held her lips together and tried not to shout back.

She was slender, brown-haired, and her skin was cragged with early wrinkles. The side effect, she presumed, of a youth spent worrying. She was beautiful and hard, while her daughter was beautiful and soft. She knew it would only be a matter of time before life hardened her little girl, as it did all women.

But what if something bad has happened? What if she's —

No. That's an extreme thought. We don't need to think it.

Maybe she is hurt . . . but it's nothing bad. It could be she twisted her ankle, or accidentally cut herself making a snack, or . . .

Or something bad happened.

"Something Bad" had become a monster in her mind. A toothsome thing with green skin and sharp talons. She imagined Something Bad attacking Ocean, tearing into her yielding skin, flaying her open with one swipe.

The windshield wipers swept back and forth in rhythmic waves. She let them hypnotize her.

Colm turned into the driveway. The rain was coming down in heavy sheets, blotting out the finer details of their home.

At least it isn't on fire!

In unison, Colm and Anne Pertwee climbed out of their car. Not caring about the rain, they rushed up the porch and to the front door. Colm joggled the doorknob, finding it locked. Usually when they went out, Ocean would leave the front door unlocked for them.

Colm went through his pockets in search of his keys. Anne opened her purse and dug around on the off chance she found hers faster.

"Shit!" Colm muttered. "I left them in the car!"

Anne saw that the car's lights were still on. Underneath the pattering of the rain, she could hear its engine purr.

She turned her purse over and dumped its contents out on the porch. The keys jangled loudly.

Colm snatched them up like they were running away from him. He pushed them in and tore the door open.

"Ocean?" Anne called.

"Oh God!" Colm roared. He charged into the house.

Anne heard a muffled cry. Her heart froze, deadened by the noise. She wasn't so sure she was prepared to go into the house and see what had happened to her daughter.

She thought of Something Bad again. The monster was drooling, its tongue hanging from its mouth like a slab of raw meat in a butcher's shop window.

We will be changed forever after this, Anne thought with mounting dismay.

"Oh God!" Colm shouted. "Oh . . ."

There was a wet sound. A grinding noise like a tire spinning in mud.

Run, Anne, the voice in her head advised.

Then Colm released a shriek. A long sound, piggish and painful. It sent her heart up her throat like a stuntman out of a cannon. Anne clutched her hands together and took a wavering step back.

You can't leave him.

He's your husband.

And your daughter is in there.

Anne had no choice. She needed to go in. She needed to save her daughter and her husband.

She stepped toward the door once again.

Something wrapped around her. Something strong and sturdy. It felt like she was being bear-hugged by a bodybuilder. Whatever it was tightened around her middle, compressing her guts. She tried to scream, but all that came out was air.

Whatever had her . . . it was invisible.

This can't be, Anne thought with mounting terror. *It can't!*

She held her arms out and put her hands on either side of the doorframe. Straining, she tried to push herself away from the house and the dark, gravitational riptide that had captured her. She braced her feet against the ground, digging her heels into the welcome mat.

Lemme go! Lemme go! Lemme go! her brain screamed.

Inside her house, she could see her husband. He lay on the floor, wet and wiggling, barely alive. The skin had been torn away from his face, exposing the red, mucousy pulp beneath. Both his eyes looked like crushed sweetener pods, leaking milky fluid down his crimson cheeks. He lifted his head up, then weakly dropped it back onto the bloodstained ground. A puddle grew beneath him, expanding from his gaping mouth. She saw that whatever had attacked him pulled his pants down to his knees. Forcefully, a fire poker had been shoved into his rear. His buttocks were clenched, but blood gushed down his thighs.

No . . . No . . . We can't die like this! Anne thought.

She was surprised to feel a flush of shame.

Everyone will talk about this. It's all we'll be remembered for. Not that we were a loving, happy family . . . but that my husband was sodomized with a fire poker.

She felt something pop inside her. Her back bent painfully.

"No!" Anne managed to project her voice. "Please, God!" Her hands began to ache. She pushed hard against the doorframe in a last-ditch effort to peel herself away from the supernatural force that had taken hold of her.

Then her back broke.

It was as if she'd been folded like a lawn chair.

Bending backward, her gut pushing forward and splitting down the middle, her heels hitting the back of her cranium, Anne screamed louder than ever before as she was *slurped* into The Home.

The door slammed shut behind her.

CHAPTER SIX

That's just how it was back then in the early '60s, before the hippies came and ruined everything. You could just pick someone up and they'd trust you to show them a decent time. Nowadays, if he'd pulled up to a curb and asked two lovely sisters and their bratty brother if they needed a ride, the best he'd get was the bird. The worst would be the cops called on his dumb ass.

We were all more trusting back then, Griffin thought as he turned over in his hospital bed and looked toward the window. *That's how Mr. Friendlyman got us . . .*

Ah, Prudence . . . if only you could see me now. A pathetic old man, all alone in the hospital . . .

He wasn't all alone, he realized. He was just throwing a pity party. Eloise was making the trip back to Starch to help him out. She'd promised to be there bright and early in the morning.

"Don't worry, Dad. Boris is gonna look after the kids. It'll be you and me for a few days, then he'll come down and help too."

Fear struck him. Griffin tried to remember how many grandkids he had. He pinched his eyes shut and thought hard on it.

Two.

Mary, who is the youngest. She has such a bright face and such long, blond hair.

Todd is the oldest. He's always all scabby and dirty because he plays rough. He's gonna be a star athlete someday.

He was relieved. Griffin Chalks didn't want to forget about the things that were most important to him.

Haven't seen 'em since Christmas. It's April now . . .

Is it?

Yes. Don't forget that, you old bastard.

Griffin heard the TV turn on.

He'd been placed in an empty room. Normally, he would have liked the solitude, but seeing an empty bed next to his reminded him of the vacant spot in his house Prudence had once occupied.

How'd we meet, Griffin? Surely you remember how you met your wife.

Sure . . . he remembered . . . He'd been driving Fincher's car and saw her standing by the curb with her sister and her little brother—

No. That was Eunice.

Prudence . . . Eunice. They aren't the exact same name, but they are pretty close.

Don't read too much into that.

His mouth felt chalky. He wondered if he ought to buzz a nurse and ask for a glass of water.

There you go. Getting all scatterbrained again.

You talked to the doctor, Griffin. Do you remember what it was that even landed you in this here hospital bed with a tube around your head and stale air being pumped into your wrinkly nose? Do you remember lying on the ground, messing yourself, thinking you were dying?

What did the doctor say?

"You've had a panic attack, Mister Chalks. It was exacerbated because you *thought* you were having a heart attack. Panic attacks feel that way, you know. It isn't rare. Has it happened to you before?"

The last time he'd felt like that . . . he'd been in The Home . . . his ankles tied to the ankles of Orville and Eunice . . . a man named Robbie Miller stalking around them . . . his face split open with his wicked smile . . .

and there was something flowing around him, like a dark cloak. A cloak with a face—

Don't think about it.

Don't think about Mr. Friendlyman . . .

"Never like this, Doc," he'd stated.

"Well, we'll wanna keep you for observation. Don't worry, Mister Chalks. Yer getting the VIP treatment today." The young doctor winked.

"I'm sorry. Do I know you?" Griffin asked.

The man frowned. "Sorry. I've grown up some. I'm Anton."

"Anton?"

"Anton Degrassi." A look of extreme pity crossed over the young man's handsome face. "I'm sorry. You're probably feeling a bit disoriented. Your daughter, Eloise, and I used to date."

"You did?"

"Yes."

"And I didn't kill ya when you broke her heart?"

Anton laughed happily. "No, Mister Chalks . . . she broke mine!"

Griffin tried to smile. "That's my girl."

The doctor set his clipboard aside and patted Griffin's knee. "Seriously, we'll take good care of you until the heartbreaker can pick you up. Anything you want, don't be afraid to ask, okay?"

Weakly, Griffin said, "I think I need some sleep."

Now, however many hours later—Griffin was struggling to keep track—he was wide awake. It was dark outside, and the window was flecked with beads of rain. Every once in a while, thunder and lightning tussled overhead.

Across from him and mounted on the wall sat a flat-screen TV. The nurses had taught him how to use the remote. He'd tried going to MeTV because they showed old shows on that channel, but he'd had a hard time focusing on the programs, so he'd muted the box and left it playing. Onscreen, Rockford was fighting a bunch of goons in front of his beachside trailer.

Griffin licked his wrinkled lips. Maybe he should've moved after retiring. He could've lived like Rockford—with fewer fights, of course—on the beach.

The image flickered.

Griffin felt his chest tighten.

Suddenly, he was looking at a bloodbath. Projected on the screen was the image of a suburban home drenched in gore. The camera traveled around the living room, first focusing on a dead man whose face had been skinned, then drifting away toward the second victim—a woman who'd been folded like laundry.

The TV was still muted. Without sound, there was something surreal about the hellish, vile images. It was as if he was watching one of his own nightmares instead of a television program.

They'd never *show something like this on regular TV. Never in a million years. This is—*

The camera floated up the stairs. Each step was decorated with splotchy gore. There were wet handprints on the wall. The killer, after destroying the man and woman, had torn through the house and ripped every picture from the wall. They lay in scattered patches, shattered and stomped.

Griffin turned and spotted the remote on the nightstand beside his bed. He lunged for it, then scrambled to turn the volume on.

He could hear heavy breathing from behind the camera. Whoever was recording this was in no rush, but his soggy breath came out in long, rattling gusts like breaking wind. It sickened Griffin to hear.

The murderer had gone into one of the bedrooms.

Oh God, Griffin thought after the camera focused on the mutilated girl on the bed.

He tried to change the channel. Nothing happened. The image stayed.

He tried muting the volume again.

The breathing seemed to get louder.

"Hey, kids." The familiar voice returned. It wasn't coming from the TV's tinny speakers. It was *in the room with him.* "I know a surefire way to summon ghosts—"

Griffin awoke with a start.

"Geez, Dad!" Eloise shouted.

"Huh?" Griffin blinked rapidly.

Outside, the sun was shining. The rain had stilled. The television was a black void.

"You scared me!" Eloise wrapped her arms around him and hugged him. "God, I'm glad you're okay!"

Still disoriented, Griffin tried to remember where he was and how he'd gotten there.

It all rushed back to him.

"C'mon, Dad. They said you can go whenever you want, but they wanna wheel you out."

Eloise ended the hug and stepped back, crossing her arms over her skinny chest. Even though she was in her early thirties, she still looked like a child to him, with her cherubic curly hair, her puffy cheeks and double chin, and her soft, dappled eyes. She looked haggard— she'd spent the whole night driving, presumably—and her skin was sticky. She was wearing a sleeveless blouse and a pair of ratty jeans.

"Eloise?" Griffin started. "It's good to see you, hon."

Smiling, she wiped a tear away. "Good to see you too, Dad."

CHAPTER SEVEN

"Yer kiddin' me," Orville muttered.

"Heard it last night," Kojak affirmed. "All those sirens. Hell, I'm surprised it didn't wake *you* up."

Maybe it did, Orville thought, remembering last night's living nightmare.

Wylie Kojak grunted, farted, then leaned forward and investigated his puzzle with his hands. He'd been working on the Eiffel Tower for three days straight, and he'd only gotten the corners and a few chunks in the middle. Kojak wasn't the smartest man in the retirement home, but he kept his cinnamon-roll-shaped ears close to the ground. When something happened, Kojak was typically the first to gossip about it.

He also knew all about The Home.

Well, not *all* about it, but he knew Orville had been there when all the "bad stuff" happened back in 1961. He'd also read *The Moon Rings of Ernth*, but he had the good graces to never make a big deal about it. Once, he'd told Orville, "It was so long ago when I read it . . . all I remember about it was the dragon. I always liked dragons." Orville had offered to lend Kojak his copy, but the old man declined, saying, "I'll just forget it all over again."

Rubbing his beard, Orville considered things.

Kojak had told him the police had gone back down Sycamore late last night. Then he said he'd heard on the radio in the kitchen—he sometimes stood by the door to listen to all the "upsetting" news when staff wasn't paying attention to him—that neighbors had reported screams from the last house on Sycamore Lane . . . 654 . . . The Devil's House.

The Home.

"They're keepin' things close to their chest," Kojak said, "but I struck up a conversation with Ernesto. You know Ernesto, right? Mexican kid? He waxes the floors and smokes like a fiend. I've never seen eyes so red. Anyways, Ernesto was telling me that he heard some high school girl and her folks were butchered . . . *butchered*, Mister North. No trace of the killer. Ernesto's theory is that it's some roaming maniac. Goes from town to town and leaves bodies in his wake. But you and I know the truth, Mister North!"

I *know the truth,* Orville thought glumly. *Yer close . . . but no cigar.*

"It's a copycat killer. Someone who's probably got himself a shrine to ol' Robbie Miller. You know, some folks a*dmire* serial killers the way others do celebrities? They see Charles Munson the same way—"

"Manson."

"—most of us'd look at Elvis! What'd I call him?"

"You said 'Munson.'"

"No, I said 'Manson.' You need ta get yer hearin' checked, Mister North." Kojak looked down at his puzzle. "Shit. I'm never gonna finish this."

"I believe in you," Orville said, clapping the old man on the back. "But I gotta piss, so I'm abandoning you."

"Everyone leaves me." Kojak put on a fake pout.

"It's because you fart like you think no one can hear it." Orville hauled himself up and waddled away.

"Yer no bed of roses either, you know?" Kojak chuckled.

"Yup. I pissed the bed just last night."

"Hey, at least no one else was in it!"

The two men honked with laughter before splitting

70

apart. Orville walked down the hall back toward his room. Sitting on the toilet, he stared at his hands and tried to organize his thoughts. The word *butchered* rang through him like a church bell.

Just like the kids Robbie Miller got his hands on . . .

Orville bared his teeth at this thought. Robbie Miller had been a monster, and now Orville felt as if they'd turned him into something so much worse.

But we didn't mean to.

We thought we were stopping *him.*

He remembered that night clearly . . . and wondered if Griffin and Eunice were even still alive.

***

Orville North was walking in the dark. His hands were tucked in his pockets, and his head was bent down, his eyes stuck on his dragging feet. Much like Griffin Chalks—who Orville had yet to meet but was fast approaching—Orville had gotten a job. He was working at the gas station as a jockey, where he spent his hours filling tanks, cleaning windows, and running back and forth under the hot sun. Every time a car pulled in, their tires rolled over a wire that rang a bell inside the station, which irritated Orville to no end.

We don't need a bell to tell us there's a car in our lot. We've got eyes!

His hands were greasy and smelled like sharp gasoline. His pits were soggy, and his eyes burned. He'd only been working a short shift because his mom had picked up the phone when his boss called to see if Orville could cover for a kid who needed to leave early. If he'd beaten Mom to the phone, he'd be sitting at his writing desk working on the next chapter of his book—at this point, the title was *Moon Dragon*.

At that moment in time, Orville and his mother lived on North Elm. That had tickled Mom when they moved in three years earlier. She'd brought Orville down to the end of the street, pointed excitedly, and declared, "Look, Orry! The Norths are on the North!" She'd smiled all day like she'd met a new man. The same drunken smile that sort of frightened him whenever she had a "fella she wanted him to be nice to."

Orville shuddered. He'd never met his real father. The man was, in Mom's words, a cad and a cheat who'd never played a good hand but kept trying either way. Someone had once told Orville there'd been rumors the old man had been butchered by gangsters to settle a gambling debt, but Orville didn't believe that. The guy probably skedaddled after soberly realizing how much of a responsibility he owed to the kicking infant in the crib beside his bed.

Mom did fine on her own. Patricia North—Orville was named after her father, who had died in a collapsed coal mine when she was twelve—was a strong, independent woman. She worked two jobs, one at the library and the other as a secretary for the elementary school. It paid a pittance. Originally, they'd lived in a shabby apartment building just outside of Starch. It was all they could afford. Until one night, after finding a cockroach in her mouth when she awoke one morning—her theory was it had fallen from the ceiling—she decided that the Norths needed a proper home.

So, she'd taken a page from Dad's book.

Patricia North walked into Dart's Tavern and made herself at home at the poker table. With what little jewelry she had, she started playing, ignoring the taunts of the men sitting around her and the jeers from the patrons at the bar.

Patricia North, who'd never gambled before and had no interest in gambling again, cleaned house.

It was a local legend, which Orville had heard from varying sources. Even his mother's own account seemed embellished. Some said she was down and out until she got a lucky card at the end of the game. Others said she mopped the floor from start to finish and that the burly guys at the table were left whimpering and crying. Too embarrassed at having been bested by a gaunt-faced single mom to try and swipe their money back the way they would have with her husband.

On their last night in the apartment, shortly after Patricia had settled her debts and purchased the house on North Elm, Orville saw her bring a book out of her bedroom and toss it into the trash. When she went back into her room to finish packing, Orville secreted the book away and studied it in the alley between their building and the pawn shop.

The book was titled *How to Win . . . Every Time!* It was subtitled *The Deepest, Darkest Secrets of Vegas and a Surefire Method to Make YOU a WINNER!*

He scanned the pages, but none of it made any sense to him.

Years later, when he was all grown, Orville would reconsider his theories on the matter. As a child, he'd assumed the book itself had been the sole reason Patricia had won her game and gotten their house. Now, as an old man, he thought the game had been as natural to her as it was evasive to his father. She'd thrown the book out because it had taught her nothing . . . and she never needed it to begin with.

He wished he could ask her about it, though. Maybe the years would have embellished the story, or perhaps she would have told him the plain and simple truth.

But at the moment, Orville was walking with his hands in his pockets, unaware that one day he'd be a bestselling author, unaware that his mother would die in a car accident.

Unaware that someday he'd be an old man.

He kicked a pebble and watched it skitter, then

zigzag ahead of him. Sighing deeply, he walked ahead and kicked the pebble again. At fifteen, he was a year away from driving. He desperately wished he could be cruising the strip like the upperclassmen. Maybe he'd pick up someone and drive out to Ponder's Point for a make-out session.

Ah, but who would want to neck with you, Orville?

He looked down at his swelling belly. He wasn't obese, but he was stout. His cheeks were cherubic, and his chin was weak—eventually, he'd grow a beard to hide it. His hands were pudgy, and his fingers were short. He smelled like engine grease and gasoline, and his nails were so grimy it looked as if he'd painted their edges with ink. Beneath the oily odor lay something swampier. If he lifted his arms now, he imagined green lines radiating from his pits.

Yeah. Cheryl Prine is just dying *to make it with you, Orville.*

The teenager couldn't help but laugh at himself. He kicked the bean-sized pebble and watched it bounce.

A horn honked behind him. He turned his head and felt his face fall.

The red convertible swooped up to the side of the road, and a leering jackal's face leaned out.

"Hey!" Orville put his hands up as if he was being accosted by the police. "I don't want any trouble."

"Too bad!" the passenger barked.

"Leave him alone!" a woman whined from the back seat.

To his horror, Orville realized it was Cheryl Prine.

It's as if I summoned her . . . and her psycho boyfriend!

Blinking, Orville processed the whole picture. Cheryl was in the back seat with Ted, who was attached to him like a defensive octopus. Ted would have been handsome if his face hadn't been beaten in over the years. He had cauliflower ears and multiple missing

Judith Sonnet

teeth. It was common knowledge that a majority of
these injuries were from the football field . . . but not
all of them. Ted went out sometimes to Dart's Tavern,
where the barkeep never cared to check IDs and
probably thought Ted deserved a drink or two because
he had a golden fuckin' arm. There, Ted got into scraps
with men twice his age. Rumor had it he sent a lot
of them home in agony. Rumor also had it that he'd
once squared away a debt by letting an old perv grope
Cheryl.

The thought sickened Orville. He'd had a crush on
the redhead for ages. At first, he'd actually been *mad* at
her for sticking by Ted's side. Now, he understood she
had no choice. If he could take down a man the size of
an elephant, just imagine what those fists could do to
her unblemished face.

Orville sometimes thought that Serffana was based
on Cheryl. In the book he was writing, she was a slave
to an evil ogre the main hero had to defeat on his quest.
The subplot felt shoehorned in, but Orville couldn't
abandon it—although eventually, he would by the time
the book was going through its ninth draft.

Ted Bracken's goons were in the front seats: Shane
Spenser, who had a rattish face and skeletal fingers and
always wore a water-damaged leather jacket, and Peter
Wayne, who was about to fall out of the passenger seat.
Peter's grin showed a mouth full of yellow planks, and
Orville was disgusted to see a clump of bloody mucus
clogging his left nostril. The right wheezed, taking
on the brunt of the work. His shoe-polish-black hair
was stringy and long. The school had a policy about
boys growing their hair too long, but no one seemed
interested in correcting Peter. He was considered a lost
cause. Everyone just hoped he'd graduate and be gone
by next year—whether he deserved to graduate or not.

Ted and his friends were more than just bullies.

Even Patrick Folk, who'd tormented Orville in the fifth grade and managed to break his wrist during a fight, was docile in comparison.

Ted detached himself from Cheryl. Like a snake, he slithered out of the seat and sat on the top of the passenger side rear door. His muscles strained to hold him steady. Ted always seemed to be *bulging*. Like a kinked garden hose.

"Whatcha gotta say, shrimp?" Ted asked.

"A-about what?" Orville answered.

"I dunno, Brain Boy. What's on yer mind? You always seem like yer on a different planet." Ted was putting up an almost-conversational front, but Orville could sense the hot rage boiling underneath each word. Orville had done nothing to Ted, but for some reason, Ted was pissed at him. As if Orville had slept with his girl, keyed his car, and left a steaming dump on his porch all on the same day.

Pocketing his hands and furtively looking down the road, Orville considered his options. He could run, but that would only make things worse. It'd give Ted an excuse to be extra cruel. He'd heard it from bullies before. "I was gonna go easy on ya, but then you had to go an' run!"

If he didn't give Ted the satisfaction, that would only infuriate the bastard more.

His options were few, so he saw no alternative other than to play along.

"I dunno. I get distracted, I guess."

Ted put his heels on the ground and lurched away from the car. On the driver's side, Shane snuck out and circled the front of the car. They were cornering Orville.

Orville looked behind him. There was a tall, white fence. He didn't think he could climb it. *If I did, I might drop down to a rabid guard dog. You never know.*

Orville blinked and saw that Peter had left the car as

well. The three bullies were approaching steadily, like praying mantises dancing down a branch.

"Hey," Orville said, his eyes pleading. "I didn't do nuthin' to you."

Ted's hand was on his shoulder. His grip was tight.

"Honest! I didn't!"

Ted punched him right in the stomach. Orville bent over and released a gust of hot wind. He coughed and snorted, then felt his knees connect with the ground. Clutching his abdomen, he whined throatily.

Ted's punch left a fireball in his gut. It coiled over his stomach and squeezed his intestines together like hair in a ponytail. His eyes swam and his teeth clacked.

"I'll tell you what you did, shrimp!" Ted cawed. "Yer stinkin' up the place!"

Orville groaned.

"You and yer whore mom!"

"Yeah, where's yer dad?" Peter snickered. "Bet he couldn't stand the *smell* on ya!"

This was projection, Orville would later realize. Peter's own dad had abandoned him and his mother before he could even stand on two legs. Only, Peter's dad's method of escape involved a shotgun and an upraised chin.

The slight against his mom hurt. Being a single mother wasn't popular in a small town like Starch, but Patricia worked hard for what she had, and she'd raised Orville better than he thought his old man ever could've.

"Leave him alone!" Cheryl cried from the car. "Please, Ted!"

Ted grabbed a fistful of Orville's hair and lifted his head. He smacked the shuddering victim on both cheeks, then honked his nose and twisted it.

Orville made a noise like a coyote.

"Little *shrimp*," Ted snarled. "Shitters like you make

me sick! Stinkin' up our streets . . . our schools . . . our churches . . . If I killed you right now, I bet the mayor would give me the key to the city! Jus' fer cleanin' up the place!"

Ted, Shane, and Peter hooted with hyperbolic laughter. The three suddenly reminded Orville of the witches from *Macbeth*. Ugly, cruel, and jeering.

Orville felt his hands curl into fists.

"You aren't gonna kill him, Ted, are you?" Cheryl shouted, seeming genuinely worried.

Ted fumed. "I oughta!"

"He didn't *do* anything!" she reiterated.

Thank you for standing up for me, Cheryl, Orville thought. *Too bad you'd probably be better off keepin' yer mouth shut. Because he's definitely gonna be pissed that yer callin' him out.*

Ted hauled Orville up to his feet, then thrust him backward until he collided with the fence. Orville started to slump down, but Ted caught him by the pits and hauled him upright. Getting close to his face, Ted sneered.

"Shit, I ain't gonna kill you, shrimp. But I *am* gonna teach ya a thing or two!"

Orville shook his head. He tried to reclaim his breath, but his lungs felt like punctured tires.

"Hold him up!" Ted barked. His cronies hopped to it, taking either side of Orville and keeping him still.

To Orville's horror, Ted reached down and began to undo his pants.

"What you doin', boss?" Shane snarked.

"Shuddup," Ted said as he hauled his penis out. It looked like a beaten rag of flesh. He peeled away the skin around the head, exposing a purple helmet.

"You ain't gonna *rape* him, are ya?" Shane asked, frightened.

"Nah! Just shuddup an' watch." Ted concentrated.

A line of yellow fluid peeled out of him and spattered against the sidewalk. He lifted his cock, aiming his stream toward Orville.

Orville felt warm filth soak his pants.

"Aw! Gross!" Shane laughed.

"Ted!" Cheryl screeched. "Ted! You can't *do that!*"

Ignoring his girlfriend, Ted pissed on Orville, laughing like he was riding down a waterslide. Orville had never seen Ted look so happy.

Squirming against Peter and Shane, Orville wished he could teleport away from this sidewalk. He knew word would spread — Ted and his goons couldn't help themselves. Soon, everyone would know that Orville had been *pissed* on. And they'd laugh at him like it was his fault, not Ted's.

Jesus. I'm dead. I'm actually dead, Orville thought with mounting agony.

Ted's stream lessened, then tapered off. Before he finished dripping, he shoved his prick back into his pants and zipped up.

"What a relief!" Ted laughed.

Orville looked down. Ted had soaked his groin and belly. He looked as if he'd been hit with puddle water by a speeding car.

Motherfucker. Orville seethed.

"What's on yer mind now, shrimp?" Ted cackled.

"He probably *liked* that!" Shane released Orville and let him slide down the fence.

"First good bath he's had in a while, I reckon!" Ted snorted.

"What do we do with him now?" Peter asked, walking toward Ted and crossing his arms like a scolding teacher. "We can't jus' leave him here!"

"Let's take him to The Home!" Ted said.

Orville's heart froze.

"Hell yeah!" Shane snickered.

"Ted! Just leave him alone!" Cheryl exclaimed.

"Shuddup!" Ted barked. "C'mon, Peter. Help me haul him into the trunk!"

Orville tried to squirm away, but Peter grabbed him by the ankles while Ted scooped him up by his armpits. Like luggage, Orville was carried to the rear of the car. Shane struggled to lift the trunk lid, and then Orville was heaved into the cramped quarters. Before he could struggle out, the lid snapped closed. He heard a fist pound against it as if to ensure it stayed locked.

In the darkness, the smell of Ted's urine was as pungent as roadkill. Orville gagged, releasing a noise like an engine's sputter. Outside, he could hear Cheyrl arguing and Ted shutting her down.

The car started, then peeled away.

I bet if anyone saw what they did . . . they'd call the cops. Then Ted would be sorry!

He knew *that* was a pipe dream. Besides, he didn't want the cops to find him like this. Crammed into the trunk of a car like a picnic basket, covered in piss, his belly all bruised, and his eyes puffy with tears. It would be mortifying.

The reality of where he was headed hit him.

Orville gulped.

The Home was notorious to everyone in Starch. It was where, eight summers ago, a young girl had once been found crucified. Someone had used rusty nails to secure her ten-year-old corpse to a wall, and then they'd bludgeoned her head with a hammer until there was nothing but pulp on the top of her neck. And he'd heard that two years before that, two young boys had been lured into the house, where they'd been slaughtered like pigs. In their blood, the culprit had written *Mr. Friendlyman Loves All God's Little Children.*

There was no *official* documentation of these events. Only rumors and hearsay. But in Starch, sometimes the rumors were more trustworthy than the papers. The town officials liked to keep a clean image, so it was no surprise they were covering up the brutal murders that had occurred at the house on the end of Sycamore Lane.

Even without this knowledge, he could tell that the house was just *bad*. A dark cloud seemed to hang over it, suspended just above the crumbling roof. The trees on the lawn were all withered and dried, and the grass looked like beard stubble. While the houses that surrounded it looked neat and friendly, The Home appeared actively hostile. Dangerous, even.

When Orville was a kid, he'd once been dared to chuck a rock through one of the windows. He'd been brave up until the moment of truth when he was standing on the lawn and looking up at The Home's glaring windows, which looked like angry eyes. He'd let the rock drop from his hand, not caring that the kids waiting by the road were going to call him a pussy. He felt that if he broke one of the windows, something evil would come crawling out of The Home . . . and it would follow him to his bedroom.

Mr. Friendlyman . . . that's what they call the thing *that lives in that house.*

Don't stay out too late . . . or Mr. Friendlyman will get you.

Don't tell any lies . . . or Mr. Friendlyman will get you.

He talks real nice. Tells you he means no harm, that you can trust him. But then, when he's lured you into The Home . . . he gets you!

When he was a child, Orville thought the worst thing that could happen was having a monster "get" you. But he'd had no concept of what "getting" meant. Now that he was growing up, he knew what people were capable of. They didn't need to be supernatural, ghostly monsters to put a person through undeserved hell.

Still, his fear was primordial. It was the same shivery sensation he'd felt when his mom forgot to check the closet before turning off the light. The same fear that made him race down the hallway after he used the bathroom at midnight.

The car hit a bump, jolting Orville . . .

***

. . . back to the present.

He'd been sitting on the toilet so long that his legs felt numb.

After a few moments, he'd finished up his business and was staring at his reflection in the mirror, not wanting to think about the single squiggly earthworm he'd left in the bowl. Part of growing old, for Orville, meant inconsistent and frustrating bowel movements. He envied his younger self, who'd maybe needed at most five minutes to produce. Now, every time he went to the can, he had to fight for his life.

It isn't fair, Orville thought, allowing himself a tidbit of self-pity.

He tried to work his brain back through his memories. Ted Bracken, who'd tormented him the night he met Griffin, Eunice, Mr. Friendlyman, and a roaming psychopath named Robbie Miller, had died suddenly a few years later. Apparently, he'd gotten drunk at Dart's, then picked a fight he was destined to lose.

The man who killed Ted Bracken was a drunken traveler named Jon Garton. He'd stopped by Dart's on a whim, had a few drinks, lost a few hands of poker, and then occupied a corner booth. When Ted and his friends came in, the boy made a beeline for Jon.

"Hey, old-timer!" Ted barked. "Yer in my spot!"

Everyone turned their heads, looking forward to the show the headstrong youth was about to put on.

"Did I now?" Jon asked. He'd been fired, folks would learn, from his assembly line job after putting his manager's head through a wall. He had a wife and child who'd run from his home due to his escalating rage. Reportedly, she'd left with bruises, and she was thankful it hadn't been worse.

Jon was a violent man by nature. Ted was violent because he believed himself to be immortal and faultless.

"Yeah! So why don't ya *git*?" Ted cocked a thumb over his shoulder.

Jon smiled. "What are you gonna do 'bout it?"

"I'm gonna *make* you move!" Ted declared, much to the excitement of his friends.

"Okay," Jon said. He then pulled out a revolver and shot Ted twice in the gut.

The whole bar went still.

Peter Wayne turned and ran. He ran out of town that night and never returned. Last Orville had heard, he was working on his grandfather's farm in Arkansas, milking cows and tilling fields.

Shane Spenser wet his pants. He would later say that this moment had been the one that forced him to find God. Shane became a functioning member of Starch's church community, devoting his life to Christ. He'd eventually become a deacon before dying suddenly in his early sixties of a brain aneurysm. His funeral was well-attended. His three children had nothing but kind things to say about their old man.

Ted fell to his knees, holding his stomach and crying loudly. For him, the future only extended ahead of him in seconds.

Jon didn't get out of his seat. He lined the revolver up, then pulled the trigger for the third and final time, planting a bullet in Ted Bracken's head.

He didn't leave his seat until the cops showed

up and the sheriff of Starch sat across from him and politely asked if he was ready to go with him back to the station.

Jon nodded and said, "I figure I oughta. Done a bad thing, din't I?"

Jon was arrested, tried, and found easily guilty for the brutal murder of Ted Bracken. Apparently, Cheryl Prine wrote him while he was in jail. She didn't tell anyone what was in the note, but the guard who'd delivered it had a big mouth and curious eyes.

"She said she forgave him, and that she hoped he could forgive himself, and that she wishes him nothing but the best. She included a Bible verse too. Can't 'member which one. Somethin' about Jesus forgiving all sins or somethin'. Either way, it was nice. I bet she was probably thankful to be rid of that Bracken kid. We all know he had a temper."

Orville sighed, hoping that Cheryl had made a decent life for herself away from Ted Bracken. She'd been such a nice and pretty girl, and she deserved better.

He had no idea what had happened to her. Cheryl had moved out of Starch months after Ted's death. She disappeared without a trace. Some folks believed a fib that went around saying she'd changed her name and done a stint in pornography, but Orville thought that was poppycock. Cheryl was too modest and private of a person to display herself in a nudie magazine.

Leaving the bathroom, Orville wondered if he should take an afternoon nap. He'd had a busy day, internally. His brain was working a mile a minute, racing up and down memory lane.

There came a soft knock on the door. It was already swinging open before Orville could finish saying, "Come in," letting him know exactly who was calling on him. Martha Plat was a busybody who lacked boundaries. She'd once barreled in his room while he was on the can just to see if he wanted chocolate or vanilla ice cream for dessert. She was intrusive but in a simple, mindless way.

"Martha didn't realize she was stepping on toes until the boot was flattened," Kojak liked to say.

Wide-hipped and mustached, she was a squat and unassuming woman. She also carried a clipboard with her everywhere, like she was in a hospital instead of a nursing home.

"Mister North, you have a visitor today!" she declared.

"A visitor?" Orville scrunched his wiry brows. "Who?"

Martha smiled. "She said she's an old lady friend of yours!"

Orville almost came uncorked with laughter. "She must be a liar, then! I haven't had a lady friend in—"

"Her name is"—Martha checked her clipboard— "Eunice Lee. I don't know much, Mister North, but I know a desperate woman when I see one . . . and she's just *aching* to see you!"

Martha didn't seem to notice that Orville's face had fallen.

Eunice Lee . . .

It can't be a coincidence.

I have nightmares about Mr. Friendlyman . . . and then Eunice Lee shows up out of nowhere.

Christ. When was the last time I saw her?

He remembered standing by the road, watching her car drive away. He saw her wave from the back window, looking longingly and sadly at him and Griffin Chalk. The spaces beside her, where Catherine and Ed should have been sitting, were hollow voids.

She'd been sixteen. It was a year after everything had happened at The Home. The Lees had tried and failed to make Starch work, but the absence of her siblings was too great a weight, and so, too, was the town's aversion toward the family. Their friends and neighbors acted like they were hexed simply because Eunice had been in The Home . . . and she told the story as it had actually happened when she came out. Everyone thought she was a lunatic.

His thoughts had become jumbled again. Shaking his head and licking his lips, Orville spoke to Martha in a calm tone.

"You're . . . certain that is her name?"

"Why wouldn't it be?" Martha looked flummoxed.

"No. I dunno. I just . . . I haven't seen Eunice in a very long time."

I didn't even know she was still alive.

CHAPTER EIGHT

It was 1954, and Robbie Miller had just killed his parents.

He was eighteen, but he already looked to be in his thirties. With his gaunt face, small mouth, and sharp widow's peak, it was often commented that he was headed toward an early retirement. Even when he'd been in school—that hadn't lasted long—a substitute teacher once mistook him for staff. He didn't act like a kid his age either, further adding to the illusion. While his peers went cruising and played sports, Robbie Miller had but one singular interest which occupied every waking moment of his life.

The desire to kill.

It lingered in him even in infancy.

When he turned seven, he'd told his dad all he wanted was a BB gun. His mother had swiftly forbidden it.

Robbie heard his parents arguing about it through their door. He often liked to army crawl down the hall and listen in on them late at night. Sometimes, they made funny grunting noises. Other times, they told each other things he wasn't supposed to know. Like how Uncle Dave was apparently an "alky," whatever that meant, and that the pastor at their church had been caught "lookin' at boys again."

More often than not, they talked about their son. On this night, his dad was proposing that instead of buying the boy a gun, he'd take him out to the range with his uncle.

"Whatever for?" his mother cawed.

"It'd be good practice for when he's old 'nough to go hunting with us."

"Yech. I don't like the idea of my son shooting and killing innocent little animals. I don't like *you* doing it either, but I can't stop you."

"Come on, Shirley," Dad said. "It's a rite of passage!"

Dad and Uncle Dave hadn't taken Robbie hunting, but that didn't stop him from trying it out himself. He'd checked out a book from the library on trap setting and put its methods to good use in the forest behind their neighborhood.

Using a shoebox, twine, and a stick, he had set a trap in a mossy meadow. The shoebox stood on the nimble, breakable stick, and the twine was tied tight around the wooden shaft. He'd set some deli meat beneath the box, hoping it'd lure in something hungry. Robbie hunkered down in the grass, holding the end of the twine and watching with wet eyes and chapped lips.

He had waited for three hours and nothing happened. When he gave up, he took the meat, chucked it angrily into the woods, then went home pouting.

But he returned to the spot the next day . . . and the day after.

On the fourth day, he used a sliced strawberry, and it pulled in a prize. A furry rabbit hopped over to the fruit, not seeming to notice the box hovering over its head.

Holding the twine, Robbie licked his chops and watched the animal as it nuzzled the fruit around and then began to chow. He was so entranced by it, he almost forgot to yank the stick away from the box and actually trap the beast! At the last minute, he did just that.

He had to be quick because the shoebox was already

moving around, and he knew it'd take the rabbit just one kick to overturn it and escape. He leaped on the box, crushing it beneath him. He could feel the rabbit squirming underneath the compressed cardboard, trapped between Robbie and the spongy ground. The animal's frantic movements sent tingles into Robbie's core.

He struggled on the ground, trapping the rabbit, scooping it, then holding it by its fur. The thing kicked, screeched, and writhed around, battling with the air. Robbie held it out at arm's length, watching its eyes go wide with panic, enjoying its twitching ears, bared teeth, and pedaling legs. Its fur was grainy. The heat coming off of it seemed as if it could burn Robbie's soft fingers.

It was just so exciting.

But what was he supposed to do with it now that he'd caught it?

Robbie Miller considered this for a few moments. In all the time he'd sat outside, poised with the twine, eyes glued on his trap, he hadn't come up with a real plan. Now that the moment had dawned, he wondered if he ought to just let the thing go. It was cruel to hold the animal in stasis, after all.

He licked his lips, then pulled his pocketknife out from near his hip. Using one hand, he opened the blade. It was dull. His mother and father didn't know he even owned a knife. He'd found it at the junkyard while playing with his pals. It was scuffed, rusty, and it squeaked when it opened.

The rabbit seemed to hang still, as if it was aware that there was no use in fighting.

I've never killed nuthin' before, Robbie thought. *Never.*

He considered things . . . then he dropped the creature and watched it scurry off, likely praying thanks to Rabbit Jesus that it lived to hop another day.

That evening, Robbie found a stream and threw the knife into it. He watched the water plonk apart as the blade dived in. The ripples were carried away, whisked down the stream's shaft, then vanishing into its eddies. He stood on the edge, looking through the water and toward its wavering bottom. The knife lay on a path of cobblestones, pebbles, and swaying greens. It would rust beyond repair since no one was ever going to look for it here.

Unless I come back for it.

But he wouldn't. Robbie turned around, kicked at the grass, then ran home. That night, his mom asked him what he'd done with his day.

"Just went 'splorin," Robbie answered. "Watched some rabbits."

"Aw," she'd purred. "I love rabbits!"

"Me too, Mom," he said.

Now, standing over Shirley Miller's cooling, steaming corpse, he felt ashamed. Not about what he'd done to his mother, but ashamed of what he *hadn't* done to that rabbit. At his childish weakness.

Killing, for Robbie Miller, was his true ambition. He could explain it no better than he could the changing tides, or the rustling of the wind, or the way his hair stood on end when he saw a picture of a naked lady. It was just how things were for him. He recalled, with clarity, the nights he'd spent reading books on the human body with a flashlight. When his little collection of hoarded medical books had been discovered, his mother had actually rejoiced, thinking he was taking an interest in medicine, that he'd grow up to be a doctor. She had no clue he'd been pleasuring himself to the black-and-white pictures of upheaved organs, which looked like glistening fruit to him. She had no idea her son closed his eyes after he'd turned his flashlight off and wondered what it would feel like to stick a knife into a squirming human body.

No, rabbits wouldn't do. That's why he'd let it live. Because if he'd killed the rabbit, he may as well have been lying to himself. The rabbit wasn't a person. It didn't have a soul. It had no ambitions or hopes or a future that could be snuffed like a candle. It could only writhe and pant. It could not plead for its life . . . the way Shirley Miller had.

Despite her hopes for him, Robbie had been a terrible student. He got distracted during class, and he picked fights when he was out of it. In the hallways, he was known as a bully. He picked on younger kids, enjoying the power he held over them. He especially enjoyed targeting young girls. The sweeter and more innocent they were, the more he seemed to be drawn toward them. After his first year of high school, he dropped out, and it was decided that his attentions were best suited for manual labor rather than academics. The dream of having a doctor for a son died, and Robbie Miller was sent to purgatory, where he bagged groceries and walked carts of food out to little old ladies' cars.

He was fired after a month when he was found in the women's bathroom with a screaming child. The little girl claimed that she'd left the stall to find him standing there, smiling at her like a clown. He insisted he had just gotten distracted and didn't realize he'd walked into the wrong restroom and that there had been nothing funny happening. No one was convinced, but there was also nothing anyone could do about it. Robbie was fired, no charges were pressed, and with great disappointment, his father told him they'd find him another job.

They never did.

Word had spread, and Robbie Miller was blacklisted.

So, while his mother and father worked, Robbie stayed home. And there, he dreamed.

He dreamed about cutting that little girl up the way he'd wanted to. He'd been hoping to catch her off guard, haul her into the stall, and whittle her like wood with the switchblade he kept in his pocket. But she'd screamed the moment she saw him, and then he'd had to play damage control.

Though the damage was done.

When people spotted Robbie, they turned their gaze away. Some even crossed the street to avoid him.

His parents, too, didn't seem to know what to do with him. They avoided any deep conversation, instead only talking with him about the weather and football, which he and his father both followed religiously.

Years passed. Eventually, Robbie was isolated totally from his community. He spent most of his time in his room, purposefully sweltering in the summer days and freezing in the cold ones.

Then, finally, the day had come. He woke up early, which was a rare occurrence for lazy Robbie Miller. Stretching, he looked toward his foggy window and saw that it was raining. Lightning crackled, illuminating the dark territory outside of his house. Standing, he walked over to the window and gazed out, his face void of expression, his eyes deep and red, his lips closed tight over his chunky teeth. Another camera flash of lightning showed the lawn and the road. Across the way, he saw the front of the neighbor's house. They'd already started decorating for Halloween despite the holiday being weeks away. Dangling from a tree branch hung a scarecrow secured by a gnarled noose. The wind battered the straw-stuffed body around, causing its limbs to sway and its head to tilt. In the darkness and the harsh weather, it looked like an actual human corpse.

That's what I need to do, Robbie thought. *I need to decorate the house.*

He turned and marched out of his room. He checked the wall clock in the hallway and saw it was three in the morning. He'd only gotten four hours of sleep. When he went by his parents' room, he could hear them both snoring loudly.

Not caring to be quiet, Robbie stalked down the stairs and toward the kitchen.

Wind buffeted the house, causing it to creak and whistle. Rain ran musical fingers over the roof.

Robbie slid into the kitchen and opened the fridge. He took out a carton of milk, popped the top, then chugged it. He didn't mind the white stream that slipped out of the side of his mouth and traveled down his chin. He put the milk back, leaving it open. He slammed the door closed loudly. It sounded like a gunshot. Even over the thunder, he bet that the neighbors heard it.

Upstairs, he heard rustling. He'd roused someone. *Good.*

Robbie opened the drawers and rootled through them. He inspected each implement before returning it. First, he studied a meat tenderizer; next, a steak knife, a wine opener with a corkscrew, and a can opener with sharp blades. By the time his father was in the kitchen, Robbie had made his choice.

"Son, what are you doing?" Garrett Miller asked. He was a fat, balding man with a thick, black mustache. His brow was constantly crinkled, and his nose looked like an expanding balloon whenever he breathed. Wearing his nightclothes, he looked like a character from a cartoon.

Saying nothing, Robbie turned, holding his tool behind his back.

"Your mother and I have work in the morning." Garrett sighed. "Please, go to bed—"

Robbie struck, driving a fist into his father's belly. The older man lurched backward, clutching himself and snorting with surprise. Robbie hit him again, aiming his punch higher. He felt his fist connect with the man's chin, forcing his jaws shut over his tongue. There was a spurt of blood followed by a sizzling cry.

Garrett fell over, hitting the ground with a house-shaking *thud*.

Robbie hopped onto him, pinning him to the floor.

"R-Rob—" Garrett tried to speak around the pain.

Saying nothing, Robbie used the wine opener to slice Garrett's throat open.

It was the first time he'd killed a human being, and it was almost too easy. He'd expected the implement to get snagged on a tendon or catch against Garrett's windpipe. He'd expected the wound to be messier, but the corkscrew of the wine opener cut a clean path through Garrett Miller's throat meat. Then there was a geyser of hot blood, which painted Robbie's face.

Robbie felt his lips curl into an involuntary smile.

He slashed the wine opener back across Garrett's gaping throat, pushing it in deeper, *hoping* to cause more of a mess.

Garrett threw a fist up and caught Robbie in the side. He yelped and leaped away, shocked by the old man's gusto.

Garrett turned over and began to crawl, dragging his legs behind him as if Robbie had broken them.

On his hands and knees, Robbie scuttled after him. Viciously, he began to carve into Garrett's back.

"No!" the old man wheezed. The word came out wet and ghastly, as if Garrett was trying to speak underwater.

Robbie clutched at the thin halo of hair around the back of his dad's skull. He pulled, lifting his head back. It was as if he'd opened a tap inside Garrett's throat. Blood *shot* out of his throat in a gulping rush. It spattered across the floor and then crawled upward, leaving a red zigzag pattern up the wall.

Garrett groaned pathetically.

Robbie reached around and inserted the corkscrew of the wine opener into the edge of the original gash. He forced it in, straining and grunting as he worked, then he tore it down and around Garrett's throat, widening the already fatal wound. More blood leaped from him. It filled Robbie's palm the way his ejaculate did when he finished masturbating. Buttery and warm, the blood made Robbie's skin dance and his prick harden.

Garrett bleated sheepishly, then rattled like a snake.

Robbie dropped his father's head, leaving the wine opener lodged in his throat. Standing, the murderer looked at his hands. They were so red he wondered if he'd ever get the color out. Not that he wanted to. He'd never felt so good in all his short life. Emotions were fleeting for Robbie, but they came on strong. It was why he struggled to control himself at the grocery store when he caught sight of the little girl entering the bathroom unsupervised. It was what had compelled him to release the rabbit. Joy and happiness were strangers to him, and so, too, were guilt and shame. Looking at his father's wet corpse, he felt only one thing. Elation.

You did it, Robbie. You actually did it.

But his job wasn't finished. He couldn't rest on his laurels when there was still work to be done.

He went back to the kitchen drawers and rifled through them, picking up each tool and investigating it with his fingers. Each implement had been used and reused by his mother until they were dulled. She didn't like to replace anything until they were in dire need. Even shoes were worn until the soles flapped like dog ears and his toes were poking through holes. The wine opener was relatively new, only because the last one had broken.

He picked out a paring knife and studied it, then shook his head and returned it to the drawer. He reappraised the meat tenderizer with a sigh. Then he felt his brain spark with inspiration. Loudly, he slammed the drawer closed and raced out the front door and into the night. Instantly, Robbie was battered with harsh winds and rain. The storm was curled around his house like a boa, tightening and constricting in squirmy, pulsating thrusts.

Picking his way around the house, Robbie sprinted toward the gardening shed. There'd been a robbery two years back, and since then, Garrett had secured the doors closed with a padlock. Rather than run back for the keys, Robbie snuck behind the shed and squatted. Using his fingers, he pried a loose plank aside, exposing a three-foot-high hole in the shed's rear, like a wooden anus. Snickering, Robbie army crawled through the hole. A snaggletoothed bit of wood grabbed his hip, causing a quick blurt of pain. Ignoring it, Robbie wiggled in.

The rain sounds were somehow louder inside the narrow, crowded shed. Robbie squinted, waiting for his eyes to adjust to the darkness. When they didn't, he shrugged and groped around until he found what he wanted.

He struggled through the hole again. By the time he was walking back into his home, Robbie was as filthy as an exhumed body. His face was streaked in crud and mud, and his hands were still dirty with blood. The rain had done little to wash away his father's death.

Stalking up the stairs, Robbie used his fingers to leave streaks up the wallpaper and over the framed pictures of his family.

He felt as if he was floating toward his parents' room.

Turning the knob, he hoped his mother wouldn't

surprise him. Perhaps she'd heard the ruckus downstairs and was brandishing a gun he didn't know they owned.

No. She was asleep. Sound asleep.

Robbie walked into the room, holding the hedge clippers by their stiff handles. The blades were rusty, but their tips were sharp. Rolling his tongue around his mouth, he walked over to his mother's side of the bed, where she loudly snoozed. Her hair was in curlers, and her nightgown was loose, exposing one of her bulbous, veiny breasts.

"Mom?" Robbie asked in a timid voice.

She turned over, honked, then snuffled.

Robbie raised the hedge clippers over his head, keeping them held in an X shape.

"Mother?" he asked in a louder tone.

"Huh?" She blinked. "Garrett . . . is that . . ."

"I hate you, Mommy!" Robbie whispered.

Shirley Miller jerked awake with a scream.

The blades swished through the air.

When he was done, his mother was a battleground. Blood covered the walls. Her face had been dismantled. Long flags of tattered flesh hung from her grinning skull. He'd managed to remove her right breast, which now lay on the floor, looking like a sand dune on the crimson-stained carpet. He'd cut her from groin to gullet and used his hands to crack her rib cage wide open. A tangled net of pulped organs stewed in the middle of the gorge. Steam rose from the corpse, heating the room like coal in a sauna.

Robbie stumbled back, leaving the clippers lodged in her naked thigh. The leg led to a stump. He'd forgotten where he'd tossed the foot after it had been removed.

The storm continued to rage outside. Robbie settled down in his mom's rocking chair, where she sat whenever the urge to knit struck her. Gently, he tilted back and forth, studying the body with wet eyes.

This was good, Robbie. It was good.

But you're destined for great *things.*

Children. All the little children. Innocent little children. You must do this to children.

The voice in his head didn't sound like his. It switched tone and tempo, going from high-pitched to baritone between words. Tensely, Robbie rubbed his sticky hands together.

"Who are you?" Robbie asked the empty room.

There was no answer.

He tried to return his attention back to his work. He was sure the police would find him soon, sitting by his mother's carcass. If they didn't, he'd blow his brains out.

Don't do that, Robbie!

Why waste such hard work by quitting early?

"Who is that?" Robbie demanded.

He heard a low chortle. A mean laugh that drew to mind images of flittering bats and creeping spiders.

In the corner, Robbie spotted a figure.

Gasping, he leaped off the chair and backed toward the window.

The figure stepped forward.

Lightning flickered, giving Robbie a brief glimpse of the intruder.

It was a man with a long, white, pale face. His lower teeth jutted out like they'd been broken, and his top gums were blackened, each tooth a yellow nub peeking out of the rotten flesh like groundhogs from their burrows.

The man had no eyes. The flesh above his nose was smooth and flat. On one side, his hair was long and black, greasy like seaweed. On the other, he was bald. Little holes dotted his scalp, making it look like he'd fused a honeycomb to his head and painted it snow-white.

His arms were too long. This somehow frightened Robbie more than the man's deformed face, nasty mouth, or his nakedness. His elongated arms bore long fingers, each one with too many joints and knuckles and ending in a smooth, reptilian pad.

His legs were short and stubby as if both thighs had been removed. He didn't have knees. His genitals hung heavily from his pelvis. Long and thick, the penis ended in twin heads, mashed together and belted with a strained strip of foreskin.

"Wh-who are you?" Robbie asked. Internally, he wondered *what* this thing was.

"I'm . . . Mr. Friendlyman . . . and I love you . . ."

It smiled, and the sight was so ghastly that Robbie about lost control of his bowels. His heart froze, and his throat tightened. Robbie hugged himself and rocked in place.

"Don't . . . be . . . afraid . . ." the creature said. Each word was spoken in a different voice. *"I'm . . . friendly . . ."*

Robbie glanced toward the door. He could dash around the creature and bolt down the hall, but he didn't want to shorten the distance between himself and this thing. He worried that its too-long arms would snake out and grab him.

"You ain't real," Robbie said. "Yer jus' a—"

"A . . . bad . . . dream?" It sounded like there was a crowd of people speaking through the creature's mouth.

"Y-yes." Robbie nodded. "Yer jus' a nightmare. I'm gonna close my eyes, and when I open them . . . you'll be—"

The creature changed shape. It happened in a blink. Suddenly, he was now a woman. Tall and slender, naked as well. She was beautiful, with teacup breasts and a neat nest of fur between her legs. Her hair was short and red, and her body was speckled with brown freckles. She smiled, showing Robbie a row of pearly teeth.

If it wasn't for her hands, she'd have stirred his libido. But once he saw what was at the ends of her wrists, Robbie felt another wave of nausea hit him.

The left hand was split down the middle. Long, green vines hung from the wound, dangling down to the floor. The right hand was totally gone, and the stump had been stuffed with bright-red roses. Blood congealed around the stems.

The woman stepped toward him, and she moved strangely. Almost as if her shapely legs were secretly broken.

"N-no!" Robbie squawked. "Don't come near me!"

The creature changed again. Now, he was an elderly man with a baby's head on his shoulders. Naked, but his penis had somehow been turned inside out. Long tubes and strips of torn skin jangled between his hairy thighs, leaving greasy stains.

"We . . . want . . . you . . . to . . . be . . . a . . . part . . . of . . . this . . . house . . ."

He didn't know what that meant. He didn't *want* to know.

Robbie spun around and fought to pry the window open. Rain spun through the room, blown in by the howling wind.

He looked over his shoulder.

The shape-shifting was happening in rapid strokes. There was a baboon's head, then a dog's, then a crying woman's, then a horse's skull decorated with stitched leather, then the whole creature was made from clay. It was as if Robbie was looking at a tornado of nightmares. As if every monster that every child had ever feared was now trying to occupy the space inhabited by Mr.

Friendlyman.

Robbie threw himself through the window, not caring when he scrabbled down the roof and fell over the edge. With a weak cry, he plummeted, hitting the ground with a hot whoosh of air. Coughing, Robbie struggled up to his feet. Muddied and bloodied, he backed away from the house, worrying that the creature—Mr. Friendlyman—was going to come after him.

He saw the creature. It stood at the window, smiling down at him. The teeth seemed to glow in the dark, each one burning with amber fire. Its eyes were now spotlights, beaming through the storm and down to the lawn.

Robbie turned and ran, vowing never to return to the house at the end of Sycamore Lane for as long as he lived.

CHAPTER NINE

Eloise dropped Griffin off at his house, then promised to be back shortly.

"Knowing you, the fridge isn't stocked," she explained. They sat side by side in the car parked on the driveway.

Hurt, Griffin bit his lower lip. "There's microwavable stuff."

Eloise gave him a scolding glance. It was bizarre seeing such a motherly look on his daughter's face. He almost wanted to remind her that not long ago, he'd been changing her diapers and wiping her runny nose. The words froze in his throat.

"It's no wonder this thing took you out if all you're eating is Hungry Man meals, or whatever they're called."

"It's better than nothing."

"You never learned to cook after Mom—"

"Mom did all the cooking," Griffin said.

Eloise looked cross, then sad, then her expression froze. "Boris and I share those responsibilities, you know."

"Mmmmph."

"It's not, like, *wrong* for a man to learn how to cook."

"I'm not an invalid, you know."

"No, but I'll bet Missus Stewart still does your laundry."

Griffin said nothing. Anna Stewart had offered to help him around the house shortly after Prudence died.

He'd politely declined, but she'd insisted, telling him that she had nothing better to do since her kids were all grown and had families of their own. Now, he left his dirties in a laundry basket by the back door, which she came over and grabbed every Tuesday. By Wednesday morning, his clothes were returned to him. Washed, folded, and even ironed! They barely spoke to each other, but she tended to his clothes.

"What'll happen when Missus Stewart dies?" Eloise pressed. "You *have* a washer and dryer, Dad."

Griffin felt like crying. His face was hot, and his guts churned.

"Do you need help getting out—"

"I'm not an invalid," he repeated before lurching out of the car and marching up the steps to his house. After entering and slamming the front door shut, he heard the car slink away.

You shouldn't be yelling at her. She's just trying to help.

Griffin shook his head. He didn't like being treated like a child. Yet he didn't want to fend for himself the way his daughter expected. He walked into his kitchen and looked through the fridge. It was barely stocked. The freezer, on the other hand, was crammed with microwavable meals. Pizzas, Salisbury steaks, and mac-and-cheese bowls.

You eat like shit. You live like shit.

He closed the freezer door, then glanced toward the back door, which led to the porch. His soggy drawers and shirts were crammed into the laundry basket, waiting for Anna Stewart's feminine touch.

Rat bastard piece of shit old man what an embarrassment goddamn I hate you.

He went back out the front door and sat in his rocking chair. Slowly, Griffin began to cry. That only made him feel worse. He'd been told a few times that crying was supposed to bring relief—especially after Prudence had passed—but he'd only ever felt embarrassed when he sprang a leak. Struggling to calm himself, he looked across the road and toward the sloping, rolling Ozark Hills.

A raspy breath of wind rustled through the trees.

He realized he'd forgotten what month it was.

April, you fool.

April showers bring May flowers.

It rained last night. He'd heard it on the way to the hospital, slapping the sides and roof of the ambulance.

It'll rain again tonight. You can feel it in the air.

From inside his house, he heard chatter. It startled him before he realized that it was the television. Although he hadn't remembered it being turned on.

Steadily, achingly, Griffin got to his feet and walked back into his house. In the living room, the TV blared, casting blue light across the carpet. Smacking his lips, he searched around for the remote.

"Hey! Hey, Griffin!" the TV said, surprising him again.

Griffin stood uncomfortably, watching the screen.

A little girl was standing in front of a playground. Behind her, children rushed around in mad circles. They swung violently from the monkey bars and zipped gaily down the slides. The playground looked brand new, as if it had only been constructed the day before this footage was taken. The young girl had pigtails, wore overalls, and she was missing her front teeth.

"Hey! Hey, Griffin! Why don't you play with us?"

Griffin shook his head. "You aren't real."

The girl closed her mouth, then opened it again. Somehow, she now had all her teeth, only they were bigger than they should have been. It looked as if her adult teeth had grown *around* her baby teeth. She began to walk toward the camera, slowly filling the screen.

He noticed more strange details.

While most of the kids were hanging from the monkey bars by their hands or legs, one kid was suspended from a rope, which was cinched snuggly around his skinny neck. He swayed as kids bumped against him, crawling over the top and bottom of the playset.

Griffin also realized that it was nighttime in the video. The moon was glowing above the playground, casting iridescent light upon the scrambling, howling, happy children.

This isn't real, Griffin thought. *I'm not actually watching this. I'm just sleeping. I nodded off on the porch, and now I'm having a bad dream.*

He looked around again for the remote, dismayed not to see it in its usual place on the sofa cushion.

"Hey, Griffin," the young girl said, drawing his attention back to the screen. *"Did you know I'm dead?"* She said it matter-of-factly, as if she was simply telling him something she'd learned at school that day.

She stepped closer toward the camera until all that could be seen was her face.

"I died in The Home. You know what happens to people who die in The Home, Griffin? We become a part of him. Of Mr. Friendlyman. We are ourselves, but we are also him. Does that make sense?"

Griffin shook his head.

"Robbie Miller is in here too. He's a part of us. As well as Ed and Catherine Lee. When they died . . . they didn't go to Heaven. You don't go to Heaven when you die in The Home. So . . . we have to make our own Heaven." Her smile almost broke her face. *"And Heaven is so fun! We've got everything we could ever want here! Candy . . . ice cream . . . puppy dogs . . . and Mr. Friendlyman lets us have all the fun we want. All the fun we can handle! So much fun, it's comin' out our ears!"*

She began to laugh. It was a desperate, pleading

sound.

"I don't . . . I don't understand!" Griffin brayed.

"Look how much fun we're having!"

The girl stepped aside.

The playground was littered with dead children. Each one had been slashed and mutilated. They lay like discarded toys on the peat moss.

Standing in the middle of the body farm was Robbie Miller. His thin lips were peeled back, exposing his yellowed teeth. He looked exactly how Griffin remembered him.

Robbie held up a switchblade knife. It shimmered in the moonlight.

A second face grew out of the side of Robbie's head. It was smiling and cartoonish, with jagged, broken-glass teeth and eyes the size of peaches. The face was there and then gone, sinking back into Robbie's pale flesh.

"Look how much fun you could be having, Griffin," Robbie said in his own voice before a chorus spoke with his mouth: *"if . . . you . . . came . . . back . . . to . . . The Home!"*

The door clattered open, startling Griffin. He expected to turn and see Robbie Miller charging into the house. Instead, it was his daughter. Eloise had returned with the groceries. Holding them in both arms, she huffed as she walked.

"What's up, Dad?" she asked.

"I was—" He saw that the TV was black. His remote was back on the cushion where it belonged. "I was just looking through the TV. Nothin' good on. Here, need help?"

"No, Dad. Please, sit down and get some rest, okay?"

"O-okay," Griffin said, fighting a frightened stammer.

"Spaghetti or lasagna?" Eloise asked as she made

her way into the kitchen.

Griffin looked back at the TV. He couldn't be so sure that it wouldn't turn back on and show him new horrors. He wondered if he ought to unplug it.

"Dad?"

Griffin shook his head. "Spaghetti sounds nice."

"I was hoping you'd say that."

CHAPTER TEN

Eunice didn't look like her old self, and Orville was surprised that he was disappointed by this. Last he'd seen her, she'd been sixteen and beautiful, with long, blonde hair and a light dusting of freckles. She'd had coltish legs, and her cheeks had been cherubic. She'd been springy, fairylike, and energetic. Even after what they'd experienced in The Home, she'd still been bright-eyed and bushy-tailed.

Now, she looked like she could have been his sister. Her scalp was balding, and her hair was dirty-white. She'd turned cumbersome and saggy, and her face was crushed with wrinkles. And yet her eyes were still youthful and twinkling. Some things changed; others stayed the same.

And who am I, anyway, to judge her for daring to age? Just look at me! Orville thought ruefully, remembering his own wrinkled face and feeling the weight of his belly.

Eunice was sitting at one of the circular tables in the commons room. Kojak's puzzle was left forgotten, and the old man was nowhere to be seen. Sitting by the TV was a small crowd of elders, one of whom was loudly yelling at the anchor as if the news was *his* fault.

"Eunice?" Orville asked.

"Aw, Orville!" She was up on her feet. Using a walker, she came toward him. As she approached, he felt like turning and running. Half of him was delighted to see her and hoped they could catch up. The other

108

half was terrified, knowing that she was back because of Mr. Friendlyman. Because of Robbie Miller.

Embarrassingly, Orville also remembered the last thing he'd done with her the day before she and her family left Starch. To this day, Eunice Lee was the only woman he'd slept with.

He'd tried before with others, but it was as if making love to Eunice had put a curse on him.

Now that you've had me . . . no one else will do.

Licking his chapped lips, Orville went to meet her. Much to his own astonishment, he wrapped her in a hug and planted a quick kiss on her brow. She giggled girlishly.

He helped her back into her seat, then sat across from her.

"How are they treating you here?" Eunice asked.

"Oh, fine. Fine. It's a nice place. Good staff. Decent food."

"Don't lie."

"Okay. The food ain't great." Orville cracked a smile.

"I could always tell when you were lying. Both of you. You and Griffin. I think maybe it had something to do with what we did. You ever think that? That we've been . . . bonded?"

So, she was going to jump right into it. Orville released a long, cold shudder. "I don't know. I spent a while trying to forget . . . then I spent too long trying to remember . . . then I tried to forget all over again."

Eunice nodded. "I felt it when Griffin's wife died. I swear it. I . . . I knew something was wrong all day. Then I saw his daughter's post on Facebook—she added me even though she has no clue who I am. Kids these days, right? Anyways . . . I saw the post and knew why I'd felt so bad. Like something had been cut out of me. It was the same way I felt after I moved out of Starch. When I realized I'd never be able to go into Ed's room to remember what he was like. There just wasn't a room that smelled like him in that new house. I hated it. I hated not having to beg my sister to get out of the bathroom so I could get ready for school too. I hated not getting wet willies from my annoying brother. I hated the way my parents didn't want to talk about it . . . but I also don't blame them."

"What happened to your parents?" Orville found himself asking.

"You remember where I moved?"

"No. I remember it being a city—"

"We first went to Kansas City. But it was still too close to Starch for Mom to be happy. So, after only a year there, we packed up and went all the way to Portland, Oregon."

"Oh."

"And then I went to New York for school, but I never graduated because my husband got me pregnant before he was my husband. Bit of a scandal there, but people have all forgotten now. I bet if you even brought my name up to my worst gossipers, they'd look confused."

"But what happened to your parents?" Orville asked again, realizing he wasn't at all ready to hear about her marriage and child

"They divorced in the seventies. You know, when divorce was slightly more acceptable. I think they would've called it quits after my siblings died if they could have. They were expected to be strong for me, I guess. I wish they didn't have to be. Anyways, Mom died in Florida. She had a stroke she never recovered from. Dad died of lung cancer. You never really met him, but he was a two-packer. Every day, I remember him screwing his first cigarette into his mouth and snapping his lighter open after his morning coffee. I thought he looked cool when I was a kid. As a grown-up, sitting by his hospital bed . . . Well, the surgeon general does his job, but I don't think he does it well. It's sad seeing someone die of tar and nicotine." Eunice sighed. She'd been talking a mile a minute. "I moved on with my life. Became a wife, then a mother . . . then a divorcee."

Orville couldn't help but admit he was somehow thankful to hear the fella had split. Not that he thought he had any lingering chance with Eunice.

"What happened, if I can ask?"

"You can. He was a hothead. I liked his spirit. A poet and a scholar, you know? We met at a coffee shop I was working at. He came in almost every day to work on a play he was writing that he never finished. Struck up a conversation with him and found him fascinating, in the way only a young girl can find a young man fascinating. Nowadays, I'd probably have been annoyed by him. He was one of those 'artist' types who was obsessed with his image. He worried constantly about finding a balance between publishing a lot and publishing only a little. Ends up . . . he published nothing at all. He lives in Vegas now, where I'm sure he's gambling away a lot of money and enjoying the heat. He was like a lizard when it was sunny out. Anyways, I don't hate him, but I wish I'd waited for Mister Right. Or Missus—I missed out by not experimenting!"

They both chuckled.

"He hated your book," Eunice added.

Orville gulped. "He read it?"

"I read all of them. Collected them the moment they started hitting the shelves. Eventually, he said he wanted to know what the big fuss was about. I gave him one, and he came back the next day and called it 'pulp trash.' I joked that you should put that on the cover. He didn't think it was a funny joke, but I did."

"Depending on the book, I might agree with him."

Eunice snickered. "I thought they were nice. Except

that horror one. Reminded me too much of— Well."

"I don't like that one either." Orville looked again at his hands. "So . . . you got married and had a kid?"

"You ever get married?" Eunice asked.

Orville had a feeling she didn't want to talk about being a mother yet. She'd suddenly turned evasive.

"No," Orville admitted. "No. I never found Missus Right either. Guess Griffin was the lucky one. I never kept in touch, but . . . I heard Prudence was a peach."

"I heard the same thing. In fact, I visited her grave the other day. Poor woman."

"I haven't been."

"You will," Eunice said. Orville didn't know what she meant by that. A small chill skittered up his back.

"So, what brings you back to Starch?" Orville asked.

Eunice bit her lower lip. "I think you know."

"I do. I saw him."

"A projection. He can't leave The Home."

Orville cocked his head. "How do you—"

"I learned a lot recently. I'll tell you everything, of course, but I think Griffin ought to be there for it."

Orville pursed his lips. "Eunice . . . I heard there was a murder on Sycamore last night."

"There was," she stated. "Three victims. A young girl and her parents. They were . . ."

Orville shuddered. "So, it has started again, has it?"

"Yes."

"And you know how to stop it, don't you?"

"I have an idea," Eunice said. "It's an ugly idea . . . but it might work."

"Tell me."

"Not without Griffin."

Orville nodded. "Eunice, did you sleep with him too?" He couldn't believe he'd asked it.

She shook her head and reached across the table. Taking his hands, she held eye contact. "No, Orville."

"I shouldn't have said anything. I don't know why that was . . . important to me. It shouldn't be."

"But it was. So I'm glad you asked."

"I know he liked you back then. You told me once that you were just friends, but I don't think I ever really believed you."

"That was before he met Prudence. And that was after I moved. No, Orville. Griffin's had his great love. I missed out on mine, if such a thing existed. I'm now guessing that I was yours?"

"Yes."

"That's . . ." She held her face still. "It's flattering. And beautiful. And a little scary. And very hopeless."

"I was never with anyone else," Orville admitted.

"I wish you had been." Eunice nodded. "I honestly do."

Orville felt a tear crawl down his face. He released her hands and wiped his cheeks with his palms. "Sorry. I'm so embarrassed."

"Don't be. Really. I'm sorry things didn't happen the way you wanted."

"It isn't your fault."

"No. But still."

"Still."

Orville looked toward the geezers surrounding the TV. He worried they were listening in.

"Do you want to go somewhere else?" she asked, looking at her wristwatch.

"I think so."

"Then we will."

Together, Eunice and Orville left the commons room and went out the back of the building. There, they steadily and slowly waded through the garden until they found a white gazebo that overlooked the lake.

"This place is beautiful," Eunice said. "Most old folks' places are stuffy and crowded."

"Yeah. I lucked out," Orville said with a smirk.

"You still writing?"

"No. I gave that up a while back. I'm happy with what I did. Didn't feel like I had any more stories to tell."

"We'll see about that," Eunice said cryptically.

"I do wish you could tell me what's happening," Orville said. "How'd he come back?"

"I don't think he ever left," Eunice said. "I think it just took Mr. Friendlyman and Mr. Miller some time to work out their issues and figure out how to kill together. You understand?"

"As much as I can."

"They're not two separate beings anymore, Orville. They're *one* . . ." Her voice trailed off. "But we'll discuss that with Griffin."

"When are we going to see him?"

"He's in town. He never left," Eunice said.

"I don't know why I never reached out to him. Maybe I was waiting for him to reach out to *me*."

Eunice looked at her watch again. "There's a dock, isn't there?"

"Yes. Sometimes, old-timers fish off it. But they have to be supervised. Last thing this place needs is a geezer taking a drink."

"Okay."

"Why?"

"Let's go to it," she said.

"We'll need to let staff know—"

"I'd rather we didn't." Her voice was firm.

"Okay."

"I mean, you won't fall, will you?"

"I won't." He pointed to her walker. "You might."

"Oh, this? Ah, I don't really need it." Eunice shook her head. "Helps when I get a li'l vertigo, though. Happens when I least expect it."

114

"Isn't that how it goes?"

"How's your health, Orville?"

"I'm on the sunny side of shitty. Things could be better, but I expect them to be worse by the time I hit eighty. I mean, I struggle a bit. The ol' memory machine doesn't always work the way I want it to. Sometimes we fight."

"I hear you. Look at this." She held out her hand. It shook. "See? Didn't used to do that!"

"I get tired easily," Orville added. "Sleep early. Except for—Well. Last night, I had a nightmare about Mr. Friendlyman. Now I think it was a dream, but it felt real. You said he projected it to me, huh?"

"Yes. He's been doing the same to me. You're prying for information, aren't you?"

"A little."

"Patience is a virtue."

"I'm an old man, Eunice. I've got no patience left."

"Walk me to the dock."

"Okay, Eunice," he said.

He helped her up to her feet and guided her down the footpath toward the dock. It was small and recently repaired, so no one had to worry about the old men who fished off of it. The water was less than calm. With the encroaching rain and blustery wind, the lake seemed to be tilting back and forth as if it was posed atop a rocking chair.

"You know what, Eunice?" Orville asked.

"Hmm?"

"It's a beautiful day. After last night, I'm surprised to be able to appreciate it. But it's just beautiful out, isn't it? And I can feel the rain coming. I know the rain is supposed to bother old folks, but it never has me. I enjoy it. The sound of it relaxes me. Makes me feel like a kid again. When I was young, I used to sit by the window in our living room and I'd read while the rain droned outside."

They'd walked onto the dock, taking each step carefully. The waves rocked them, but only slightly. Still, Orville secured his grip on Eunice, worrying she'd tip over the edge if they weren't careful.

"Hmm." She looked again at her watch.

"Eunice, dear?"

"Yes?"

"What are we waiting for?"

Eunice looked out over the lake, studying the waves. "Our getaway."

"What do you mean?"

"I'm taking you away from here. They wouldn't approve of any of the things we have to do, so it's best we simply vanish."

She could be evasive sometimes, but she could also be so startlingly upfront that it felt as if she was playing a joke on him.

"Are you being serious?" Orville asked.

"Yes. Here he comes . . . right on time."

Orville followed her gaze. He caught sight of a motorboat speeding toward them. Manning the vehicle was a young man in a tank top with curly brown hair. He was wearing sunglasses and a backward ballcap. The closer the boat got, the more alarmed Orville became.

"Eunice, who is this young man?" Orville asked. "He's got *tattoos!*"

Eunice laughed.

"Is this your . . . son?"

"Good heavens, no. My child died, Orville."

This news dropped down on him like a hammer. "Oh, I'm so sorry, Eunice."

"We'll talk about it later. You're going to have to help me onto the boat."

"We can't *run away*."

"We can and we are."

"Oh God!" Orville marveled.

The boat rocked toward the dock, freezing beside them. The young man smiled and waved.

"C'mon, Orville, you dolt! Help me!" Eunice spurred him on.

Against his own will, Orville found himself helping the old lady onto the motorboat. After she was aboard, he folded up her walker and passed it to her.

The boat was a sleek vehicle with flames drawn on the sides and plenty of seats. The driver was, Orville guessed, in his twenties. He was handsome, but he'd ruined his face and arms with tattoos. He had a phoenix burning on one cheek and a skull and crossbones on the other.

"Jesus!" Orville muttered, glancing up toward The Old Folks' Home. No one was running down to stop them. It seemed as if no one even noticed that Orville was being abducted.

Not abducted. You can still choose to walk away. What's Eunice gonna do? Hold you at gunpoint?

Orville sighed and climbed onto the boat.

"Hey, dude!" the young man said. "I'm yer captain!"

"I'm sure you are," Orville mumbled.

"Russell Carver. Good ta meet ya!" The man smiled, then kicked the boat away from the dock. They tore through the lake, leaving Orville's home and friends in its wake.

He looked over to Eunice, who was smiling and had her head tipped over the side of the boat. Like a dog hanging from a car window, she seemed to be enjoying the wind that caressed her and threw her thinning hair into a tizzy.

"Where are we going?" Orville asked over the chopping wind and slapping waves.

"Away!" Eunice said.

He looked hopelessly toward Russell, who was laughing to himself.

"Who are you?" Orville cried.

"I told you . . . name's Russell Carver."

"No. I mean . . . *who* are you?"

Russell seemed flummoxed.

"How do you know Eunice?" Orville demanded.

"Who's that?"

Frustrated, Orville pointed to the old lady.

"Oh. Forgot her name. I dunno her at all. I work at the marina. Business was slow as shit today. She came in and told me she'd pay me two hundred bucks just to grab her and you from that dock. I'm supposed to take you back to the marina on the other side of the lake, then she's givin' me another two hundred to drive you to some other guy's place."

Orville looked back toward Eunice, wondering what her plan was.

"Hey, four hundred bucks just to cart y'all around? That's more than I make in a day!"

Russell was, Orville realized, too stupid to know that he was breaking some laws by taking an old man away from his residence without notifying the staff.

Scrutinizing her, Orville wondered why Eunice was spending so much money on their escape. And where did the money come from? Four hundred bucks may not have been that big a deal in the scheme of things, but an Uber would've cost about twenty dollars. Besides, old people such as themselves were often stingy with their money.

She's not leaving anything to chance, Orville thought.

CHAPTER ELEVEN

Robbie Miller ran away from Starch the night he killed his parents.

He sat in the passenger seat of a flatbed truck, holding his hands together and praying that if he did get caught, they wouldn't take him back to Sycamore Lane. For some reason, he believed that the cops would do that. They'd march him right back to the front door, knock, and wait for that . . . thing . . . to answer.

Robbie barely believed that what he'd seen had actually happened. It had been a few days since he'd seen the creature in his parents' room, and still, the cold, nightmarish feeling hadn't left him. It lingered like a bad smell, corroding his nerves and frying his brain like meat on a skillet.

Robbie had done his best to clean up. After running out of Sycamore, he had hightailed it into the hills. There, he slept on leaves and rootled around for grub. He found a private pond and took a bath, scrubbing the crusty blood out from beneath his fingernails and clearing the mud from his face. Despite this, Robbie still stank. The undercurrent of blood was there, steamy and sneaky beneath the tart scent of pond water and sweat.

He had come out to the road hoping to hitch a ride out of Missouri. Thankfully, the first man who stopped for him was headed into Arkansas. It wasn't far, but it was far enough for the moment.

"I appreciate you," Robbie said while climbing into the cab. He had to play nicely, or else he wouldn't get

119

anywhere.

"No problem at all," the old man replied. He looked like a stereotypical farmer, with a ratty ballcap, shredded overalls, and a stark farmer's tan. Old, white, and brittle, the man would have made an easy target. Robbie couldn't help but muse that the man was too trusting.

If he'd had a knife with him, Robbie would have pounced on the geezer and cut his throat. But then he reconsidered. What use was a stolen car if there was blood all over the windshield? Besides, he hadn't brought any weapons with him. He'd made such a hasty retreat from his home, after all.

So Robbie sat as close to the open window as he could, hoping the breeze seeping through the car would curtail his odors.

"Where you headed, son?" the old man asked.

Robbie stated a practiced lie: "I'm trying to see my sweetheart. She lives all the way clear on the other side of Arkansas. Her parents moved her out there, and I've been missin' her somethin' awful."

The old man smirked. "Young love, huh? Lemme ask ya somethin', son. Yer parents know yer runnin' out this way?"

Robbie nodded. "I left a note tacked to the fridge."

"Well, God love ya fer it, but you oughta reconsider, I'd say. I mean, what if she's moved on to 'nother feller?"

Robbie smiled. The old man had a charming way of talking. Much to Robbie's surprise, he was glad he didn't have an opportunity to kill the geezer.

"She won't," Robbie said. "She said she'd be loyal ta me. That her heart is mine."

"Maybe. You never know." The old man turned off the highway and onto a back road. "This way's shorter," he said.

Robbie nodded.

"I'm Flint Jacobs, by the way."

"Patrick Kirk," Robbie Miller lied. "Pleased to meet ya."

"You like a little radio?"

"Sure. Just as long as it ain't rock." He was taking a risk here.

"You hate that shit too? Thought you kids were all about that *negro* music."

"Not me," Robbie said. "I'm more of a country type of guy."

"American music." The racist man beamed.

The truth was that Robbie didn't like any music. Black or white, country or rock, classical or modern . . . he didn't care to listen to any of it. He'd have rather spent his time imagining using the musical instruments to break child skulls open.

Just imagine the damage one of those guitars could do to a toddler's head!

"Well, Patrick," Flint said, "you might just be all right! Gives me hope in the younger generation ta hear that at least some of you are resisting the Black plague."

"The Black plague?"

"The coloreds. They're tryna put themselves everywhere. Can't even go ta the supermarket without one of 'em staring at ya from the shelves. An' the TV is fulla 'em too."

"It's a shame," Robbie agreed.

"A god-damn shame. You know the town we just went past?"

"Starch?"

"Was a sundown town back in my day. Used to be the white man could go there, put his feet up, and feel safe. But of course, they had to rebrand. Why, they even tore down the ol' sycamore tree they used to lynch 'em on!"

"Sycamore?" Robbie asked with a gulp.

"Yeah. Sycamore Street. I think it's Sycamore Lane now. I could be wrong. Anyways, used to be, if you caught a blackie out and about after sundown, you took 'em down to the ol' sycamore and put him on it."

Robbie didn't want to hear about this.

"I can't explain it," Flint added.

"Explain what?"

"Something about the land there. Death felt like it belonged there, you know?"

Robbie didn't.

But he also did.

He remembered the thing he'd seen in the room after he'd killed his mother. The thing that changed shapes and spoke in multiple voices. What had it said to him?

We . . . want . . . you . . . to . . . be . . . a . . . part . . . of . . . this . . . house . . .

Shuddering, Robbie found himself asking a question he didn't want to know the answer to.

"Isn't that place . . . haunted?"

"Haunted? Not that I know of. They razed the whole lot and put up a suburban neighborhood, didn't they? But I'll say, there may not be ghosts . . . but there *is* a history."

"A history?" Robbie repeated.

Flint turned up an incline and they were back onto a highway, which slipped through the hills like stream water over waggling toes.

"I dunno the whole story, so I won't tell it right. But back in the pioneer days, back when Starch wasn't even called Starch, it was Nibley's Way, there was talk of an old witch that lived out there. A woman of . . . Whatcha call it? Ill repute?" Flint shook his head. "I drive through Starch a lot. I hear stories the old-timers tell. They all kinda go cold when they talk about that old hag. As if they knew her themselves and were afraid of her."

"What was her name?"

"Abigail. Abigail Friend. Funny name, huh?"

Robbie closed his eyes. He pictured a dirty shack in the woods surrounded by animal bones and warning signs. On the porch stood a raggedy old hag with a crooked nose, warts along the edges of her smile, and green skin. He imagined her hair looked like burnt straw, and she was wearing a tall, pointed hat with a wide, black brim.

"She lived out there with her son. Reclusive, they were. You know, some of these old-timers like to speculate, and they claim she and her boy was lovers, if'n you buy it."

The image changed. The door to the shack swung open, and a tall man came out. Gaunt, skeletal, and monstrous. He kissed his mother on the cheek before stalking into the woods to hunt for dinner.

"The place always attracted death. So when witchcraft was being persecuted back then . . . ain't no surprise the townsfolk of Nibley's Way turned on the old witch and her boy. They came out with pitchforks and torches. Lit the shack on fire, hung her, then nailed him to the tree and left him to die. Some folks claim the residents came back the next day, separated their hearts from their chests, and buried them apart. Others say they let the wildlife feast on 'em. Either way, they claim that's when the land got cursed."

"Cursed?"

"Yeah. I'm surprised you ain't heard 'bout it. Yer from Starch, ain't you?"

Robbie didn't want to admit that. He didn't want to give Flint a reason to tie him to the murders when he heard about them. And yet he couldn't come up with a convincing lie, so he told the truth. "Yes. I'm actually from Sycamore Lane."

"You are, huh?" Flint asked.

"Yes."

"You think it's cursed?"

"No," Robbie said, trying not to think about the *thing* he'd seen.

"I think it is. But not cursed the way folks often think when they hear the word." Flint looked at Robbie with a knowing smile. "You liked it, didn't you?"

"Liked what?"

"Killing."

Robbie's heart froze.

"Hey, I'm not gonna turn you in." Flint looked back at the road. "I done my own share of blood spilling. It's a smell I'll never forget. I liked it too. Liked watching 'em squirm from their ropes, knowing that they weren't *actually* inferior to me, but somehow, I was superior to them because I was alive and they was about to die. You understand?"

Robbie found himself nodding. "Yes. I do."

"I see that. I see you liked it." Flint rolled down his window and rested his arm on the frame. "If you'd killed anywhere else, you'd've been horrified with yerself. You'd have felt shame and guilt. But on that land . . . in that house . . . it feels better than sex, don't it?"

"I—"

"I tried killing again. Tried killing in Arkansas and Texas. It wasn't the same as it was in Starch. And it's the thing that lives on that land that does it, ain't it?"

Robbie frowned. "What thing?"

"The thing that told me to drive out here and pick you up," Flint said. "He calls himself Mr. Friendlyman."

Robbie's blood turned to sludge.

"You saw him, didn't you?"

"I—I dunno what I saw."

"I saw him myself. Only once, but I'll never forget it." Flint's eyes grew misty. "We'd caught this fella trying to sneak through town. He was a hobo with a knapsack. Blacker than night. We rounded him up and brought him over to the tree. We'd hung so many folks from it, the air around the tree smelled like roadkill. After we put him up . . . I saw Mr. Friendlyman. He was sitting on the limb, looking down at the dying man, salivating like a thirsty dog."

'Did he—"

"Change shape?"

"Yes."

"Oh, you bet he did, Robbie. One second, he was a giant lizard, then a monkey, then he was a naked man with an itty-bitty sparrow's head. Then he looked down at me and he said—and this I'll never forget—he said, '*Bring me more*.' Gave me goose bumps. Also gave me a stiffy you wouldn't believe."

Robbie couldn't believe they were having this conversation. He also realized the old man had called him by his real name.

"It feeds on it, you know?" Flint asked.

"On what?"

"On the souls of people. The moment they die, it absorbs them. Sucks 'em up and keeps 'em. It can speak in their voices, take their shapes, and I think they even *live* inside it. Like bees in a hive."

"Wh-what is it?" Robbie asked.

Flint shrugged. "It's old. It's always hungry. And it calls itself Mr. Friendlyman."

"Why?"

Flint spat out the window. "It's *very* friendly to folks who bring it victims. I'd know. I was its friend for a while. Eventually, I didn't even care if my victims were Black or white. I brought him little girls. He likes children a lot. He never showed himself to me again, but he did speak to me. Hell, he speaks to me to this day. Whenever I turn on the radio, he talks to me. Told me all about you. How happy he was when you were born, you know."

"When I was born?"

"Yes. You were born *in* The Home, weren't you?"

Robbie nodded. "Mom had me by surprise in the kitchen. I was premature."

Flint snickered. "That was probably Mr. Friendlyman's doin' too."

"What'd he tell you about me?"

"Told me you were growing up fine and evil," Flint said. "He told me about the rabbit."

The rabbit.

"Said you shouldn't beat yerself up over it. The first kill is always the hardest."

Robbie swallowed a lump. "He told you what I did to my mom and dad?"

"Yes. Said you ran away too. He understands. You were frightened. You weren't ready to see him yet."

Robbie shook his head. "I'm not going back."

"No. Of course not. You go back now, you'll get caught. Mr. Friendlyman doesn't want that. You can't feed him if yer in jail, can you?"

"I don't *want* to kill for him."

"But you do want to kill again, don't you?"

Robbie held his lips closed.

"Yeah . . . you do," Flint purred. "You were thinking of killing me, weren't you?"

"I wasn't—"

"Don't lie to me!" Flint barked.

Robbie shuddered. His palms were slick, and his knees felt hollow. Something slithered through his guts.

"Here. There's a lesson to be learned if'n yer willin' ta hear it." Flint started down another back road. The gravel crunched and rumbled beneath the flatbed.

"Where are you taking me?" Robbie asked.

"Don't worry, son. *You* ain't in no danger." Flint

laughed.

In silence, they sped through the backcountry. Soon, the gravel thinned and became overpopulated with weeds. Robbie hastily rolled his window up when tree limbs started to reach for him.

Flint pulled to a stop in a sunlit meadow. In the distance, Robbie could hear a gurgling creek. The trees were crowded and shaggy, and the grass grew high.

The old man crawled out of his seat and went to the back of the truck.

Robbie awkwardly opened his door and stepped out. The grass tickled his ankles.

Flint came back, carrying a hammer with him.

Robbie was briefly startled before the old man dropped the tool on the ground and pointed at it. "Pick it up, son."

Robbie shook his head. "I don't understand."

"You will. Pick it up."

He stooped over and hefted the hammer up. The head was rusty, and the wooden handle was splintery. He felt a shard pierce his palm like a bee's stinger. Wincing, he switched hands and used his teeth to dig the sliver out. He spat it over his shoulder.

Flint started into the meadow, walking leisurely.

"What do you want me to do?" Robbie asked.

"I want you to bash my brains in," Flint said matter-of-factly.

Robbie stood stiffly, then released an uncomfortable wheeze. "You're kidding me."

"Nope."

Flint went down to his knees. He straightened his back and rolled his shoulders. Diligently, he removed his hat, exposing a small rat's nest of thinning hair.

"You want me to kill you?" Robbie asked. "Why?"

"When I was feeding Mr. Friendlyman, he fed me as well. I've eaten my fill, and this is all he asks of me. This is my final debt, and I'm paying it. And when you kill me, Robbie, I'll go to Hell. I won't be a part of him the way my victims are. And that, my son, will make Hell as good as Heaven."

Robbie didn't understand what this old coot was saying. He scratched his head and ground his teeth together.

"You hit me, boy, and I'll move on. And after yer done, you turn on my radio." Flint smiled. "I promise it won't be playing no rock and roll."

Robbie stalked toward him, testing the weight of the hammer. He'd never considered the act of life-taking to ever be consensual. He felt strange, like he'd been dunked underwater. The meadow was suddenly hazy and distant. It took a long time for Robbie to walk through the grass and take his position behind Flint.

"Do it 'fore you lose yer nerve, kid," Flint said.

Robbie held the hammer over his head, clutching the handle with both of his shaking hands.

"You're gonna do well, son. You're gonna kill so beautifully—"

Robbie brought the hammer down. The claw end struck the back of Flint's skull. It punched in like a fist through a plaster wall. The skin around the wound dimpled, then swelled, and blood spewed from the hole.

Robbie tore the hammer loose and brought it down again, burying it in deep. He heard something whistle and whine inside Flint. Then it was as if a sandbag had dropped on the old man. He slumped and fell forward, dragging the hammer out of Robbie's hands.

He took a step back.

He looked at the body, hardly believing it was there and that he'd been responsible for killing it.

This doesn't feel right at all, Robbie thought. *Where's the joy I felt when I killed my folks? Where's the thrill? Why does my skin feel so goddamn tight? Why does—Oh God. This is* wrong. *They'll catch me and fry me for this! Oh God! I don't want to die!*

Robbie backpedaled, wanting the grass to swallow Flint's body so he could convince himself it wasn't there, that he hadn't committed this crime.

Turn on the radio. Do what he said.

Oh Christ! OhGodOhChristOhJesusGod!

Robbie sulked away from the corpse, leaving it to lie in the meadow, where it would stay. As far as he knew, later on, no one found Flint's body. He was never buried properly. He was simply consumed by the earth and its creatures.

He sat in the driver's seat. Holding the steering wheel, Robbie sucked in a shallow breath. His eyes were hazy, and his stomach had been crimped into swollen knots. He felt like weeping. He wanted to scream until his throat broke. His lungs were inflated with salt and pepper. His grip on the wheel was so tight his knuckles looked like snowballs.

Time passed. It could have been seconds, but it felt like hours. Then, so casual it seemed surreal, he reached over and turned the radio on.

"*Robbie?*" a deep voice crooned. "*Is that you?*"

Robbie shook his head. "I don't know who you are. I don't know . . . what you are."

"*I'm Mr. Friendlyman.*"

"That's not your real name." Robbie pushed his tongue against his teeth.

"*I don't have a* real *name.*" The voice chortled. "*I am The Hive. I am The Beast of Hungry Teeth. I am The Core. I am—*"

"I don't understand what that means," Robbie whined. "I don't understand you!"

The voice continued. This time, it sounded like his mother.

129

The Home

"I am The Eater of Ghosts. Come . . . let me show you."

There was pain and beauty and sudden waves of pleasure and Robbie felt his face slide away from his skull and his arms twist around like ropes and his teeth ground down over his tongue and instead of blood he felt honey dribble from between his shaking lips while below him the earth quaked and shook rumbling and roiling and driving shafts of wood up through the bottom of the car and into the soles of his feet and Robbie was falling falling falling falling falling falling he was ...

fallingforeverandhecouldn'tseehewasblindandtherewasjoyinbeingblindinbeinghungryinbeingaghostandingivingghoststoTheEaterofGhoststhewayChristwasgivengiftsinhismangerandRobbiecouldn'tstopcryingandlaughingandcryingandcryingandcry—

PART TWO
LURK THERE IN THE DARK

CHAPTER ONE

Eunice looked over at Griffin. As they drove toward Sycamore, she couldn't help but find him handsome. He looked slick all over, and his smirk was permanent. Plus, he'd been willing to buy her and her siblings dinner. That was a gentlemanly thing to do. Still, a creeping fear worried her. What if, after all this niceness, Griffin turned out to be rotten?

Eunice had become interested in boys only recently, and she was both enamored and terrified of them. They seemed less human to her and more like wandering, roving beasts. And they were not as simple as television made them appear. Take, for instance, her father. A pleasant man on the outside, but he had a tendency to yell. And he did so without caring who was in the next room. Unlike Griffin, her mother's smile was a façade, painted on with worry. It never lingered and was always forced, and Eunice knew that this was due to the things her father said to her. The shocking, dark, cold, cruel things.

But from the outside looking in, the Lee family appeared as hunky-dory as white suburbanites could be. It had even been remarked upon that they looked exactly like the cheerful, giddy, constantly beaming families from the catalogs.

Is Griffin two-faced? Was it a mistake to get into his car? Or is he genuine?

She hoped he was.

She did think he was handsome.

And funny.

And she liked how he handled Ed. The little kid could be a handful, and demanding to go see The Home was sort of a big ask. But Griffin had been cool about it.

They turned down Sycamore. Eunice caught sight of The Home immediately. It stood at the end of the lane, looking stern and rotten. She'd been by the place before, but she'd never been brave enough to chuck a rock at it. She'd feared that doing so would somehow make The Home angry at her, and that was the last thing she wanted.

You sound superstitious.

Well, maybe I am!

Eunice wrung her hands. She didn't dare reach over and take Griffin's hand in hers. Ed would've spotted it and called them out. He probably would have said something like, "Gross! I'm tellin' Mo-o-o-om!" Little brat.

She felt her heart soften. Ed was a good kid. Sure, it was annoying having him tag along when Eunice and her twin sister wanted to go out and do "grown-up stuff," like riding in cars with boys, but he was a good kid at the end of the day. Ed was always quick to tell a joke to soften the mood when Dad was feeling snappy, and when it came to ribbing, he gave as good as he got. Plus, he didn't insist on doing lame kiddie stuff. He was content hanging with older kids and engaging in their conversations.

And suggesting they go to The Home was actually a good idea. Even if it was a scary one.

Maybe it would give Eunice an excuse to get closer to Griffin.

"You ever toss stones at this place?" Ed asked.

Griffin considered this. "No."

"It's a tradition! All the kids do it at least once."

"Guess I never got around to it."

"You'll need to do it tonight," Ed said.

"Sure."

"I mean it!"

Griffin chuckled. "Whatever you say, Captain!"

Eunice laughed too.

Catherine drew her arms over her chest. "This place gives me the creeps. Let's go somewhere else."

Griffin parked the car on the street, right next to The Home. All four of the kids looked out the passenger side windows toward the ominous abode.

By all accounts, there was nothing *scary* about The Home. It was just a vacant two-story suburban house. The same as any other. But there was a *wrongness* to it that couldn't be defined. The air above it seemed darker. The windows looked foggy, spiderwebbed by thrown pebbles. The door was somehow warped. The lawn was overgrown with tall grass. It used to be that the realtors had kept The Home looking spiffy, but when it became clear that no one wanted it . . . they let The Home fester.

A sign was posted at the end of the drive. It read *FOR SALE* in bold, red lettering. The sign was replaced frequently, but it never changed. The house had been for sale ever since that Robbie Miller kid had killed his folks before vanishing into thin air.

"You know the story, right?" Griffin asked.

"I don't want to hear it!" Catherine insisted.

Ignoring her, Ed chirped up: "Yeah. Back in the fifties . . . some guy killed his parents. Then, every year since, someone else has died in that house!"

"Well, not *every* year," Catherine said.

"Uh-huh. Last year, it was Tim Michigan! He was found with his head cut off and his eyes poked out and—"

"The Michigan family moved. They live in Nebraska now," Catherine asserted.

"Because Tim was killed!"

"No. Because Mister Michigan got a new job. We s*aw* them move out of their house, Eddie. Tim was complaining the whole time to his mom, remember? She got fed up with him and put him over her knee on the front lawn—"

"Oh. I got confused. It wasn't Tim Michigan. It was Rudy Sparks—"

"Rudy was held back a grade. He isn't *dead*." Catherine sighed deeply. "Okay, you want the real story? Because I know it. And I'll tell it so long as you don't pipe in every time you feel like it."

"And how do *you* know so much?" Ed crossed his arms.

"Because when Mister Adderton came over for supper last week, he talked about it with Mom and Dad. You were too busy picking yer nose to hear it."

Eunice frowned. "I don't remember them talking about The Home over dinner."

Catherine hesitated. "Well . . . they talked about it after we were supposed to be in bed."

"You were s*nooping*?"

"I just went to the bathroom. I overheard them."

"Now I'm interested," Griffin said. "There's plenty of rumors but . . . Mister Adderton is a cop, ain't he?"

"Yeah. He and our dad were friends when they were kids."

"Mister Adderton was never a kid!" Ed said.

"Uh-huh. Everyone was a kid once." Catherine rolled her eyes.

"Nah-uh!"

"Yer bein' a menace, Ed." Griffin smirked.

Ed slumped back in his seat.

"Anyways, I heard him talking about it. Dad brought it up. Asked when the city was gonna flatten The Home and rebuild on the property. Mister Adderton said something like, 'They never will. Not in a million years. It's the ground itself people are worried about. Putting a new house on that property would be like polishing a turd with spit.'"

Everyone giggled at that.

"Mom wasn't too impressed with that language, but she didn't say anything about it. Just meowed a little, and I heard her shuffle her silverware around. Anyways, Dad asked him how many folks had died there. Adderton said, 'Not as much as the kids like to say. Half their stories are make-believe. I think they get 'em from comic books.'"

"I bet that's where Ed gets most of *his* stories anyhow," Eunice jibed.

Ed bared his teeth. "Hey, at least I can read!"

"Took you long enough!"

"Ha-ha! That's so funny, I forgot to—"

"Anyways," Catherine cut in, "Mister Adderton said that the first murders were back in nineteen fifty-four when Robbie Miller killed his parents. He left town and vanished. 'Probably livin' large in Mexico,' Mister Adderton said. The next death wasn't until nineteen fifty-seven. It was a homeless woman."

"A hobo?" Ed asked.

"Whatever you call 'em. The police had run her out of town a couple times. They figured they'd scared her off for good when she stopped showing up on Main Street, bothering folks. Then, neighbors reported an awful smell comin' out of the house at the end of Sycamore. Adderton said she was in the bedroom where Missus Miller had been killed. He didn't say much, but he said it was obvious she didn't die of natural causes. A few months went by, and then there was *another* murder. And this one was a kid."

"Was his head chopped off?" Ed asked.

"I dunno. I didn't go out and ask." Catherine

136

shrugged. "Anyways, Mister Adderton's voice got a little shaky. The kid went missing a day or two before they found him in The Home. He was also left in the bedroom. Adderton said the poor kid had been murdered. Said he was only four years old too."

"Christ," Griffin said.

"Yeah. You could tell he was rattled. Anyways, he said the next murder wasn't until nineteen fifty-nine. It was a young couple. They were found tied together in the living room. Mister Adderton said they were barely recognizable. Mom told him not to explain what he meant by that, and he didn't. So . . . that's it. Those are the *real* murders that took place in The Home. Every other week, someone comes up with a morbid story about it. But the truth is . . . The Home is responsible for"—she did a quick tally—"six murders."

But Catherine didn't know about the murders that had occurred before the Millers moved in. The Home itself had been built on the lot in 1944. The house was fresh, but the land itself was rotten to its core. She didn't know about the innocent men who'd been strung from the sycamore tree for the sick amusement of a dark creature, or about the witch and her son who'd been slaughtered on the property. She didn't know that in 1930, eight children had been found sitting in a circle on the lot, holding hands, their throats slit so wide it looked as if they'd grown extra mouths.

"And no one ever got caught for 'em?" Griffin asked.

"Some folks think it's still Robbie Miller. That he comes back to his old stomping grounds every once in a while. Others think it's a satanic cult."

"Devil worshippers?" Ed was aghast.

"But that's just a rumor. Like the thousands of other rumors that surround this creepy place."

"God, Catherine." Eunice shuddered. "You're spooking me!"

"Hey, y'all wanted to see the place. I'm just telling you what happened." She shrugged again.

"You think it's haunted?" Ed asked. "I mean . . . all them dead people—"

"There's no such thing as ghosts," Catherine said.

Eunice thought her twin sister didn't sound so confident.

"You wanna go somewhere else?"

Eunice looked over, surprised to see that Griffin was addressing her alone, as if Ed and Catherine weren't in the back seat of his borrowed car.

"No!" Ed shouted from the back seat. "You *gotta* throw a rock at it, Grif! Or else yer a pansy!"

"I've never thrown a rock at The Home," Catherine said. "What does that make *me*?"

"A girl." Ed shrugged.

Griffin chuckled.

"Girls don't *gotta* throw rocks at it. Boys do!" Ed declared.

"Gee. I never knew," Griffin said.

"It's true! Ask anyone!"

"Well, I reckon I better, then. But afterwards, let's go somewhere else," Griffin said.

"Where?" Eunice found herself asking.

"I dunno. We can make up our minds on the way." Griffin popped his door open.

"You don't have to throw a rock at that spooky ol' house just because my brother's a—" Catherine started.

"Nah. It's fine. Besides," Griffin said, turning his eyes back toward Eunice, who fluttered under his gaze, "it's tradition."

***

The boat rocked, knocking Eunice out of her memories and back to the present. She was feeling a little seasick, even though they hadn't been on the lake for very long. Ahead of her, Russell manned the vessel, steering them toward the marina—toward freedom for Orville. He looked so worried in his seat. He knitted his fingers together and talked to himself as if he was alone in the dark.

Poor old man. He certainly has changed a lot since we were kids. In some ways but not in others.

For the short time she'd known him, Orville had been a Nervous Nelly. She attributed that to his creativeness. You had to be, assumed Eunice, a bit high-strung to lose yourself in the world of your imagination. Creative types also saw things through "worst-case-scenario-scope," in Technicolor too!

And that's not a bad thing, she thought. *We'll need caution where we're going.*

Where we're going . . . where we've been before . . . where no one else has ever gone . . .

Eunice shuddered. Forgetfulness was common among people her age, and so was confusion. But there was something insidious about the confusion she'd recently experienced. It was as if something had slipped into her head and set up obstacles in her brain. Hurdles that she needed to jump through to organize her scattered thoughts.

Mr. Friendlyman . . .
I know a surefire way to summon ghosts . . .
God can't help us now . . .
We can only help ourselves . . .
And we'll start in the cemetery . . .
That will feel like the worst part . . .
But it only gets worse from there . . .
Mr. Friendlyman . . .
He's missed us . . .
All of him . . .

CHAPTER TWO

Robbie Miller came back to Starch earlier that day. He returned periodically just to feed Mr. Friendlyman. The creature was good to him. Ever since he'd shown him *The Way*—and he always thought of it like that. Italicized. Official. Not simply the way but *The Way*.

And *The Way* was simple. *The Way* was this: So long as Mr. Friendlyman was fed, life would be easy for Robbie Miller. So long as life was easy for Robbie Miller, Mr. Friendlyman would be fed. They were symbiotic in this respect. Mr. Friendlyman was Dracula, and Robbie Miller was his Renfield.

Robbie traveled frequently, easily evading the police. He camped, and he found himself sleeping in the guest rooms of friends of the entity who lived in The Home. He had many friends, which was a surprise to Robbie. The craziest place he'd stayed was in New Mexico, where he found a convent of females who had all secretly "married" Mr. Friendlyman. They wore white robes and basked in the sun like lizards. They'd also been more than willing to meet and match his every pleasure. Robbie spent seven nights fucking around with the younger girls in the convent, while in the mornings, he rested and the older women told him stories.

He'd become, in his travels, something of a history buff. In his glove compartment, he kept his notes, which traced the long and storied timeline of the creature, plus every theory he had discovered of its origins.

"Someday, Mr. Miller, your writings will be worshipped like the Bible," an old lady named Agnes Weatherby told him while he rested near the pool, slowly eating grapes from a teenager's hand like a Roman emperor.

"You think so?" Robbie asked around a mouthful.

"I know so. It's your purpose. The truth is, Mr. Miller, that we will die, and Mr. Friendlyman will live on. And the more who die in his house, the bigger and stronger he'll become. Eventually, he will be unavoidable. He'll be public."

"You mean . . . eventually, everyone will know about him?"

"I'm saying that eventually . . . everyone will *see* him, but they will not know him or accept him until you *teach them*."

Agnes was a batty old crone. She'd become a wife of the entity when she was a child, or so she claimed. Back then, she'd lived in Starch and found the old sycamore tree. For no real reason, she'd cut her palm and smeared the blood upon the bark. She watched the blood tremble, then dissipate, slurped up by an invisible force that had coalesced around the firm tree. She had run away screaming, only to be drawn back by multiple nights of fractured sleep and strange dreams. When she returned, she said that Mr. Friendlyman appeared to her as a smiling dragon with a multitude of faces growing along his scaly belly, which popped like froth in the mouth of a rabid dog. His voice, she told Robbie, was the most calming and frightening thing she'd ever heard.

The women used to travel to Starch to hold an annual orgy on the property. Then houses had been built on the land and bought before the wives had a chance to stake a claim on it. So they'd moved away to New Mexico in the hopes they could survive without

141

the entity's touch. Many of the women in the convent were starved without him. Some went crazy and were kept under lock and key—Robbie had only heard stories of these poor damsels.

"The house is abandoned now," Robbie had told them. "I killed my parents there, and it's been for sale ever since."

Agnes shook her head. "We can't go back."

"Why not?"

"Because we'd raise too much suspicion, and he's not ready for that yet. Besides, he'd kill us. He's power-hungry right now, and we'd no longer be wives to him . . . we'd simply be bodies."

Many of the younger women in the community had never met Mr. Friendlyman. They simply believed in him. He assumed many were runaways who'd have found a home in any community . . . even the ones that worshipped a ghost-eating monster.

Ghost-eating monster . . .

Even now, in the house where the creature dwelled, he thought the situation was absurd.

A hand landed on Robbie's shoulder. He startled, almost yelled.

Multiple voices spoke from one ever-changing mouth: "*Do . . . not . . . be . . . afraid.*"

Mr. Friendlyman sounded content. He got that way after a good feeding.

He'd found the woman on the outskirts of town on his way in. She'd been camped in the tree line, visible from the road but only to those hawkeyed enough to look. Robbie had pulled into the ditch, then walked over to the woods, following the musky scent of sweat and the crackling noises of her tiny fire. When he approached the camp, he found the area cluttered. The woman had been posted here for quite some time. She must have been just outside Starch city limits, which meant the cops wouldn't bother her any more than they wanted to. As far as they were concerned, she was someone else's problem.

The camp also smelled a bit like a zoo, which meant she wasn't going far to use the toilet. Wrinkling his nose with disgust, Robbie considered simply pouncing on the tent and stamping on it until she was unconscious. But he couldn't afford to get sloppy, especially so close to the road.

He vaguely remembered having killed another homeless woman some time back. This one had been sleeping under a bridge, and she'd been a helluva fighter. It'd been no easy task getting her to The Home and killing her.

He had a feeling things were going to go smoother this time around. He didn't believe he was a total psychic, like those scam artists on TV, but he got a good or bad feeling about things too often to ignore. His theory was that it was a side effect of proximity to The Ghost Eater.

"Hello?" Robbie asked.

A crabby old voice leaked out from the tent flaps. "Whozzit?"

"Just a friend. And a stranger."

"There two of you out there?"

"No, ma'am, jus' the one," Robbie said.

The woman peered out. Her face was sunbaked and mushy. She hadn't any teeth, merely a line of black gums behind her craggy lips. Her brown hair was in a messy topknot, so unwashed it appeared stiff.

"You can't be both!" the woman said.

"Both?"

"Both a friend and a stranger. It's one or the other!"

Robbie grinned. "What if I'm a friendly stranger."

"I got a gun," she said.

No . . . she doesn't. Robbie heard Mr. Friendlyman's

voice in his head. Sighing heavily, he held his hands up in mock surrender.

"I don't," he said.

"Don't what?" she demanded.

"Have a gun."

The woman scurried out. She was wearing a thick sweater and a pair of men's jeans secured to her scrawny hips with a length of rope.

The sun was just setting behind the hills, and the air felt chilled.

"You really friendly, huh?" the woman asked.

"Where's yer gun?" Robbie sneered.

The woman balked. "I got it hidden where you can't grab it." She put a hand behind her back.

Robbie took a step toward her. "What are you doin' out here . . . all alone?"

She'd been easy to subdue. Easier even to kill, but of course, this action had to wait. He'd driven down to Sycamore, parked down the lane, then lugged her body over his shoulder, praying the house lights around him would stay dark. Then, after walking the old woman into the house—Mr. Friendlyman always left the door unlocked for him—Robbie sat down and huffed a great big sigh. All of the furniture had been moved out of The Home except for a rickety rocking chair, which seemed to change location every time Robbie came inside. He took it as an indication from Mr. Friendlyman as to where he'd like the death/feeding to occur.

When the woman awoke, she groaned and rubbed her head.

"Wha-happen?" she asked with a moan.

"I about beat your head in," Robbie said.

She looked around. The house was vacant and dirty, yet it looked as if the place had been scrubbed clean since the last batch of murders Robbie had committed within its walls.

"Wh-why'd you go an' do a thing like that?" the woman asked. "I ain't done nuthin' to you."

"That's right," Robbie said.

He stood. The chair tilted back and forth, creaking like an old tree in a harsh storm.

"You ain't done nuthin' to me. Nor have you done anything to our host."

"Host?"

"The man who owns this house."

"Who's that?" she asked, breathless with fear. She was lying in the middle of a room that had once been the kitchen. Aside from the countertop, there was nothing about the area that indicated it as the room where Robbie had, years prior, slaughtered his own father.

"Who's who?" Robbie snickered.

"Who's that man you're talkin' about?"

"He's a devil, not a man," Robbie said.

"Please. Please, jus' lemme go and I won't tell no—"

Robbie crouched down over her and unsheathed his sleek hunting knife from its holster. She watched the blade with wide, unblinking eyes.

"Before I go ruining what little life you had, how about you do me a favor, huh?"

"Please, mister," she said. "Anything."

"How about you try and scream?"

Before she could, he sliced her throat wide open. All that came out of her was blood.

After she'd been drained, he cut her head off.

While Mr. Friendlyman fed, consuming the spirit that had escaped the old woman's dead body, Robbie Miller walked over to the living room, stared out the window, and watched the streets. It was a quiet night in Starch. A perfect night, he thought, for a killing.

Maybe multiple.

A car stopped by the house. Inside, he could see

a group of young people. They didn't realize that the interior lighting of the car illuminated them for Robbie's viewing pleasure. They talked, gawked, and pointed, obviously there to look at The Home.

It must be legendary by now, after all we've done, Robbie thought.

Mr. Friendlyman shifted behind him. "*The woman . . . was . . . good . . . but they'd . . . be . . . better . . .*"

"I know." Robbie licked his lips. "I'm just trying to think of a good enough excuse to get them all in here."

Much to his glee, he saw the driver—a strapping young boy—crawl out of the car and head toward the lawn.

C'mon, kid. Did they dare you? Did they double-dog-dare you? Come on up the steps and into The Home. I promise you it's warm and cozy in here.

The teenager stepped up to the lawn. He pocketed his hands and kicked his feet, then looked down at the ground with a keen eye. He stooped over and came back up with a pebble. Just a tiny one. He investigated it with his fingers, then tossed it and stooped over again. This time, he returned with a bigger and better prize. A rock the size of two quarters.

He reeled back and tossed the stone.

It struck the window.

Robbie ran toward the door, flung it open, and was halfway down the walkway before the kid even realized that The Home was occupied.

CHAPTER THREE

Orville remembered hearing the homeless woman dying. He squirmed around, hoping to break free.

After taking him off the road, Ted and his goons brought him to The Home, as promised. He figured they'd drag him inside, close the door, then ditch him. But they'd gone the extra mile.

Orville North had been trussed up with ropes, then brought upstairs and crammed into a closet. Before leaving, Ted had leaned in so close that Orville could smell the peanut butter on his breath.

"You know what happened in this room, shrimp?" Ted asked.

Orville shook his head. A dirty sock had been shoved into his mouth, and then a bandana was tied around his face, keeping the obstruction secured. He wanted so badly to spit the sock out. The longer it lingered in his mouth, the more worried he became that it was a "cum rag," like the dress socks he tossed underneath his own bed and prayed his mother would never find. He could just imagine someone as nasty as Ted wiping the sperm off his belly, then keeping the sock around just on the off chance he could torment someone with it.

"This is the room where the Millers were *butchered*. Did you know that?"

He didn't. Shaking his head, Orville pleaded with his eyes, begging Ted to show some humanity.

Behind the bully, Shane and Peter chirruped like goblins in a dark cave. Obviously, they weren't merely along for the ride. They were enjoying Orville's agony at the exact same perverse level as their leader.

"Fuck . . . you!" Orville mouthed.

"What was that, bud?" Ted asked. "Couldn't hear ya over all that shit in yer mouth!"

"Hey, we oughta go," Peter said. "Cheryl might run her mouth if anyone stops by the car."

"Yeah." Shane nodded.

"You think my girl would *tell* on me?" Ted rasped.

"No, but—"

Ted grabbed Orville by his hair and thrashed him around. "She won't tell . . . cuz she knows if she did, I'll do worse to her than I'd ever do ta this shrimp!"

Peter snickered. "Yeah, what would you do to her?"

Ted ignored him and stared deeply into Orville's eyes. "Listen, shrimp. I know you like my girl. Guess what? You ain't gonna get her. She's *mine*."

Orville's face flushed bright red.

"If no one finds you in the next two days . . . I'll come back and untie you," Ted said. "If I feel like it."

Ted stood, then slammed the door shut. Orville was instantly drowned in darkness.

He listened to the boys as they marched out of The Home. He heard the car peel away and vanish down the road.

Then . . . mere minutes later . . . he heard someone walk into The Home.

He'd been relieved. Orville believed that Cheryl had somehow talked Ted into coming back and letting him go. He heard something big and heavy hit the floor of the first story—probably near or in the kitchen, he wagered.

He heard muffled voices.

Then he heard something wet and sloppy, as if a pipe had burst, followed by grunting and hacking.

Orville tried to stay frozen, knowing that any move

he made would cause The Home to creak. It would alert whoever or whatever was in The Home to his presence, and he was quite confident he didn't want this noisy animal to find him.

Did he . . . kill someone?

It had sounded like it, but Orville wasn't too sure whether he believed that. He might have just been so frightened by Ted's assault that he'd misheard a simple, everyday noise as a death rattle.

He squirmed slightly. Ted's urine was sticky on his groin and belly.

He could smell his own fear leaking out of his pores.

God, please, save me. If you do, I promise I'll stop writing silly-fantasy books and I'll go to church and I'll worship you and I'll—

"*Hello?*" The voice's sudden appearance startled him.

Orville turned his head and squinted, but there was no light in the closet. Not even a strip of it below the door. It was the sort of all-dark he pictured when he worried about being accidentally blinded.

Around his gag, Orville mouthed, "Hello?"

"*Do you see me?*" The voice was chipper and childlike.

Orville shook his head.

"*I see you.*" The voice tittered.

Orville felt his blood freeze and his heart stall. Gulping, he tried to turn away from the voice, as if no longer acknowledging it would render it useless.

"*I see you!*" the voice said. "*I see you . . . Orville North.*"

How does it know my name?

Is it Ted? Did he come back just to mess with me?

No . . . the voice isn't outside the closet. It's in here. With me!

"*You promise you'll go to church?*"

Orville nodded. *Please, God . . . Please.*

"*You'll say your prayers?*"

"Y-yes," Orville mumbled.

"Say them. Say your prayers. Say them now!"

Our Father, Orville thought, *who art in Heaven—*

A deep, growling voice penetrated the darkness. *"Howling be thy name—"*

Orville began to weep with fear.

"And burning be thy tongue, you hungry thing—"

Orville turned his head over.

Despite the darkness, he saw the creature's face.

It looked like a human head that had been hollowed out. The skin hung off the skull like a hat dangling from a rack. The mouth drooped like laundry on a clothesline, exposing the emptiness behind it. The eyes were wide, obsidian pools.

Maggots came streaming from the open mouth, followed by the next words in the creature's unholy prayer.

"And feed forever on the flesh of man!"

Orville screamed around his gag. He pulled at the ropes that held his hands behind his back, wriggling wormishly on the ground inside the closet, wishing each time he closed his eyes that the creature would go away . . . go away . . . *go away!*

***

Orville thought of the first time he'd seen Mr. Friendlyman. He wished it had been the last.

Sitting in Russell's car, being shuttled away from the nursing home and toward Griffin Chalks—toward destiny, he decided to think—he wished to God he'd *only* seen the beast that one horrifying time. He remembered thinking that night couldn't get any worse after Ted Bracken had left him behind. Ha! If only!

Ted had been awful, but he was no Mr. Friendlyman. He was no Robbie Miller either. He was just a bad apple festering with spiritual worms, lashing out at others before they had the chance to lash out at him.

Orville had even considered attending his funeral after he'd been shot, but he decided against it at the last minute.

Orville may have been able to forgive Ted for what he'd done to him, but he could never forgive him for the torment he'd laid upon poor Cheryl. Once again, Orville hoped the young girl had found peace and happiness in her life without Ted. She'd be as old as he was now, he thought. Maybe even a touch older. He couldn't quite remember if they'd been peers or if she was an upperclassman. Still, it was bizarre enough seeing Eunice as an old bitty; he didn't think he wanted to see Cheryl at this age.

This train of thought made him feel guilty, so he returned to the present. He was in the back seat of Russell's car, his head leaning toward the window. Outside, trees and hills swept by in fast motion, becoming a green blur. Russell's radio had been blaring when they stepped into his car, and Eunice had been the one to turn it down, but she hadn't spun the volume dial until it stopped. Faintly, Orville could hear electric guitar and the thump of drums.

Russell had explained that it was his band they were hearing.

"We're pretty good, but the problem is finding an audience, you know?"

"Do you play live shows?" Eunice asked. "I used to love going to see live music when I was young. Can't handle it nowadays, of course. Too loud."

"Yeah, but that doesn't get you fans the way it used to. You gotta be online nowadays for that. You know, most music anymore is shorter than it was a couple years back because everyone is trying to make it big on TikTok. I guess you could say I'm an old soul because I'd rather *die* than go viral on TikTok. Led Zeppelin would be toast if they'd started today. Their songs are

151

too long for my generation."

"What's a TikTok?" Orville asked, slightly peeved by the "old soul" comment. He hated that phrase.

Russell rolled his eyes. "You don't wanna know, man. Best you don't."

Believing him, Orville looked back out the window at the hills. They were driving toward the outskirts of Starch, where Eunice promised Griffin lived. "Out on his lonesome, like some hermit," she'd chided.

"Is that where he used to live? When we were young?" Orville asked.

"No. He lived in town. After his mom passed, his dad moved out of Starch. I think Griffin considered leaving, but he wound up with his own place in the hills. Half in and half out, you know? Anyways, I only know this because the damn fool put his address on his Facebook page."

Now, they were halfway there, and Russell was talking about things Orville didn't understand, and all he wanted to do was go back to the nursing home and vanish into his room. He was tired, he'd left his medication behind, and he was starting to think that Eunice was a crazy woman for putting all of this into motion.

But she's our *crazy woman . . . just as Griffin and I are* her *doddering old fools.*

Orville swallowed another lump. They were developing fast.

"How far away are we?" he asked.

Russell looked over at his phone, which was perched on something that looked like a miniature music stand with a suction cup. Orville couldn't believe that a product had actually been fashioned to make it easier for drivers to look at their phones while they were cruising. As if things weren't dangerous enough! Thankfully, Russell was only using it to look for directions on Google.

"Ten minutes. Damn, this guy lives out in the boonies."

"He's very private, I imagine," Eunice said.

"You don't know for sure?"

"Well, I haven't seen him since . . . Oh, I was younger than you. Probably a hundred years?"

Russell laughed. "You're still fine, momma. Don't fret."

"Thank you, I think."

"So y'all knew each other when you were kids, huh? Grow up together?"

"We grew up in the same town. Right here in Starch. But we didn't exactly grow up together. In fact, we didn't know each other until we ran into each other one night in sixty-two."

"It was nineteen sixty-one, Eunice," Orville cut in.

"Oh, that's right. Sorry. Sixty-one. I moved a few months after we met, so we only really knew each other briefly. You'll understand when you're older, Mister Russell. Some of your briefest memories are your brightest."

A*nd darkest*, Orville thought with a deep shiver. He recalled, once again, his first glimpse at Mr. Friendlyman. The maggot-encrusted face in the darkness, howling at him, speaking in multiple voices—

He didn't want to think about that anymore, so he didn't. Instead, he thought of the weeks that followed their experience in The Home.

Of the day he ran into Eunice at the library.
***

He'd been coming to the library a lot since seeing what had happened in The Home. He couldn't stand being in his own empty house, waiting for his mother to come back from work. His own job had insisted he take time off. His boss, a weathered old man who was actually proud to be nicknamed "Snot," had frowned at him when he came into work.

"Nah, son. You may hate me fer it now, but you need time before yer back at the pumps. You need to process what you seen. Trust me on this, huh? I'm a veteran. I seen shit that'd make yer toes curl."

And Orville had thought, *Unlikely. You don't know all of it. All you think happened was that a killer got us and butchered two kids in front of us. You don't know about—*

But even thinking about it brought tears to his eyes, and he had to admit that Snot was right. He *didn't* know how to process what he'd seen, and it struck him at the most inconvenient times.

"But . . . we need the money. I've already been out of work for a few weeks now and—" Orville started, fighting back the swelling in his throat.

"It's a paid vacation. I'll give you a week's worth of money. You need more time and it'll be on you. Best I can offer you. Wish I could do you better, son, but that's how it is."

"No. That's fine. Better than fine. It's—"

"I just try and walk with God, son. It ain't much, but it's the best we fool humans can do."

"I'm sure you're right." Orville didn't want to admit to him that he no longer believed in God.

Snot walked into the station and came back with a small amount of money. After paying Orville, Snot waved him off.

"Go rest. Read the Good Book. Pray a little. I know it's hard, seeing what you saw, but God is with you, son. God loves you."

"Yes, sir. Thank you, sir."

He went off.

When he walked back the usual route, he remembered Ted Bracken's car appearing by the curb. He remembered even kicking the pebble ahead of him beforehand. He remembered how dark the night surrounding him had been and that he wished he had a car to cruise in.

He no longer wanted to walk this path, so he turned and went back into town, figuring no one would blame him if he used a little of his money as spending cash. A milkshake, in fact, sounded very therapeutic indeed.

Being in an empty home was nightmarish to him, but there was very little comfort to be found in public. Word had spread of what had happened in The Home, and everyone looked at him from the corners of their curious eyes. Lots of church people came up to Orville to let him know they were praying for him and his mother. He thanked them all as if he could personally feel the good energy they were sending to him. Though, in reality, all he felt was cold. There was an iciness that had burrowed its way right into the core of his mind and spirit. It made him shiver even when the sun was out. He even hated blinking because in those quick bits of darkness, he saw Robbie Miller and the ghoulish thing that surrounded him.

He walked down the main strip of town and found the drugstore, which also served as a soda shop. The man who ran the counter, Mr. O'Leary, was a tall, gaunt man who always wore a paper cap. His left eye was slightly lazy, and Orville figured kids would have made fun of him if he didn't make the best damn milkshakes in all of Missouri.

When Orville walked in, he spotted two boys sitting at the counter reading the same comic book together, their legs kicking as if they were running somewhere special. They were young kids, both bright-eyed and bucktoothed.

Like a patron at a dark bar, Orville sat sullenly on the opposite end of the counter and waited to tell O'Leary — who, thankfully, didn't tell him he was praying every night for him—that he wanted a chocolate shake with cookie crumbles. O'Leary brought it over quickly, crossed his arms, and stood waiting for Orville's approval. An odd habit, which Orville's mother had a theory about.

"You ever see that man rubbing a little chipped pin he keeps in his pocket?" she asked.

"No. Wait, yes! What's that about?"

"It means O'Leary used to be a drunk, but he ain't anymore. You know, he came to town a few years back and wouldn't tell a soul where he came from. Just appeared one day and started making milkshakes."

"Yeah?"

"Yeah. I think he used to be a barkeep, but the drink got the best of him. It's why he asks each kid their opinion before he moves on to the next one. I bet he worked for some high-paying customers that liked their drinks mixed *just r*ight."

"It's a habit he hasn't broken?"

"Breaking one habit is hard enough, believe me."

And he was more of a bartender than a soda jockey, Orville thought. He just tended to a different clientele. One that wouldn't convince him to take a drink with them or spill something on his table he couldn't clean up—like blood. Orville wanted to know what had happened to O'Leary, but he also knew, from recent experience, that the man probably never wanted to be asked. So he didn't. He just said it was a damn fine milkshake, as always, and watched as O'Leary walked off to check on the comic book readers.

The milkshake was good, but it couldn't soothe the aching inside Orville's chest. He drank as much as he could, then left, leaving behind a small sum of cash for O'Leary to pick through.

Wish I was old enough for a drink. I could use it.

When he stepped out of the drugstore and turned

156

around, he was shocked to see Peter Wayne standing a few yards ahead of him. The bully was walking down the street, running a branch along the surface of a wall of fences. He froze, catching sight of Orville.

The boy braced himself, expecting Peter to dash toward him, to harass him. Always, when he saw one of Ted's goons, they took the opportunity to give him hell, as if on behalf of their cruel master. Like dogs who barked at the door when their owners weren't home.

Orville prepared himself to run.

Much to his surprise, Peter frowned, then turned and strode away. Before rounding the corner, Peter took a quick glance behind him. Orville saw that his face was beet red.

He feels bad about what happened. He's just too chicken to say it.

Orville's heart jumped in his chest. He wanted to run after the bigger boy, let him know that he forgave him, that he didn't exactly blame him. What Peter had done was rotten, sure, but no one was supposed to die. None of his bullies had known what would happen in The Home, and if they had . . . Orville liked to think they would've pulled a different trick. He wondered if this was weighing heavily on all their consciences. Maybe even big, bad Ted Bracken was feeling guilty for the hand he'd played in Mr. Friendlyman's game.

Orville decided that he was too chicken himself to go confront Peter, so he turned and walked the other way, heading even farther away from home. Toward the center of town, he had two options: one was the Baptist church, and the other was the library. The choice was obvious.

Walking up the stone steps toward the library, Orville wondered if he'd ever be able to write again. He'd been working on a pretty cool book about a dragon and a distant moon, but the idea had shriveled up after his experience in The Home. When he tried to escape reality, all he saw were demons.

He thought that it would take some concerted effort to get back into the swing of things. More than just with writing, it would take a while for Orville to start breathing right again. Every intake of air was hurried as though it was his last. He constantly sounded winded, as if he'd just gotten done doing laps around the gym.

As if there's still a sock shoved down my throat.

He wondered if maybe he could escape into a book. It used to be that he'd devour books from the school library, but he'd read about every fantasy and science fiction book they had on their shelves—there were precious few. And although he and his mother both had cards for the town library, it was rare that they went.

Even if all they have is The Hobbit, *I wouldn't feel bad rereading that.*

He pushed through the double doors and found himself in the lobby. Behind a desk sat a little old lady, who looked at him pathetically, instantly recognizing him as "the boy from the news." There'd been an article about the whole happening, and much to Patricia and Orville's chagrin, the article included the full names of all involved. *Orville North, Griffin Chalks, and Eunice Lee appear to be the only survivors from the horrific scene at the house on Sycamore Lane.* He was thankful that at least the article didn't include his home address! Maybe that had been left on the editing room floor.

He tried to smile at the librarian, to reassure her everything was okay and he wasn't some sort of head case. He was just a normal teenager, hoping to do the things normal teenagers did. Instead, his smile must have looked more like a grimace because the woman flinched and looked down at her desk, where she was stamping new books.

Orville hurried past her toward the library shelves.

He ducked through them, hoping no one would notice him. That he could skate by without being perceived while also not going home to the empty void where his intrusive thoughts were at their loudest.

He found the fantasy section, located near the children's aisle. He perused the books, seeing old familiars such as Tolkien and Lewis. His eyes fell upon a book he didn't recognize: *The Worm Ouroboros* by E.R. Eddison. He glanced through it but found the prose a little too complicated—almost Shakespearean. He needed something easy to pull himself away from his own thoughts. Something that would slip in and consume his imagination totally.

As he suspected, he returned to Tolkien. Picking up *The Hobbit*, he walked around the aisle toward the work tables, where students often came to complete assignments or read books for class. They were empty today, save for one girl sitting by her lonesome.

But it couldn't be.

Orville stood still, shocked by the sight of Eunice Lee.

After losing her brother and sister, how could she come here and—No. I'm in the same position, aren't I? I can't stand being home. I'll bet Eunice can't either. I'll bet she sees the emptiness where her siblings once lived the way I see monsters when I close my—

She was already looking up at him. It was too late to turn tail and run.

She smiled. Like her face, the expression was soft and gentle. *Fawn-like*, Orville thought. Years later, when he wrote his fourth fantasy book, *Paraflex*, he had described the nymph queen's smile the same way. But he wouldn't realize that he was actually describing Eunice until the second round of edits came back to him for approval.

He wondered, now, in Russell's car, if Eunice had

noticed that he'd based a character on her.

Back to the past, to his memories in the library, she smiled at him, and he couldn't help but return the gesture. He made to leave, and she shook her head, mouthing a single word that speared through his heart.

"Stay."

He scootched into the seat across from her and opened his book on the table.

"What are you reading?" he asked in a whisper.

She showed him the cover of the book. *Ghosts of Missouri.*

He shook his head, too shocked to be polite. "I don't know how you can—"

"It's all I can think about. My sister knew a little about the house on Sycamore, but . . . the story goes deep. A lot of it is just rumor, but . . . I don't know. I'm trying to learn what I can."

"Why?" Orville asked, aghast. "It's over, isn't it?"

"We don't know that. We only think it is. Hope it is." She shivered. "If that thing comes back . . . I want to stop it."

He swallowed uncomfortably, wishing he could draw her away from it. As far as he was concerned, the three of them needed to move on.

But we can't . . . because we've been apart. Already, being near her, even now, I feel better. More focused. Less worried. Maybe we'll keep each other strong.

He sighed. "I'm sorry. I shouldn't have questioned you like that. I was just surprised."

"Griffin was too."

"You've seen Griffin?"

"He's here. In the bathroom now. Should be back in a moment."

"How long have you two been—"

"We aren't dating, Orville."

"I didn't mean—"

160

"We tried. We went out together, thinking we could have a nice, romantic evening . . . but all we talked about was what happened. All we did was cry. So we're just friends, Orville."

"I didn't mean that. I'm sorry," Orville muttered.

"I know, but I thought I'd let you know anyways."

"Okay." Orville blushed.

"What are you reading?"

Feeling childish, he showed her the cover. "It's a favorite of mine. I figured it would distract me."

"Nice. I've read that."

"You have?"

"Yes. Although I worry it won't do the trick."

"How so?"

"The Barrow-wight is pretty similar to that . . . thing we saw."

Orville smiled. "Maybe to you. But I'd say our thing is ten times worse. All it took was Tom Bombadil to scare the Barrow-wight off."

Our thing.

He hadn't meant to call it that, but that was how it felt. A thing they had shared together. A secret the three of them kept, which Catherine and Ed had taken to their graves.

She smiled. "If only it were that easy."

"Besides," Orville added, "the Barrow-wight doesn't show up until *The Fellowship of the Ring*. He isn't in *The Hobbit* at all."

Eunice nodded. "I get 'em mixed up."

"*The Hobbit* has a dragon, though."

"Smaug," she said.

"You really think it's not gone?" Orville asked, shifting the conversation back to what had occurred in The Home.

"Ghosts rarely just *leave*. I'll bet it's hiding in there, waiting for someone like Robbie Miller to show up again. They were working together, you know."

He did. That had been easy enough to decipher.

"Now, Robbie is just a part of it . . . and no one is going to dare enter The Home until what happened to us is forgotten."

"You think that'll ever happen?" Orville asked.

"Sooner than you think."

Griffin came walking back to the table. He seemed flummoxed to find Orville there.

"Hello," Orville said slowly.

Not saying anything, Griffin sat beside Eunice. "Was this your doing?"

"No. He just showed up."

Orville felt uncomfortable, like a kid who'd just walked in on his parents fighting.

"I could leave if—"

Griffin turned and gave Orville his full attention. "She's crazy, you know. I had to convince her yesterday not to go back."

"Go back?" Orville shuddered. "Where?"

"You know. Back to The Home. She was convinced she'd found some ritual in an old book that would 'seal Mr. Friendlyman away for good.' If you can believe it." Griffin rolled his eyes.

"I still think we should try it," Eunice said. "All of us."

"We aren't. It's morbid."

"What is?" Orville asked.

Eunice went to say something, then stopped herself. "It was just an idea," she stated.

"You should've heard her, Orville." Griffin seemed genuinely unnerved. "I told her it'd just make trouble."

"What?" He still wanted to know.

Orville suddenly got another visual of what had happened between Griffin and Eunice. They hadn't just decided to become friends, he theorized. Instead,

Eunice had brought this plan up to him, and it had ruined things.

Orville decided all of a sudden that he didn't want to know about the ritual. That he wanted to instead go back to normal life as he'd originally intended. Whether she could sense this or not, Eunice hung her head and looked at her ghost book, refusing to elaborate despite Orville's hanging, unwanted question.

"I'm not crazy," she eventually muttered.

Griffin, looking guilty, rubbed his brow. "Sorry. I'm sorry. We've all been through the wringer, haven't we?"

Happy to have something they all agreed on, Orville nodded. "Have you guys struggled with sleeping? I sure have."

"We've all got bags under our eyes, don't we?" Griffin asked.

"God. I can't cover them up. I never wore so much makeup until recently!" Eunice chuckled.

Both boys started to laugh as well, helplessly. From her desk, the elderly librarian looked up pensively, then decided not to bother them. Still, Orville held up an apologetic hand and covered his mouth until the laughter subsided.

"This feels right, doesn't it?" Eunice whispered. "Being together? After all we've been through?"

"I can't explain it," Orville said. "But I'm starting to feel better than I have in . . . days."

"It's been three weeks since it happened," Griffin reminded them. "In the hospital, I felt like dying. I wished I had. And you scare me, Eunice. I won't lie. The idea you have . . . is frightening. But I don't want to be apart from you. I can't even control it at this point. I wake up and I worry."

"You think it'll always feel like that?" Eunice asked.

"Lord. How can I know? All I know is that I don't like the way other people look at me." Griffin turned in his seat and gazed toward the busy librarian. "Like I'm some charity case."

"So, what do we do, then?" Orville asked. "Just stay together?"

Eunice put her tongue against her cheek. "You know, I heard once that soldiers feel bonded after surviving battles. Maybe that's just what's happened to us. We went to war, and now we're back. We can't adjust yet . . . we're just going to have to stick it out together. Because no one else will understand exactly what we went through. No one can. Even if we told them all of it, they'd say we just went crazy, right?"

"Right," Orville agreed.

"And Griffin may call me crazy, but I know he doesn't mean it."

"No. Not like *that*, at least." Griffin said. "And if anyone other than me called you that, I don't know what I'd do. Something stupid. Hell, something *crazy*."

Orville looked down at his open book. The words looked fuzzy to him.

"I don't wanna be alone. Every time I go home and no one's there, I feel like crying."

Eunice reached across the table and took his hand. He blanched, knowing just how sweaty his palm was, how sticky the lining was between his fingers. Gulping, he looked cautiously toward her and found himself mystified by her smile.

"You don't have to be alone," she reassured him. "We've got each other, Orville."

None of them knew that at that moment, Eunice's parents were planning to move out of Starch. When they did, taking their surviving daughter with them, Orville and Griffin would grow distant. They'd try to spend time together, just as Eunice and Griffin had tried dating, but it wasn't the same.

You couldn't have a Holy Trinity without the Father,

the Son, *and* the Holy Ghost, after all. And if any of them was a Holy Ghost, it was Eunice. She bound them together, more so than their trauma and heartache.

***

And now . . . she was bringing them back together.

Licking his lips, sitting in the back seat of Russell's speeding car, Orville wondered if he'd now learn what terrifying ritual she'd proposed to Griffin all those years ago. The one that paled his face and caused him to lash out at her. The one that Orville never wanted to know about, no matter how curious his wandering mind became.

CHAPTER FOUR

Griffin took a nap, and when he was finished, the house smelled like cooking pasta and spicy sauce. He stepped out of his bedroom, fully dressed and blinking blearily. Eloise was working like a madwoman in the kitchen.

He considered going in and offering to help, but he assumed she'd snap at him and tell him he needed to rest.

I've had enough rest, thank you, Griffin thought as he stepped into his living room. Instinctually, he picked up the remote and went to turn on the TV, stopping when he recalled the awful thing he'd seen the last time the tube was on.

All those dead children and Robbie Miller. God, I'd be thankful to never see his *ugly mug again. Even in my nightmares! Especially there!*

Still dazed from last night's excitement and today's napping, he sat down on the sofa with a gusty groan, then tried his best to lie back and relax. His head thumped like it had a heartbeat, and his nerves were splintered. He felt like he did when he was a child and he knew he was in trouble but hadn't yet been found out by his teachers.

Eloise came into the living room a few moments later. "Supper's about ready, Dad," she said.

Griffin blinked and looked at her wearily. "Thank you."

"I'll set the table."

166

"No, I shou—"

"You won't," she said with a pesky smile. It was the first time she'd really smiled at him since arriving.

Prudence would get the same way, Griffin thought. *She worried so much over others, and then she'd try and tell a joke or crack wise, just so you knew she wasn't actually frustrated with you . . . just worried. Nothing wrong with being worried, Griffin, you see.*

Eloise slid away, leaving him alone in the living room. He struggled to get off the sofa, then followed behind her. When he entered the dining area—they used to have a great big table when Eloise was small and Prudence was alive and well, but it had been replaced with a circular folding table since the only person who tended to eat in this house now was Griffin and maybe Mrs. Stewart if she brought something over with the laundry—Griffin took a whiff of the meal. It was delightful.

"You inherited your skills from Mom, didn't ya?" It was something he always said whenever Eloise made food for him.

She nodded. "She was the best."

"Remember, when you were a kid, how much you complained about her cooking?"

Snickering, Eloise pulled out a chair and helped Griffin sit down. "Because I didn't have any *culture* back then."

Griffin snorted.

"She was making five-star meals, and all I wanted was chicken nuggets."

"You were easy to please," Griffin said. "When Mom was gone to visit her folks, I'd feel relieved. A whole week and all I needed to do for food was make sure you had enough marshmallows in your breakfast cereal and that there was frozen pizza in the freezer."

"If you were a single dad, I'd've been a very fat

girl." She went over to the stove and prepared Griffin's plate. A small pile of spaghetti smothered in sauce with Italian sausage chunks and a side of steamed broccoli. Thinking back on the frozen meals he'd been eating the last few years of his life, Griffin felt his mouth salivate.

"You're too kind to me, Eloise," he said as the plate was set before him.

She hesitated. "I love you, Dad. I just worry about you."

Just like Prudence.

With her own plate ready, they said grace before eating.

"How are the kids? I haven't even thought to ask!" Griffin said around a mouthful.

Even though she had finished chewing, Eloise cupped a hand over her mouth while she spoke. "Fine, Dad. Just fine."

"How's school been treating Todd?"

"Oh, you know. He struggles with math. And reading. But he's great at sports. He's decided to try out for JV football next year. He's even become a Chiefs fan! Just like his grandpa."

Griffin sneered. "It's infectious, isn't it?"

"You riled him up with that jersey you bought him for Christmas," Eloise said.

"And Mary?"

"Full of herself. Like I was when I was her age."

"Prima donna."

"She watches *Frozen* almost every day. The sing-along version. Someday, she'll be on Broadway, I'm sure . . . but for now, she sounds like a bat screeching. If I never hear those songs again—"

"You'll miss it when she's grown," Griffin said. He speared a large chunk of meat with his fork and ate it happily. "Hell, you used to sing every morning like no one in the house could hear you."

"Was I any good?"

"You were awful."

"I guess these are my just desserts, then," Eloise said.

"Well earned, I'd say."

"Didn't I suffer enough with potty training?"

"Please. Some memories are best left unremarked on! Especially over dinner!"

Again, father and daughter laughed.

"I dunno, Dad," Eloise said. "I wish Mom was around. Wish she could see her grandkids. They were babies when she passed."

Griffin nodded. "They're still babies."

"They are and they aren't. It's incredible . . . but I see the *people* they are becoming, and it's almost enough to stop my heart. Like, Todd . . . he's such a firecracker. I can already tell that in college, he's just going to party even harder than I did. And I'm helpless to stop it—"

"He's only nine."

"But it's there. Like I'm some sort of psychic. I can see Mary getting her heart broken once . . . and using that as an excuse to break every heart she can for a few years. Again, like me. God. Is parenting really so . . . helpless? Did you and Mom just stand around and watch me, knowing you couldn't stop me?"

Griffin continued nodding. "They don't put that in the handbook. When you were a teenager, especially. Don't you remember the fights we got into?"

Eloise blushed. "Sometimes. Although I don't remember what they were about."

"You were becoming a woman. It terrified me."

"Really? Is that all it boiled down to?"

"Awful, isn't it? Especially in hindsight, when I see how well-off you are."

"Well-off?" Eloise sighed. "God. I was going to wait to tell you—"

"Tell me what?"

Eloise looked at her plate. She'd only eaten a few bites. "Boris and I are having trouble."

"Oh dear." Griffin set his fork down.

"I dunno. I didn't wanna bring it up. I shouldn't have. You're already dealing with so much and—"

"Listen to me, Elly. I'm your old man. I don't care if I had a knife to my throat and a gun against my back. If you have a problem, I'm all ears."

Eloise smiled. There was something furtive about her eyes.

"He's a good guy, Dad, and I don't want you to get the wrong impression about him just because—"

"Just because of what, dear?" Griffin prodded.

She sighed heavily. Slowly, she lifted her chin. "He's just been talking strange lately."

"Strange how?" Griffin didn't want to be pushy or insistent, but he needed to know what was happening to his daughter. In his mind's eye, he saw Boris putting hands on her despite her insistence that he was a "good guy." He'd always been fearful for his daughter when she took to boys. The first time she'd gone on an actual date—which wasn't chaperoned—he'd stayed by the door biting his nails, fearing that she'd come back raped, or wouldn't even come back at all.

A warm flush roared through him. He focused intently on his daughter, while inside, he thought, *I'll kill him if he hurt her.*

"He's been talking in his sleep," Eloise admitted.

Griffin scrunched his brow. It was peculiar, sure, but it wasn't concerning. Unless, of course, he was saying *horrible* things in his sleep. Like how he wanted to burn the house down with Eloise and the kids in it.

"What does he say?" Griffin asked, realizing he'd need to pry this information out of her.

"Just weird stuff," Eloise said. "He talks a lot about

. . . Well, I try and wake him up when it gets bad, but it's like he's locked in. Like he can't wake up until his dream is over. And he never feels rested either. It's put us on edge. We've been fighting a lot. Thankfully, not in front of the kids, but you know Mary. She's perceptive. She can tell. Last week, she came up and asked me if Daddy was going to leave because one of her pals at school has split parents and—"

"But what is it that he says, Eloise?" Griffin pushed. "What could be so bad that it's . . . driving a wedge between you?"

Eloise took a sip of water. Her throat clicked; it sounded like the hammer being pushed back on a revolver.

"He says . . ." Her voice suddenly and alarmingly changed. It was as if Boris was talking *through* her mouth. If it was an imitation of her husband, it was an eerily good one. "*I . . . know . . . a . . . sure . . . fire . . . way . . . to . . . summon . . . ghosts . . .*"

Griffin's mouth dropped open. It was Boris's voice, in Eloise's mouth, speaking words that Griffin had last heard uttered . . . by the serial killer Robbie Miller on the night that Griffin's reality had been shaken. The night he'd gone into The Home.

Eloise's face cracked into a gruesome smile. Her lips pulled back so far that he could see her molars. It happened suddenly, loudly, and wetly. The skin didn't tear, but it was as malleable as moist clay in the hands of a demented potter.

"Elly—" Griffin started.

Her head began to bob like it was attached to a spring. It bounced back and forth, up and down, and then began to circle around and around, steadily gaining speed. Fervently, breathing harshly, she planted her hands against the table to balance herself. Soon, her head was a tornado between her shoulders, thrashing inhumanly fast. So fast it *blurred.*

This isn't my daughter, Griffin thought *It's not her . . . it's him! It's Robbie Miller!*

She stood unexpectedly, knocking her chair over. Her hands remained firmly secured to the table, but something was happening to them. Her fingers split down the middle, and white tendrils began to seep out from the wounds. Soon, the tendrils expanded until they covered the surface of the table, a web of sticky, glue-colored twine, which wriggled and wormed like an organic *thing*. Griffin pushed himself away from the table, not wanting to be anywhere near the substance that was rapidly pouring out of his daughter's bisected fingers.

Multiple voices eked out of her blurry mouth.

"*It . . . burns . . . in . . . Hell!*" Somehow, her head was whirling around faster than it had before. He could see, in the fuzzy motions, changes taking place. Sharp, snaggled teeth, writhing tongues, and eyes that glowed bright orange. "*Come . . . burn . . . with . . . me!*"

Griffin cried out. He held his hands up defensively just as his daughter *grew*. She was no longer a diminutive five feet tall. Now, she towered over him, her growth spurt resulting in a succession of bone-splintering pops. Her clothes ripped open, revealing pale, snow-white flesh. Featureless and formless, like a drawing created by a child. Her head stopped whirling, finally taking on a horrible shape.

The sight of it made Griffin scream.

"*Burn with me in Hell!*" the distorted creature said, maggots dripping from its infected, bloody gums. Its teeth were removed, replaced with flat razor blades that had been forcefully shoved into place. Robbie Miller's mouth was a vortex of sharp edges and dripping ropes of gore. His eye sockets were stuffed with brightly colored gumballs shoved in so haphazardly that his orbital bones were bulging. His head was covered in tangled weeds and long stalks of corn that brushed against the ceiling. *"Burn and die, Griffin Chalks! Burn and DIE!"*

And then he was awake. It felt like being punched in the gut. He was lying on his back, holding himself, weeping loudly. It all came to him like a wave rushing through a sandcastle.

I didn't go to the hospital last night, he thought. *Eloise is safe at home. I've been here this whole time, lying on the ground, seeing what Mr. Friendlyman has wanted me to see! Oh God! I've been lying on the floor this whole time!*

His weeping screams wouldn't cease. They flew out of him like pigeons from their roost, drowning out the reassuring voices around him. He was surrounded by strangers—probably some friends of Mrs. Stewart. She'd found him here and called for help, bless her heart.

One of them, an old, portly man with a beard, was wringing his hands into knots. "Is he crazy?" the man asked in a vaguely familiar voice.

"Shit, man! Snap out of it!" a younger male said, holding Griffin by his shoulders. "Oh God! Get him some water, y'all! Get him some water!"

His pleas were unnecessary. An elderly woman was hobbling toward him with a glass in hand.

Abruptly, the screams were replaced with raspy coughs. He turned around in the young man's hands and threw up, splattering last night's frozen meal onto the floor.

"Oh shit!" the young man muttered.

Griffin fell limp, not unconscious but too shocked and weary to struggle.

The woman knelt beside him and tipped the glass toward his mouth. He drank gladly, relieved to feel the water slide over his bile-drenched tongue. He sputtered, swallowed, then struggled to speak. Nothing came out aside from exasperated pants.

"Hey, man," the young guy said, "I didn't sign up for this! I said I'd drive you and that's it. I'm technically breakin' and enterin', you know? I shouldn't have kicked that goddamn door down. Fuck! This guy needs a hospital!"

"No," the woman said simply. Griffin was surprised to recognize her voice as well. "He just needs us."

Griffin closed his eyes—

—and was taken back to The Home.

CHAPTER FIVE

Ed howled the second the man came barreling out of The Home. Eunice clasped a hand over her mouth and watched as the redheaded man sped toward Griffin, who seemed too startled to move.

"Run!" Ed shouted. "It's a ghost!"

A ghost? No. Ghosts don't exist, silly! Eunice thought. *It's something worse! A squatter! A killer! A crazy! It's—*

But then the man slowed down, keeping his distance from Griffin. He smiled. His thin lips seemed to struggle to peel back over his teeth, but it was a smile nonetheless. Slowly, he held up his hands and spoke loud enough to be heard, even through the car doors.

"Whoa there," the man said.

Griffin juked to the side, then froze. He didn't seem sure what to do. Eunice could see his hands were shaking.

"Sorry, bud!" the man apologized. "Didn't mean to startle ya so! But, hey! You scared me! Throwing rocks at my house!" He chuckled, letting them all know he wasn't actually mad at Griffin for his transgression.

"Y-your house?" Griffin asked.

"Yup." The redheaded man pocketed his hands. "As of today! Just bought the puppy!"

Eunice blinked. Who would be sick enough to buy The Home? Slowly, she rolled down the window and poked her head out, feeling a cool breeze against her cheeks.

"*You* own this place?" she shouted, perplexed.

"Don't you know it's—"

His smile broadened. "Howdy, ma'am! Yep! I know. This place has a pretty nasty history to it! Maybe y'all know more than me, you bein' local and all." He walked toward the car. His movements were jaunty and strange but nonthreatening.

"Name's Flint Jacobs." Later on, she'd wonder how Robbie Miller had used this false name so easily. Usually, when someone made up a name, they stalled a bit to think it through. Otherwise, they'd come up with something like John Johnsonsmitt.

Griffin let out a whoosh of exasperated air. "Jesus. You scared the tar outta me!"

Flint Jacobs smiled knowingly. "My apologies. Really, I just wanted to catch ya before ya scampered off. That's a nice car you got there."

Griffin blanched. "It isn't mine. A friend loaned it to me."

"So's you could take yer girlfriend out?"

Now it was Eunice's turn to blush.

"A couple friends. Her sister and brother—"

"Ah, howdy folks! Didn't see ya there!"

The back window came down. Before it was even halfway, Ed stuck his face out and asked, "You ain't a ghost?"

Flint laughed heartily. "No, but I know a surefire way to summon ghosts!"

"Really?"

Flint laughed, although no one else seemed to get the joke. When he finished, Griffin stepped closer.

"Why *did* you buy this place, mister? I mean, if you know what happened—"

Flint pawed a dismissive hand ahead of him. "Listen, this property is a *steal* because of what happened. I know it's morbid, but I figure I could raze the place, rebuild from the ground up, and it'll be like it never happened. Sure, it's weird for now . . . but I'd rather build something new than let a good deal like this fester. Besides, I'm not scared of ghosts!"

"I guess yer right," Griffin muttered.

"The realtor haggled me so much—I never saw a realtor try his darndest *not* to sell a house! I think it goes against their nature! His head looked 'bout to pop!" He clapped his hands together for emphasis.

Griffin rolled his eyes. "Sorry again, mister. Seriously, we'll get out of your hair and—"

"Now hold up a mite, bud," Flint said, his tone commanding and very adult. Eunice had tried to sound like a grown-up before in the privacy of her room, in front of her mirror, but she could never pull it off. She figured kids weren't capable of authority, except among other kids.

Griffin looked sheepish under Flint's gaze.

"Now, I'm not mad at you or nothin', but it don't change the fact you threw a rock right at my property!"

"Oh, jeez," Griffin started. "I'm—"

"And I've got enough on my hands without having to deal with kids vandalizing what's mine."

"I didn't mean nuthin' by—"

"And if I let this infraction go, well then, it'll set a bad example. Before I know it, kids all over will be trying their luck." He tucked his hands beneath his pits and sighed. "So, what do we do about it?"

Everyone in the car was silent. Even Ed.

"We didn't throw anything. Just Griffin," Catherine whispered. "Why are we all in trouble?"

"He didn't say we were," Eunice whispered back.

Flint grinned and snapped his fingers. "I know! How about we clear things up the old-fashioned way?"

"How's that?"

"Community service!" Flint declared.

Eunice narrowed her eyes. What could he possibly

mean by that?

"Yeah. Sure!" Flint said. "Listen, I'm gutting this place. It's been a *hell* of a job. Lots of leftover furniture, old clothes, and just a bunch of bits and parts. I've been struggling with the dining room table. It's not too bad, it's just—What's the word? Cumbersome!"

"What's that mean?" Ed asked.

Ignoring him, Flint continued. "How about this, y'all? You help me get that table moved out of the house, and we can keep tonight's little mishap between friends, yes?"

"Well." Griffin seemed strained. "Ed's pretty little—"

"Hey!" Ed shouted.

"He doesn't have to carry the table. That's a man's job! You and me'll get either side of it. We'll let the gals and the young'un get the chairs. In fact, there's only three of them, and they're pretty beat up! Wouldn't take long at all!"

"Okay!" Ed was already opening his door, happy to be called upon.

"Wait! Ed!" Catherine grappled with his arm, but he shrugged her away.

"I mean," Griffin cut in loudly, "we really oughta be going. Their parents have a pretty strict curfew."

Flint sighed. "I hate to insist, but if we can't cut a deal . . . Well, maybe the authorities can make one for us."

"No sweat!" Ed said, hopping onto the curb and balancing with outstretched arms. "We'll get that table out in a jiffy! Easy-peasy!" He flapped his arms like a bird and bounced off the curb, onto the street, and over to the lawn.

Eunice found herself opening the door, not entirely sure if she was confident with her decision or not. But she knew she'd rather die than let Ed go into The Home alone. Besides, there were four of them and only one

Flint Jacobs. If he *was* up to something funny, they could easily overpower him! Besides, she didn't want him calling the cops on Griffin because he threw a puny little rock at The Home just like every other boy in town.

Catherine was the last out of the car. She moved reluctantly, as if she'd been soaked in cold water. Striding up next to Ed, she took his hand and whispered harshly to him, "You don't leave my side, okay?"

"Gee, sis! It's not like we'll be in there long."

"No exploring. We'll help Mister Jacobs, and then we're dust. Got it?"

Ed seemed to sense the severity in her tone. Eunice thought Catherine could sound pretty close to grown-up when she wanted to.

"Okay." Ed capitulated. "You got it."

Together, they all walked toward The Home, following Flint Jacobs's lead.

He held the door open for them, allowing them to enter first. When Ed went by, he paused and looked up at the smiling adult.

"Do you really know how to summon ghosts?"

Flint Jacobs/Robbie Miller winked. "Stick around and you'll find out."

CHAPTER SIX

Griffin was conscious, and for that, Orville was thankful. He allowed a long breath to stream through him, then he sat down on Griffin's sofa and buried his face in his hands.

"What happened?" Griffin asked.

"We came up to knock on the door and heard you . . . screaming. My friend here, Mister Russell, broke your door down."

"Sorry, man," Russell muttered, lying on his back and covering his eyes with his elbow. "Fuck, dude. You about gave *me* a heart attack."

"I did, huh?" Griffin scowled. "Yer too . . . young for that."

Eunice was sitting on the floor next to Griffin, inching away from the slowly spreading pool of vomit when she could. The whole house stank of sweat and human filth.

"I guess I need to clean up, huh?" Griffin blinked. "I'm sorry, folks. I must have had an—"

"Griffin," Eunice said.

He looked at her.

"It's me."

Confused, he tilted his head.

"Eunice."

Griffin hesitated. "I might've guessed. So that would mean that old man on my sofa is Orville North, huh?"

"Old, and tired, and very scared," Orville cracked.

"But who's the kid?" Griffin asked.

180

"Outta here," Russell said as he lurched to his feet. "Taking my money and leaving . . . and I hope I never see the three of you for as long as I live."

"Hopefully, that's a long time," Eunice said. "My purse is on the porch where I dropped it. Take as much as you're worth, Russell. Not a penny less."

The young man backed out of the house. They heard him rustle through the purse, then descend the steps. Soon enough, his car started, and Russell was gone. Orville was both sorry to see him go and happy to be rid of him. If, God forbid, he'd followed them to The Home, he might have been slaughtered. Although Orville thought him something of a dim bulb, he didn't think the young man deserved such a terrible fate.

"Now that he's gone, I guess I can speak freely and ask, what the fuck are you two doing here?" Griffin wanted to know.

"I'm wondering the same thing myself," Orville said. "This was Eunice's doing."

Griffin turned and stared at the old lady. "No."

"Yes, Griffin. It's time."

"But . . . no. I told you then and I'll tell you now . . . it's *insane.*"

"This brings back memories," Orville chittered. "Mostly of sitting in the library, wondering what on earth you two were talking about."

"You still want to perform the ritual, you crazy bat? Jesus!" Griffin rolled over and struggled up to his feet.

"Ah, yes. So many wonderful memories," Orville muttered.

"It's our only shot!" Eunice said.

"It wasn't. Our best shot is to get *away* from it all."

"And how's that worked for you so far?" Eunice asked. "Or are we supposed to believe you weren't lying on the ground, speaking in thirteen different voices when we showed up?"

181

Griffin stopped. "I was?"

"It sounded like there was a crowd in here," Orville said. "It was scary. Russell is probably going to have nightmares forever, poor kid."

Griffin stepped over his puddle and went toward the hallway. "I'm going to take a shower. Maybe you should tell Orville everything before he agrees to follow you to hell and back."

"I want to discuss it with both of you," Eunice said.

"Orville,"—Griffin turned on his heels—"it really is good to see you again. Maybe after we laugh all this off, you and I can have a beer and reminisce about the good ol' days."

Griffin vanished down the hall. In a few short seconds, they heard the blast of the shower.

Orville looked down at the ruined carpet. "Christ, Eunice, I thought he was dying. I thought—"

"That Mr. Friendlyman had him?"

"I'm not going nuts, am I? He really was speaking in different voices. Did Mr. Friendlyman—I dunno—Possess him?"

Eunice shook her head, then nodded. "He's stronger than I thought. I guess he wasn't just recovering all this time . . . he was waiting too."

"Can he do that to all of us?" Orville asked.

"My guess is that he'll only be able to do it with Griffin. Griffin's the only one of us who *stayed in* Starch. You came back, but you were gone for a good while. I left for good until the other day."

"Christ," Orville repeated.

"Turn on the television. I want to see the news." Eunice groaned her way up to her feet and sat beside Orville, facing the tube. It took some searching to find the remote.

"Local station," Eunice said.

"I know. You wanna see if there's any word on

Sycamore, don't you?"

"Yes."

"I heard someone died there last night. A couple someones."

Much to their annoyance, the news didn't make much of the murders on Sycamore. There was a lot of weather and sports chatter and then a brief clip of a reporter in front of The Home stating that tragedy struck late last night during the storm when an entire family was found dead in their home. She didn't call it a murder, but the implication was there.

"Most folks don't know The Home's legacy. So many of our crowd died or moved on, and we took our stories with us. I can't believe a family was *living* there," Eunice stated.

"The Home looks different. More modern."

"But it's the same place. It's still The Home."

The news moved on to a political panel. Eunice asked Orville to turn the television off, and he was all too happy to oblige. By the time the screen went dark, Griffin was back. He wore a tight bathrobe, a pair of trunks, and his stringy hair was dripping. His eyes looked hollow, as if he'd just finished crying.

"She tell you much?"

"No."

"Figures. She's probably hoping I'll handle the hard stuff. Fine. Fuck it," Griffin spat ruefully.

"Manners," Eunice scolded.

"Forgive me, toots. I'm in a bad mood." Griffin waddled over to the sofa, staring down at his mess. Flinching, he looked away. "God. That's a shame, isn't it?"

"You were in a bad way. No one holds it against you," Orville stated.

"You know, I started reading your book. I actually picked it up by random. Had no idea why the name was so familiar until I got a few chapters in," Griffin said.

"You like it?"

Griffin shrugged. "I couldn't keep track of all the names."

"Most can't. You're skirting around the issue at hand, Griffin."

"Yeah. Guess I'm a pussy too. I don't want to talk about it because it's—unhinged. Scoot."

They did, and Griffin plopped beside them. He stared ahead, looking past the TV and through the wall.

"Eunice thinks there's a ritual that will lock Mr. Friendlyman up for good."

"It will. I don't think, Griffin, I know."

"It's called *ghost eating*."

"Isn't that what—"

"Yes. Mr. Friendlyman himself is a ghost eater. The ritual . . . would give us his powers." He sat upright. "Orville, Eunice is saying that *we* need to *eat* him if we want to be rid of him."

CHAPTER SEVEN

Griffin awoke on the floor. He couldn't remember what had happened after walking into The Home. He'd heard Ed ask Flint if he could summon ghosts, and Flint had said something snarky back. And then there was darkness. It was as if breathing in the air inside The Home had poisoned him.

He tried to sit up, but there was a powerful weight on his chest.

Blinking, Griffin lifted his head and looked around.

He was shocked by what he saw.

They were lying in a circle in the center of the living room, their legs spread and bound to each other by the ankles. The ropes were secured with viciousness, digging into his bare flesh. Around Ed's ankles, Griffin saw blood pooling as if the ropes had cut *through* him.

Griffin took a head count of the members of their crude circlet. Eunice was on his left; Catherine was to his right. Ahead of him was Ed and . . . someone else. A boy around his age. Portly, with curly hair cut very short. It took Griffin a moment to recognize him as Orville North, the quiet kid who sat behind him in Algebra and lived with his single mother. Lots of kids picked on Orville because he was somewhat spacy, but Griffin had never had a problem with him.

But what's he doin' here? How'd we end up—

He heard a soft sound to his left. Eunice had woken up.

One by one, the rest of them joined her.

"Where are we?" Catherine asked blearily.

"I wanna go home!" Ed shouted.

"Shush!" Orville said, knocking Ed with his knee.

"Hey! Don't pick on him!" Eunice shouted. Griffin doubted she was actually mad at Orville. She just needed *someone* to yell at since their captor was nowhere in sight.

Orville lifted his head. The look of terror on his face caused Griffin's heart to skip.

"You don't understand . . . there's something in this house!" His voice was raspy like he'd been screaming for hours.

*Not some*one. *Some*thing. The difference between the two seemed slight but purposeful.

"What happened?" Griffin asked.

"That man who lives here—he's a killer!" Orville said. "I heard him *kill* someone earlier."

Ed began to mewl like a lost kitten.

"We have to get out of here," Catherine said.

Everyone tried to move. They could wiggle and lift their heads, but their limbs were locked to the ground despite having nothing to bind them. Each motion aggravated the rope burns around their ankles.

Ed was weeping now. "Stop it! Stop it . . . it hurts!"

"I'm sorry," Orville apologized. "Really."

"Okay, we can't move . . . What *can* we do?" Catherine asked.

"We could beg," Eunice muttered.

"It might be all we've got," Griffin said, trying his best to stay cool. The tremor in his voice told him he was failing.

Orville sucked in a deep breath. "I mean it. There's something in this house."

"We have his name . . . Jacob Flint, right?" Catherine asked.

"Flint Jacobs," Griffin amended.

186

"We could tell the police—"

"What if that's a fake name?" Eunice reasoned.

"He's not the only thing we've gotta worry about," Orville said.

"What do you mean?" Griffin asked.

"I mean, there's *something* in this house."

"What . . . do . . . you . . . mean?" Griffin repeated, growing weary of Orville's chatter.

The boy hesitated—as if he was about to begin a speech but had forgotten the first line. After a few muted seconds, he spoke in a conspiratorial whisper, "I saw something. A ghost . . ."

"No." Catherine shook her head, jostling their collective ankles. "You didn't."

"I did!" Orville insisted. "I got shoved in one of the closets by, by some bullies. While I was in the dark, I saw—"

"You saw something in the dark. Something scary, sure, but not something *real*."

"Oh, he's real!" Flint's familiar voice cracked through the shadows.

Everyone screamed when he stepped out of the corner, smiling down at them with his thin lips and sharp teeth. He'd stripped his clothing off and was naked, but not exactly *nude*. He had so many tattoos on his body that he may as well have been wearing a shirt and pants. Griffin noted that all the tattoos depicted giant, leering eyeballs of varying shapes and colors. It looked like a tornado of ocular horror swirling up his skinny frame.

"And you were right; Flint ain't my real name. It's Robbie Miller. You know that one?"

Everyone did.

The boy who killed his parents . . . then vanished into thin air.

Robbie keyed in on Griffin. "You like 'em?" he

asked, pointing a scrawny finger toward the cluster of eyes between his pecs. "I got 'em slowly, building it up over time. You know what they are?"

Griffin didn't know how to speak anymore.

"They're the *eyes of Hell*," he said.

"Please, mister, just let us go!" Catherine exclaimed.

"Hush now, darlin'. Daddy's talkin'." Robbie snickered. He strolled around the circle of bound children. "My, my, my. What a lovely crop." He froze. "Yes, I'll get to killin' them. Don't you worry. You're hungry? So am I."

Was he having a conversation with himself?

That's what crazy people did, right?

Griffin shook his head, hoping this was just some big joke. That it was a put-on devised by the bullies who'd been tormenting Orville. Maybe someone would jump out in a Halloween mask and get them screaming, and then it would all be over. Just a cheap and quick scare.

Robbie stood over Griffin, looking down at him. "You woulda been all right . . . if you'd just gotten in yer car and drove off."

Griffin felt bile rise in his throat.

"I'm gonna kill the little one first. Just so y'all can hear him die."

"Lay a finger on him and I'll *kill you!*" Catherine cried.

"So much gumption." Robbie smirked.

"Please! Please, no!" Ed wailed.

Robbie stepped away and started toward the corner where he'd been hiding. "But we can't start yet. No sir . . . not till Mr. Friendlyman is ready."

What the fuck is he talking about? Griffin thought. The reality of the situation was still dawning on him. He'd been scared of adults before, but usually of justifiable punishment. There was no logic or sound reason behind Robbie Miller doing what he was doing to them. No cause other than a thrown pebble.

And we were so damn gullible too. We walked right into his trap, didn't we? Like idiots!

He heard something rumble. It sounded like distant thunder. Then it got closer . . . and closer . . . until the house was shaking. It felt as if a train was speeding right through the backyard.

Robbie Miller stood in the corner, facing away from them, his arms hanging low and his head tilted down. His shoulders began to roll and writhe as if he was stretching before a workout.

"Please!" Ed cried. "I didn't do nuthin' wrong! I'm—I'm so-orry!"

His cries hurt Griffin's heart. Each one was a spear launched directly at his chest. And what made things worse was that he could do nothing to help the little kid. He couldn't defend him, or comfort him, or protect him. In fact, Ed being here was Griffin's fault, the more he pondered on it.

If I hadn't picked them up . . .

If I hadn't driven out here . . .

If I'd been an adult and said no when Ed asked me to chuck a rock at this stupid house . . .

I was in charge, and I walked them right into the chomping jaws of—

A long, aching moan rose from the corner.

Robbie turned around.

The sight of his face caused instant panic.

To the left, it was Robbie Miller. Reptilian, grinning, and hollow-eyed. To the right . . .

It was like flipping through the pages of the world's worst horror comic at high speed. One second, it was a pig with curled tusks, and the next, a sunken ghoul with a toothless mouth. And then a laughing jester, and then an alien, and then a—then the faces were changing too fast to keep track of. It was simply a *blur* of monster masks.

The right arm was normal. Long and bony, sure, but coiled in muscle. The left was skeletal, soaked in dripping gore, and the fingers were changing from one weapon to another as well.

Griffin had never seen anything like this.

Never dreamed anything like this.

Crying like a child, he jerked against his invisible restraints, wishing like hell he could stand and run. He didn't even care anymore about the others. Maybe the thing would be so distracted eating them that it would forget all about Griffin Chalks.

And then it spoke, and that was somehow worse than all the faces and distortions and weapons combined. *"Be . . . not . . . afraid . . . of . . . The . . . Eater . . . of . . . GHOSTS!"*

Ed was crying so hard that his throat was torn. His eyes were sealed shut, and he begged for his life, not caring about the front he'd put up earlier—the tough kid persona had died even before the body.

"Help me!" Ed brayed. "Help me, Mommy! Please, God! Please, Mommy! Help me!"

And then . . . the creature was upon him.

There was another blur and then a splatter of blood. It went everywhere, like a chipmunk tossed into a wood chipper. Griffin felt it soak his front, fill his mouth, and tint his vision red. It splayed over the walls in nasty spiderweb patterns. Huge chunks of flesh flopped out of the mess.

And Ed was no longer screaming.

He couldn't.

The silence was like being plunged under the ocean. Griffin felt as if he was falling through the depths, his feet tied to cinder blocks, his arms cut from his shoulders so he couldn't even paddle.

Dead . . . Oh God . . . Oh Jesus . . . He's DEAD.

Robbie was on his feet again. Whatever had overtaken him was gone, and all that was left was a naked, tattooed, bloodstained killer. He sucked on his fingers one by one like he'd just dipped them in a tub of cream. Afterward, he smiled at Griffin, showing the poor boy a mouth full of —

Razors.

"You ever see a ghost, kid?"

Griffin shook his head.

"You just did." He strolled across the circle of bodies toward Griffin, zeroing in on him. "You saw, actually, a *whole lotta ghosts*. All at once. Beautiful, wasn't it? Terrible, even."

"E-Ed?" Catherine sniffled. "Ed?"

There was no use in even saying his name, thought Griffin. Ed was dead.

"Let us go," Orville muttered. In the commotion of blood, the bigger boy had vomited down his front. His chin was slick with glistening bile.

"NO!" Robbie roared, spinning on his heels and facing the cowering child. His voice was suddenly changed. It flipped back and forth from Robbie's to — another. A deeper, growling voice that could have bubbled up from the bottom of a swamp. "*I'll . . . NEVER . . . let . . . YOU . . . go!*"

The house began to rumble and tremble once more. Griffin heard something *snap* deep inside Robbie's body. Like a decayed tree finally splintering and falling.

Orville began to scream, getting a full look at Robbie's changing, distorted face.

Robbie swept toward Orville, hands morphing into scissors. Just before he landed on the boy, he changed direction. The shift was jarring, like a radio station switching from classical to rock. Then, before Griffin could comprehend what was happening, he was on top of Catherine.

Catherine screamed once, but the sound was cut apart by Robbie's flurry of slicing limbs.

"No!" Eunice cried. "Please, no! No! God, no!"

Catherine's head rolled away like a kicked soccer ball, followed by a train of bloodied hair.

Griffin saw what was happening. In the storm of violence and spraying blood, one half of Robbie's head was lapping up the fluids. The other—the shifting side—was consuming *something else*: a thin blue gas that rose from Catherine's steaming corpse. It wavered like seaweed before becoming vacuumed up into the monstrous side of Robbie's face.

It's just like he said, Griffin thought. *He's eating our ghosts. He's killing us . . . then he's eating our spirits before they can go to Heaven.*

He said we've ve seen a whole lotta ghosts. *Those were his words.*

Are they . . .?

Is he made *of the ghosts he eats?*

Trying to parse this logically was boring a hole through Griffin's brow. He gave up and collapsed into hysterics, crying and shuddering while Robbie finished with what was left of Catherine.

And then, when he closed his eyes . . . everything changed.

He was surprised there was no darkness behind his lids. Instead, Griffin saw flashes of bright, white lightning, which illuminated—

Griffin blinked.

Had he woken up from a bad dream, or had his brain shut down? Was he so traumatized by everything he'd been struggling to comprehend that something inside of *him* had snapped with the same bone-crunching sound that had emanated from Robbie Miller?

Unsure of himself, he took a juddering breath and tried to take in the sparse sights presented by the flickering light.

There was a landscape all around him. He was no longer *in* The Home, although he was also somehow confident that this place could *only* exist in The Home.

One at a time, Griffin. Just take a breath again. Focus on that. Then sort through this.

Five seconds crept by. Each one felt like an hour. In that time, he saw that the ground he sat on was smooth and flat, like the surface of an oil slick. There were no walls around him, only foggy barriers that climbed like smoke. He squinted upward, hoping to see a ceiling. Instead, there were storm clouds, which the lightning crawled through—spiderlike and whip-quick.

Griffin looked at his hands. They were clean. All of Ed and Catherine's blood had been washed away from him. If he tried, he could almost believe their deaths had been part of a dark dream, that they were alive and well, just waiting for him to wake up.

In the distance, he heard a sharp scream. He blinked, then was startled when he saw Eunice sitting on the ground across from him.

"E-Eunice?" Griffin asked, mouth agape.

"Griffin!" Her eyeballs were so weepy they looked as if they'd been boiled. She stood and ran to him, collapsing into his arms.

Together, they remained in their embrace, crying and clutching each other as if frightened the other would float away.

"Wh-where are we?" Eunice asked, glancing around at the void.

"I don't know," Griffin responded.

"Are we—"

"Guys?" a meek voice cracked through the darkness. It was Orville. He'd joined them.

Griffin had been so distracted he hadn't even realized that their bonds had dissipated until he opened the embrace and Orville joined them.

Griffin wasn't an introvert, but he was reserved. He'd never before opened his arms to a stranger, but now he held on to Orville as if they were long-lost brothers.

"Where are we?" Eunice asked again when their tears dwindled.

"I dunno," Griffin said. "This place is—"

"It's scary," Orville interrupted.

It's better than where we were just a few minutes ago! Griffin thought.

"Where's Catherine? And . . . and Ed?" Eunice sniffled.

"I dunno," Griffin repeated.

"They should be here if we're—"

"Don't say that!" Griffin snapped.

Flinching, Eunice bowed her head.

"Say what?" Orville asked.

"Don't say we're . . . dead."

"Dead?" Orville gasped.

"We aren't. We'd know if we were."

"I don't know what happened," Eunice said. "I closed my eyes, opened them, and now—"

"Now we're here." Griffin looked toward the nearest wall of fog.

"What do we do?" Orville asked.

Griffin closed his eyes and took another deep breath. Before he could make the observation himself, Orville spoke up: "The air tastes weird."

Eunice sucked in a breath. "You're right."

"It tastes like—like it's—" Griffin struggled to find the right word.

"Sour," Orville said.

"Yeah. Like . . . diesel fumes."

But it was more than that. It was spicier, tangier, and the taste tattooed his tongue and refused to leave, no matter how hard he worked it around his mouth. It was

194

as if each breath was clogging his pipes with more of the taste, turning solid inside him.

Orville walked toward the wall of fog, separating himself from the group.

"Orville!" Eunice shouted. "Come back! It's not safe!"

"We won't know if we don't try," Orville said.

"Try what?" Griffin cried.

Before they could stop him, Orville reached out and pressed his finger against the fog. It slipped in easily, but Orville's body seemed to shake like he'd been electrocuted. He pulled away with a sharp yowl and scurried back to them.

"What's it like?" Eunice asked.

"It hurts!" Orville proclaimed, showing them his finger. It was red and raw. A few layers of skin had been shaved away from the digit, but the result was bloodless. As if the wall had consumed the flesh and then the blood before it had a chance to spill.

"We can't go through it," Orville whimpered, holding his hand against his chest. "It'll kill us."

"So, we aren't dead, right?" Eunice asked. "If we can get hurt, that means we aren't dead!"

Orville held up his right hand and inspected his finger. Griffin shuddered at the sight of it. Even the fingernail had been extracted.

"It doesn't hurt the way it should," Orville said. "If this had happened to me . . . before . . . I'd be crying. This is like a bee sting."

"Even if we aren't dead," Griffin said, "Robbie is alone with our bodies."

Eunice began to cry again. "He killed them, didn't he? That wasn't just a bad dream, was it? He actually—"

Seeing no point in lying, Griffin nodded.

"What should we do?" Orville reiterated.

"I don't know." Griffin sighed. "We could try . . .

walking."

"Where?" Eunice asked.

"Forward. Follow the walls . . . see where this place leads."

Orville peered ahead. "I dunno, man. This place is— It looks like it could go on forever."

"What other option do we have? Come here, Orville."

Orville froze. "How do you know my name?"

"We have a few classes together, don't we?"

"I don't know you guys."

"I'm Griffin Chalks. This is Eunice Lee."

Orville looked back and forth, as if he was suspicious of them. Then, he warmed and leaned toward Eunice, who was still sobbing.

"You need a hand?" he asked.

She nodded and put her arm over his shoulder.

"Here, I'll help too," Griffin said as he took her other side.

CHAPTER EIGHT

Orville let Eunice lean her head against his shoulder. Soon, his shirt was sopping wet with her tears. *At least it'll cover up all the piss stains Ted left on me. Har-har*, Orville thought sardonically. Hauling Eunice around was a struggle, but she'd been much more scared than either of them. Orville was an only child, so he couldn't even fathom the loss she'd just experienced in The Home.

If I see that Robbie guy again . . . I'll clobber him.

No, I won't. I'll tuck my tail between my legs and run off like a kicked dog.

No way I'd face up to that guy.

He's not even a human being anymore, is he? He probably was once upon a time . . . before he killed his parents. Now, he's as much a part of The Home as that . . . creature is. The . . . Ghost Eater.

He'd never heard of such a thing before, even though he had two encyclopedias at home that were dedicated to mystical creatures and folklore. He knew all about water monsters—like the Afanc and the Kraken—and he knew about dragons and goblins and orcs . . . but he'd *never* read about ghost eaters before.

There was, he recalled, a religious ritual called "sin eating," where the eater would consume the sins of a dead person who'd not yet been forgiven. In essence, the ritual was supposed to purify the soul of the deceased so that they may enter Heaven. But it marred the soul of the sin eater, who took on and then bore the sins of the dead until they themselves died and their apprentice ate their sins. It was a bizarre thing to consider, but Orville wondered if that wasn't quite dissimilar to what a ghost eater was.

What if it started as a person?

He went from town to town, eating ghosts from haunted houses . . . haunting himself so that houses would be clean of dark spirits. He carried all these ghosts around with him so that good Christian families could sleep soundly at night with no poltergeists to interrupt their prayers.

Then he ate one ghost too many, and now, he's a vortex of angry spirits.

Theorizing could only do so much. Besides, Orville doubted any answer would truly satisfy him. What he knew already was enough to give him nightmares until he was a very old man—if he survived that long. Especially now that they were walking down a long stretch of nothingness, surrounded on all sides by swirling fog, their path lit only by flickering lightning, answers seemed unnecessary. All he wanted was to be back home, tucked in bed with a book, blissfully unaware of the horrors that lurked there in the dark with him.

"See anything up ahead?" Griffin asked.

"No," Orville answered. "Just more of the same—Wait!"

"I see it too! Eunice!" Griffin jostled her—a bit unkindly.

She lifted her head and blinked away a fresh crop of tears. Her arm left Griffin's side, and she wiped her face with her palm.

"What is it?"

"It looks like . . ." Orville squinted.

Ahead of them, the darkness seemed to *part*. What he first figured was a totem pole was, in actuality, a lighthouse. It stood tall, a strong shaft of stone that stretched up to the storm clouds. On its top, a beam of light swirled back and around, rotating like an owl's head.

"A lighthouse?" Eunice asked. "But . . . how?"

"Maybe there's an ocean behind it," Griffin said.

"I mean, we aren't anywhere *real*. Who would build a lighthouse in a . . ." Orville fought to find the right word. "Netherworld!"

"A what?" Griffin asked.

Ignoring him, Orville stepped forward, dragging Eunice with him.

"Wait, what if it's a trap of some kind?" Griffin started. "What if we knock on the door and Robbie answers?"

The three of them froze. Orville could envision it perfectly. He saw half of Robbie's face shape-shifting, becoming that of The Ghost Eater.

Mr. Friendlyman. That's what Robbie said. The Ghost Eater has a name . . . and it's Mr. Friendlyman. That old urban legend our parents used to tell us about not accepting any invitations from "Mr. Friendlyman," they were talking about The Ghost Eater—about that thing *in The Home! And when kids teased each other, saying Mr. Friendlyman would "getcha," they didn't know what that meant. They didn't know what he* did *after he got you! It wasn't a boogeyman . . . it wasn't a stranger . . . it was The Ghost Eater!*

Orville heard Ed and Catherine's screams again. They clanged in his head like cowbells.

"I don't know if we have any other choice," Eunice said. "I think if we turn around and walk all the way back . . . the lighthouse will just show up again."

"How do you know that?" Griffin asked.

Eunice shook her head. "I just do."

She just does.

Just like how you know what a ghost eater is.

It ate more than human ghosts . . .

It ate the ghosts of . . . old things . . .

It ate the ghosts of the things that crawled on Earth before man could walk. Before man was even a seedling or a sprout. It consumed the ghosts of gods.

ANCIENT TERRIBLE AWFUL GODS WITH CHOMPING MOUTHS AND MILLIONS OF HUNGRY EYES AND—

Orville realized it was not his voice that was speaking to him. It was coming from the light. It grew stronger and louder when the beam swept over him. Softer and quieter when it shied away.

He looked toward Eunice and Griffin, wondering if they, too, were experiencing the same phenomena.

"Do you hear that?" Orville asked.

"Hear what?"

"The voice in my head. It's—"

"I hear it too," Eunice confirmed.

"I've been trying to ignore it." Griffin snorted.

"What's it saying?" Orville asked.

"That The Ghost Eater isn't . . . it wasn't human. When it was alive, before it became what it is now . . . it was . . ."

"What was it?" Eunice asked.

"I think if we go to the lighthouse . . . it will tell us," Griffin said.

The beam fell upon them again.

Orville shuddered at the words in his head.

Come, Orville . . . Come and learn the great and terrible things I must teach you.

Come . . .

CHAPTER NINE

At the front of the lighthouse, Eunice held her breath. She stood back, allowing the boys to go ahead and knock on the old, oily wooden door. Around the lighthouse, the flat, black landscape turned into rock and moss. Homosporous growths bloomed along the base of the structure. Barnacles and crusty coral skittered with bright crabs and slithering things. She spotted a creature that looked like a lizard with folded bat wings and jewels for eyes. It crawled leisurely out from beneath a stone, glared toward her, then scurried back, hiding in the dark. The sour taste of the air had turned rotten around the lighthouse, as if the building was packed with spoiled meat and painted with sun-dried milk. Right behind the edifice was a towering wall of roiling fog. Not an ocean but a flat, white slate. To Eunice, the place beyond the lighthouse looked like an unending blizzard. The sort that would make Alaska look like a summer retreat.

They could not go onward. The lighthouse was, it seemed, their final destination.

Orville was about to knock with his uninjured hand when Griffin stopped him. "Let me," he said.

Orville relented, stepping back.

Griffin went to knock. Just as his fist grazed the wood, the door fell open. A hot gust of air blew out of the building like breath from the mouth of a hungry tiger. Eunice took a hesitant step back. Orville gagged and put his uninjured hand over his mouth, pressing the other to his chest.

"Oh God!" Griffin moaned. "It stinks!"

"That's like . . ."

"Death." Eunice finished the thought, stepping forward.

"I don't wanna go in," Griffin said. "Let's leave! Let's try the other way! Come on! I don't want to—"

Something uncoiled from the darkness. It looked like a mass of hair swirling around a drain. Eunice's heart froze in her chest, and she felt her stomach cramp at the sight of it.

An inhuman voice boomed from within the dark chambers of the lighthouse. It reverberated over the ground, causing the rocks to tremble and the sea creatures to hide. Even the foggy walls that surrounded them seemed to flex and bend, pushed by the voice's force.

Force, Eunice thought with fascination. *It's not a voice attached to a body. It's not a human spirit. It's a FORCE.*

And it said to them a simple sentence, which warmed their blood until they felt as if they were boiling: "*Come . . . and . . . learn . . .*"

Learn? Eunice thought, frightened. *Learn what?*

Learn what he is , , , what it is . . . what Mr. Friendlyman is . . . what Robbie Miller is becoming . . . what consumed my siblings and brought us to this terrible place?

We are trading one nightmare for another.

To know is to commit suicide. Nothing will be the same for us. Nothing! We may find our way back to our world, but we will be changed forever. Mutated by the things this creature wants in our heads.

No!

I refuse!

Eunice took another step back, wishing she could spin on her heels and run. Not even caring if she collided with one of the eating walls which had taken the skin from Orville's finger. She wanted to be away from this lighthouse, from the voice within, from the knowledge that grasped for her.

I just want to go back to the real world.
To being stupid, happy, and unaware!

But it was too late to turn back.

Against her will, her feet began to take her forward. She wanted to fight them. To fall down on her rump, pull her shoes off, and scrape the bottoms of her feet raw with a broken seashell. But she was helpless—hopeless. Instead, she watched as she was carried, almost lullingly, toward the door.

"What are you doing?" Griffin asked.

"Eunice? Don't go near there!" Orville shouted.

She shook her head, a single bead of moisture falling from her left eye while her right turned upside down in her head, becoming as white as fresh paper. Zombielike, she approached the door.

"Stop her!" Orville screamed.

"I can't move!" Griffin said.

Overhead, the light began to swing back and forth, flicking like a horse's tail. Every time the beam swept over Eunice, she felt something *grow* inside her. It pushed against her flesh with ragged fingers and sucked in its breath deeply, cramping her organs. It felt like she had become pregnant . . . but not with a fetus. Whatever was inside her was somehow *bigger* than she was. And it spoke in her head, whispering deep and dark secrets to her. Things that no human ear had heard before without going mad. It told her the names of gods and aliens, of planets man would never discover, of the guards that stood outside the boundaries of time and space, their scepters adorned with swirling comets, their heads crowned with glittery stars. She heard their voices, and they boomed louder than thunder . . . louder, even, than Mr. Friendlyman. And she knew now that that wasn't his real name.

His name was unpronounceable. It did not cater to the restraints of the human tongue. His name was the sound of a galaxy dying, of stars clashing, of millions braying in agony. His name was a shriek that pierced through the heavens and corrupted even the ears of God.

"I am . . . I was . . . I shall be . . . And you . . . you will serve . . . you will worship—"

"No!" Eunice cried. "No! Please, GOD!"

She saw a massive skeleton. A creature with huge, leathery wings on its back and dried tentacles bearding its titanic skull. The corpse of the demon god—Cthulhu was its name—lay supine on the bed of Earth's dry crust, and on it crawled worms. One of the worms wriggled into the creature's skull and chewed on its husky brain, and that worm became a ghost. A ghost which was eventually eaten . . . by a man.

A man called The Ghost Eater, who came to the haunted land to purify it before it was settled, before it was named Starch. The man, a shambling ghoul, consumed the ghosts that lay in the soil. He dug them up with his fingers and shoveled them into his gaping, toothless maw. He'd removed his teeth himself, knowing the ghosts inside him would rot them anyway.

Then he chewed on the worm—it changed him. Twisted him. Infected not only him but every spirit that possessed him. Instead of simply swallowing the ghost, the man knelt on the ground and tore himself open with his bare hands, allowing his steaming guts to tattoo the ground that The Home would eventually be built upon.

You won't find this in their history books. Starch forgot about me as soon as I was buried—in the same ground you now rest upon. They forgot about me . . . but I still fester here. I still rot!

204

She realized who was speaking to her. That man, who now lived in a lighthouse in the Netherworld of its own construction, was the being that spoke to her now. That worm, which called itself The Core . . . The Hive . . . The Beast of Hungry Teeth . . . That amalgamation of spirits which was known as Mr. Friendlyman. The boogeyman of Sycamore Lane. That demon, which had killed and swallowed the spirits of Ed and Catherine Lee, denying them the afterlife they deserved, fed now on their screams. Screams which drove nails into Eunice's head and she was falling falling falling forever and ever and she found the ground made from the same dense fog that surrounded the lighthouse and she wished to God it would devour her so she didn't have to feel the pain of knowing and her tears streamed out of her in rivers and cities grew and died on her belly and her skull cracked open while her flesh melted from her bones only to slide back into place centuries later—

And then she awoke.

And she was back in The Home.

Orville, Griffin, and the corpses of her siblings were there as well, anchoring her feet.

She sat up, surprised her invisible bonds were broken. Her eyes were bleeding tears, and her nose was wet. Sick dribbled out of her mouth and collapsed onto her lap like a warm cat. She glanced around, frightened and relieved all at once.

Robbie was in the middle of their circle. Naked, tattooed, and weeping.

"Wh-what happened?" she asked.

"You were chosen," Robbie said. His face crumpled like that of a child who'd been gifted prunes for Christmas. Gone were the ghostly aura and the monstrous mutations that had overtaken half of his body. Eunice saw that Robbie was just as he'd been before he'd killed his parents, before Mr. Friendlyman had laid claim to his soul.

"Please, let us go—" Eunice started, just as Griffin and Orville were shocked awake.

"You were chosen," Robbie cried again. "I wasn't."

He held up a switchblade knife. It gleamed in the dark, smiling at Eunice.

But she wasn't afraid.

Not anymore.

She remembered what was in the lighthouse and the things she'd been told.

She smiled back.

"Do it," Eunice said.

Robbie speared himself through the throat with the blade. It slid in quietly, but the blood that came out of him roared.

PART THREE
A MOUTH FULL OF HUNGER

CHAPTER ONE

Orville looked at his hand. Funny, the finger on his right hand was smarting. A phantom pain, he knew. He'd recovered after leaving The Home, and the finger had never bothered him before. But now, on the drive from Griffin's house to the cemetery, his finger felt as if it was filled with needles.

"What did you see?" Griffin asked from behind the wheel. He wasn't a great driver, but with Russell hightailing it, they didn't have another option. Griffin was hard on his brakes and tended to nudge the gas like he was afraid it would fall asleep.

"Nothing now. It's too dark," Eunice replied.

"No . . . I mean, do you remember what you saw in the lighthouse?"

"No." Eunice's voice was firm.

"I remember you were the only one that walked into it. Then I remember waking up right when Robbie killed himself. We all started screaming then, and shortly after . . . the police came."

"Covered in blood, all tangled up in those ropes," Orville remarked from the back seat. "It felt like years before the police barged in and freed us from that—"

"I don't remember," Eunice said. "I remember walking up to the lighthouse, and I remember feeling all kinds of sick. Then there was . . . I don't know. Something like a dream. You remember how it feels but you can't recall a single detail. Then I woke up."

A beat of stalled silence passed between them.

"Then I got the book."

"The book?" Orville repeated.

"The one that told me about the ritual." She passed her purse to him. "Dig around. You'll find it."

Orville fumbled with her purse, a little embarrassed to be allowed access to it. Indeed, there was a small, leather-bound book within. No bigger than the palm-sized New Testament Bibles that Orville often found in his mail.

He opened it and read the title aloud. "*The Worshipping of The Core.*"

"The Core? That was a name he used, wasn't it?" Griffin asked.

"Yes," Eunice said. "I did some research. Did you know there was a cult of women who actually believed they were *married* to that beast in The Home?"

Griffin snorted. "Crazies."

"They committed group suicide. Just like those folks in Jonestown, 'member? The folks that all drank cyanide or somethin'?"

Orville shivered. "When?"

"Three days after we made the national news in nineteen sixty-one," Eunice intoned. "'Teenagers Survive Brutal Satanic Slaying in Missouri' was the popular headline, I think. I always liked that one. Sounded like the plot to a movie instead of . . . what actually happened."

"Christ," Griffin said.

"In those three days, their leader—a woman named Agnes Weatherby—wrote this little manifesto. It was never printed or put into circulation. She simply wrote it out, then mailed it to me the day she and her cult offed themselves."

"Jesus!" Orville shook his head. "What is this? Some kind of Bible?"

"It came with a note. Apparently, they were

expecting Robbie to write their Bible," Eunice said.

"They bet on the wrong horse."

"So they cobbled this together at the last minute. It's not their Bible, Orville. It's the rough draft."

Orville flipped through the pages. They were covered in chicken scratch, which had blurred and smudged. In the back of the car, in the dark, the handwriting was impossible to read.

"I'll look through it later," he said before shoving the book back in the purse and passing it to Eunice.

"I know it by heart," Eunice announced. "I read it front to back, repeatedly, when I got it. Then I brought it up to Griffin, and he called me crazy. He told me I oughta burn it."

"I still think you should."

"After this is over, I might take you up on that," Eunice said. "In fact, I promise you this . . . I'll burn the damn thing as soon as we've finished our business tonight."

"Damn right, you will." Griffin scowled. "I still can't believe we're doing this, anyways."

Orville looked out the window. The trees appeared to be crawling toward Griffin's car like stalking panthers. He shivered, held himself, and wished again that he was back at Everly. He wondered if the police had been called yet, or if the nurses had simply decided that one missing old man wasn't worth their time. Besides, who was going to call in and ask for his whereabouts? Maybe they were forging a death certificate at this very moment.

He heard Kojak's voice. *Daft old fool. Yer imagination will be the death of you.*

His arms felt tight, and his stomach hurt. He'd been missing his pills, which he seemed to need on a nearly hourly basis.

If I hadn't followed Eunice to the dock . . . none of this would be happening. I'd be tucked into bed and—

And I'd be having nightmares about Mr. Friendlyman.

Until, eventually, he would get strong enough to attack me the way he did Griffin.

Maybe that's what's happening now. All of this is a hallucination, and I'll wake up to a heart attack and a stroke in no time at all.

Orville thought to a few hours back when he and Griffin and Eunice had been arguing in Griffin's living room, which still stank of his "attack."

Eunice had been convincing then, telling them things would only get worse if Griffin and Orville didn't follow her commands . . .

"What is this?" Orville had asked. "How can *we* become ghost eaters?"

"It's nonsense!" Griffin exclaimed. "Can't you hear yourself? See how ridiculous you sound!"

"I need both of you for it to work," Eunice said, her tone calm and collected. "It won't work with just me. I tried—"

"You *tried*?" Griffin was genuinely shocked.

"It wasn't right. I thought maybe the instructions were symbolic . . . but no. They're literal."

"God!" Griffin put his knuckles against his teeth.

"I need your help, guys. Both of you. Otherwise, Mr. Friendlyman is just going to—" For the first time, Eunice's voice wavered. "He's gonna get bold. He won't be satisfied just spooking us old people. He'll become a black hole in the middle of Starch, and everything we know and love will be consumed by him."

Orville held his breath before speaking. "I'm with you, Eunice. I wish you'd tell me more about this ritual . . . but I'm with you."

"You know what she's proposing, Orville? You know what you just agreed to?" Griffin rasped.

"Tell him. Tell him, Griffin, and get it over with."

"*Grave robbing*," Griffin blurted angrily. "This ritual . . . involves *digging up* Ed and Catherine!"

Orville blanched. He looked at Eunice, hoping Griffin was being hyperbolic or that he'd simply misinterpreted the ritual. She gazed back at him seriously, her jaw set and her eyes narrowed.

Orville could hear Ed crying for his mommy as he was torn to pieces, and heard Catherine's final scream as Mr. Friendlyman/Robbie Miller cut her life short.

"W-we have to dig them up?" Orville asked, still struggling to believe what he'd been told. "Eunice, I can't do that . . . I'm . . . Besides . . . I'm too old to go *digging up graves* at night."

"You don't have to dig up my siblings, Orville," Eunice said. "It's been taken care of."

"It's . . . Wait . . . it's a*lready happened*?" Griffin asked.

"It's happening. The second it gets dark."

Orville glanced toward the window, at the land across from Griffin's house. The sun was already setting behind the hills. He imagined cloaked ghouls slinking through an old, gothic graveyard, shovels and picks in hand, faces masked with broken skulls.

"I hired a few people to do it for us," Eunice said. "All we need to do is . . . pick them up and take them to The Home."

"We can't do that," Griffin said.

"Besides," Orville added, "The Home is probably crawling with police."

Griffin frowned. "How many people died there last night?"

"Three. A family," Eunice answered.

Orville felt his heart deflate. "Christ. We have no choice, do we? I don't even know what this family *looks* like and . . . I feel like if I say no, I'm disappointing them."

"It'll be more than just one family if we don't do

212

this," Eunice said. "Eventually, Mr. Friendlyman will get hungry enough and not care who sees him. And who'll stop him, anyways?"

"We stopped Robbie, didn't we?" Griffin asked. "I can't remember how but . . . somehow . . ."

Orville remembered. "We didn't stop him. Eunice did."

Griffin moaned to himself, as if he was struggling to hold back a justifiable complaint.

"I don't know *how* she stopped him . . . but *she* told him to kill himself and he fuckin' did." Orville continued. "I'm in, Eunice. You know this shit better than I do. Better than any human being on the planet. Hell, you're the ONLY person who's ever been in the lighthouse, I'd wager! I think it's disgusting and terrifying what you want us to do. I think digging Ed and Catherine out of their graves is *wrong* on every level . . . but I trust you."

"So do I, damn my stupid heart!" Griffin angrily admitted. "And after everything I've been through today, everything I saw . . . Shit! There's just no other option, is there?"

"I wish I was wrong, but I know I'm not," Eunice said. "You think I *want* to pull poor Ed up from the earth? No. He belongs there. He should be resting. But he's not . . . because he's still in The Home. He's still being . . . *digested* by that awful, terrible thing."

Griffin stood and walked around his living room, pacing deliberately.

"I've had visions too, you know. Maybe even more realistic ones than the vision you just endured, Mister Chalks," Eunice scolded. "Mr. Friendlyman sends me dreams about Ed. I dream I'm walking through The Home, and I know Ed is around every corner, but when I turn, he's just escaped my eyesight. And when I chase after him, the ground around my feet becomes

213

sticky. When I look down . . . I see I'm walking on faces. I'm walking on the faces of every single man, woman, child, and alien that *beast* has eaten. And then they're on the walls and the ceiling, their mouths open, dripping blood. And then they close around me, and I feel like I'm not in The Home anymore, Griffin . . . I'm in a s*tomach.*" She was panting.

"I believe you," Griffin said, his voice small and defeated.

"I wish I'd never gone in that lighthouse. I wish I'd never heard his voice—his *true* voice. I wish I'd let Robbie Miller kill me, most days. And life hasn't been easy. Hell, it's barely been worth living. My husband left me because I became obsessed with my memories . . . My son—" She began to weep.

Orville wrapped his arms around her as best he could, and shushed her . . .

Thinking back on it, in the present, in the back seat, he wondered why she'd lied.

She'd mentioned her husband before, at Everly. The portrait she'd painted hadn't been a flattering one. In it, her husband had been a hothead layabout who'd wasted her time after getting her pregnant with a doomed child. She'd even mentioned that he'd run to Vegas to waste his money gambling.

But now, Orville saw a different image. A bedraggled man, coming home to find a maniac waiting. A woman obsessed with ancient gods, haunted houses, and digging up corpses.

She was probably embarrassed, Orville figured. *Too embarrassed to tell the truth until it became necessary, poor dear. Poor Eunice . . .*

When Eunice's tears had cleared, Orville had patted her on the shoulder reassuringly.

"I'm sorry," she muttered.

"No need to apologize." Orville smiled.

214

"We'll do it, Eunice," Griffin said. "We'll follow you to Hell and back, I guess."

Eunice reached over and held Griffin's hand. "Thank you. Both of you."

"Yeah. Sure thing. Besides, what are friends for?" Orville asked . . .

Friends are for grave robbing, he thought as he returned to the present.

The car trundled through the hills and toward the cemetery.

"I can't believe it's taken all this to bring us back together," Eunice said.

"You'd have liked Prudence," Griffin stated. "Both of you. She'd have liked you too. Although I doubt she would have approved of what we're up to."

"I'm sorry I never got a chance to meet her," Orville said. "I should have made some effort to see you both."

"Hell, I never even finished reading your book," Griffin smirked.

"I did," Eunice admitted.

"Any good?"

"Great. But *you* wouldn't have liked it." She laughed.

"Too much make-believe. No cars." Orville snickered.

Griffin pretended to snore.

At once, the interior of the car felt brighter and happier as the three old friends laughed. The moment was an island in the middle of a tempest. A soft touch after life's hard slaps. Orville felt the cramps flee his belly, and his finger stopped twitching with imaginary pain.

The good feelings were dashed away when the car rose over a hill and the headlights shone down on the gates of a desolate cemetery.

CHAPTER TWO

The graveyard looked abandoned. There was no night watchman, no office building bright with lights, and no lock on the gate, which stood ajar. Inside, the headstones were moss-laden and tilted. The walls surrounding the graveyard were acrawl with lichen and ivy. Standing at the entry of the cemetery, in full view of whoever might approach, was a rough, cross-armed man. Tall, bearded, tattoos, a red bandana, and sunglasses—despite the lateness of the hour. He wore a frayed denim jacket and faded Levi's, which were sullied with mud. There were another four men behind him, but they were so shadow-cloaked they may as well have been inkblots.

"Let me talk to Pierce," Eunice said. "He doesn't look happy."

"Where'd you meet this guy?" Griffin asked.

Orville swallowed a lump. He didn't like the looks of this at all.

"Some people are desperate enough to do anything if you give them the right figure," Eunice explained. It wasn't a real answer, but it was all she seemed willing to offer.

"You hired him?" Griffin asked. "Where? At a biker bar? On the dark web? Did you post a fuckin' want ad?"

Ignoring him, Eunice opened her car door before the vehicle came to a stop.

"Get my walker, dear," she said to Orville. "And stay close by me. Just in case."

In case of what?

Orville exited quickly out of the passenger side. He rounded the car, opened the trunk, and got Eunice's walker out. By the time he brought it to her, she had stumbled halfway toward the graverobber and his clan.

"We didn't agree on diggin' up no kids!" Pierce spat, his voice tainted with a smoker's cough.

"I gave you the names. You never asked their ages," Eunice said firmly. "If you didn't do what was asked of you . . ."

"We did, lady. But we think we need to renegotiate a few things. Who's this?" He nodded toward Orville.

Before Orville could answer, Eunice spoke up. "Friend of mine. His lips are sealed."

"They better be," Pierce growled.

Eunice continued. "I think I offered you a fair price for fair work."

"That wadn't fair work. One of 'em was just 'bout nine or ten."

"He was my brother," Eunice explained. "If anyone's got a claim to him, it's me. Now, I hired you for a job and we agreed on the price. Seems to me we oughta shake hands and be done!"

"How much did she pay you?" Orville found himself asking.

Pierce turned his head owlishly. "Oh. It speaks, huh?"

Orville didn't know how to respond. He crossed his arms and looked at his feet.

"Eight thousand. Total. Four grand for each corpse."

Orville looked at Eunice with pure shock splashed across his sagging face.

"I wanted to incentivize them," she explained. "Now, it looks like they just want to milk me for all I'm worth. Fine, Pierce. You win. How does an extra two thousand sound?"

"Th-that's ten thousand dollars, Eunice!" Orville jabbered.

"I don't love it . . . but I like it," Pierce said.

"Where'd you get that kind of money?" Orville moaned.

She shook her head. "We have a deal, then?"

"We have a deal."

"Orville, be a dear and fetch my purse."

Slack-jawed, Orville bumbled back to the car. The purse was left on Eunice's seat.

"What's happening?" Griffin asked. "Do y'all need me out there?"

None of us could take these bastards in a fight. Each one of his goons looks about bear-sized, Orville thought.

"We'll tell you later. Just keep the car running," he muttered, taking the purse and walking back. He left the passenger door open so Griffin could better hear what was happening.

Does Griffin own a gun? He's always been a bit more conservative than me. Maybe he has a concealed carry permit. I hope so.

Orville shivered before handing Eunice's purse to her, feeling less like a friend and more like a manservant.

She dug around in the bag until she revealed a stack of greenbacks. Orville was shocked. He assumed she'd be writing a check.

Do grave robbers take checks? Is that Mary Poppins' bag? It seems to be bigger on the inside than the outside! Orville thought incredulously.

"Here." Eunice passed the money to the hulking man.

Pierce inspected the bills quickly. Slowly, he nodded and turned around. "Bring 'em out!" he shouted.

The goons slunk out of the shadows. They were as ugly as Orville had worried they'd be. They looked like motorcyclists who had just stumbled away from a road-clogging pileup. Black eyes, torn lips, bloody knuckles, and long gashes down their bare, hairy chests. Orville couldn't help but notice that all of them were white, and a few prominently displayed Nazi symbols on their arms, either as tattoos or a red armband. He shivered again, frightened to think of Eunice conspiring with Nazis to dig up long-dead bodies.

This has to be a dream, Orville thought whimsically. *Nothing like this happens in the real world, to real people like me. No. This is the stuff of movies. Silly-fantasy, as my mother would say.*

The lumbering racists brought out two small sacks. At first, Orville thought they were plastic garbage bags, but then he realized they were actual body bags—the sort he'd only ever seen on cop shows. Their contents seemed light.

Hell, there wasn't even much left of Ed to bury, was there?

He hadn't attended Ed and Catherine's funeral. His mother forbade it, thinking that reflecting on what had happened would do more harm than good. Griffin had gone, and later, he told Orville that the caskets were kept closed.

"They were simple pine boxes," Griffin had explained in a shallow voice. "Missus Lee started crying. Her husband was holding on to her as if he was scared she'd jump up and dive into the grave with her kids. God. It was uncomfortable. It was sad. Be glad you weren't there, man."

I didn't see the funeral . . . but I'm gonna get a good look at the bodies!

Orville felt repulsed. His stomach gurgled loudly, and he felt his knees press together. Sweat bloomed like orchids in his cracks and crevices. Shaking his head, he watched as the Nazis hauled the corpses over to the car.

Pierce opened the trunk, then pointed a stubby finger. His men worked quietly, placing the bodies inside with surprising care and gentleness. After they were laid together side by side, Pierce shut the trunk, then circled around the car again, leading his pack of goons behind him. He looked disdainfully at Eunice.

"Yer about as fucked-up as they get, lady."

Orville almost laughed.

Eunice did. "You're one to talk, Pierce."

"Forget my name. Forget my face. Forget Dart's Tavern. You ain't welcome there no more."

"Pleasure doing business with you!" Eunice jeered as the Nazis sank into the darkness.

Orville grabbed her arm and hurried her back to the car. Since there were obstructions in the trunk–it was better he didn't think about them as corpses, when he was able–Orville hastily folded Eunice's walker and crammed it into the backseat. He had to squeeze himself in next to it.

Griffin looked paler than a ghost. "Was that—Did they put—In the trunk?" he muttered.

No one answered him.

Orville fastened his seat belt, then leaned back and covered his eyes with his fists.

He could smell the dirt and rot behind him in the trunk. It was a hard odor, like alcohol and gasoline. It drilled through his nose and speared his quivering brain, filling his head with dark and awful things.

CHAPTER THREE

Rodney Hoh glared through the darkness. The air was turning and it would rain soon, but nothing short of fire would remove the stink from the air. It clung to him, he realized, the second he'd entered The Home. There he was, calling it The Home, just like he had when he was nothing more than a scared little kid. In actuality, The Home was simply 654 Sycamore Lane. *Missed opportunity,* Hoh thought. *Should've been six-six-six!* He frowned and looked back at his lap. He truthfully hated that he'd drawn the short straw and was now posted outside the infamous murder house. At least he wasn't alone.

"Whaddya think?" Darnell Cole asked.

"About what?" Hoh returned.

"This shit." Darnell shoved a phone in Hoh's face. He took it and held it at arm's length, squinting to see. "You need glasses," Darnell commented.

"I've got glasses," Hoh said. "I just don't wear them. Christ, what is this?"

"It's an article about what happened here last night," Darnell answered. "They mention you."

"Why?"

"Because you were first on the scene."

"What an honor." Hoh passed the phone back to his partner. Where Hoh was stout, sturdy, and gray-faced, Darnell was a chubby redneck with blond stubble, rosy cheeks, and a seemingly endless smile. The two made somewhat of an odd couple, but they got along well enough.

"I was there too," Darnell said. "But they don't mention me at all."

"Your fifteen minutes were over before they even started."

"Lucy said she saw me on the TV, but I watched the news coverage and didn't see myself at all."

"How is Lucy?" Hoh asked, realizing that it'd been a minute since he'd last seen Darnell's wife.

"She's fine. She's Lucy. You know . . . chatty . . . mad as hell half the time, usually over nuthin'. Beautiful as the day I met her."

"She's from here, ain't she?' Hoh asked.

"Yep. She knew all about The Home when she was a kid. Says she was always told that all the stories were just that. Most folks in Starch wanted to forget about it."

"Guess they can't do that now."

"You know, the realtor never even *told* the Pertwee family about The Home's past? They found out from townsfolk. I bet they kept it hidden from their daughter. I couldn't imagine sleeping in a place like that. Surprised if that realtor doesn't wind up sued."

Hoh frowned. "It still looks like a normal house to me. But that's what makes it creepy, I guess."

"Yeah. Smack-dab in the middle of town, we've got a little piece of Hell." Darnell shook his head. "Tourism is gonna go up when folks outside of Missouri hear about it."

"No."

"Yes. It happened the last time. When those two kids got killed and that murderer offed himself."

"There were people who traveled here just to see where people died?"

"Your problem is that you expect better of the human race, man."

"Shit."

"Shit, indeed. Hey, you got any more of those cheese sticks?"

"All out."

"Damn."

"I've got an apple."

"Fine. I'll eat it."

"Who said I'm offering?"

Darnell grinned and leaned forward, lifting up his little lunch bag. "Bag of chips says you'll trade."

"You're a child, Darnell."

"But you'll trade?'

"Absolutely."

They swapped treats and ate silently, both keeping their keen eyes on The Home as if it would run away the second they turned their backs.

Might be better for everyone if it did, Hoh thought as he used his tongue to compress a salty chip against the roof of his mouth.

"You believe it's haunted?" Darnell asked.

"Are you crazy?"

"I didn't say *I* believed that. But, hey, I'm not a local. Lucy does. She says she'll never go to Sycamore because of it."

Hoh nodded. "I don't think it's haunted, no. But I do think it's *bad*."

"Bad," Darnell repeated.

Their job was simple tonight. Darnell Cole and Rodney Hoh were supposed to watch The Home and make sure no one fucked with it. In Sheriff Barker's words, "We gotta ensure that no one *mo*-lests the crime scene."

Outside, a light drizzle began. The window was pattered with glittering droplets, and the sky flexed with lightning.

"We could use the rain. Poor Lucy has been

complaining about the garden lately," Darnell started.

"Hey." Hoh sat upright.

"Turn on the wipers. I can't see shit."

"Hey!" Hoh pointed.

"What?" Darnell asked dumbly.

"Look!"

Darnell squeezed his eyes. "Jesus. Is that—"

Hoh flicked on the wipers, clearing a path.

Their eyes weren't playing tricks on them; there was a light on in one of the rooms on the top floor. Standing at the window was a vaguely feminine shape, only it was too tall to be an average girl. It seemed stooped, hunched over so that it could peer out the window at the car.

"Which room is that?" Darnell asked.

"That's Ocean's!"

"Christ!" Hoh recalled finding Ocean Pertwee's demolished body in her bedroom. She'd been smeared across the bed like a bug against a windshield. The flashes of remembrance were like hot needles in his heart. "Someone snuck in from the back, I guess." He tried to sound unperturbed, but he failed. His voice was clipped.

They saw the figure vanish, slinking into the room.

"What if it's the killer?" Darnell asked.

"It's not," Hoh replied.

"But what if? You know, some of them come back to places where—"

The front door fell open, the yellow crime scene tape tattered. A long block of light spilled out of The Home and illuminated the yard. The light wavered as if it was turning on an axis. The rain fell harder, but it could not mute the beam.

Hoh felt his eyes swell with tears. He could hear something gnawing at his ear like a pesky mosquito. It switched from one side of his head to the other, speaking in a language he didn't recognize.

What's happening to me? Hoh wondered as he felt something coil up inside his guts.

"We gotta call this in!" Darnell said. "Something *weird* is goin' on here!"

Not weird . . . bad! Hoh thought. His mouth went dry, and his fingernails began to buzz.

Surprising himself, Rodney Hoh pulled his gun out from his holster and pointed it at Darnell's head. The gun popped in his hand, and then there was a blow of thunder so loud it sounded like fabric ripping inside Hoh's head.

Wait . . . what? Hoh thought, dumbfounded. He turned his gaze toward his partner, who had crumpled over. Blood painted the passenger side window and the windshield. Darnell's skull looked like a broken vase.

Why'd I do that? Hoh thought before he realized he'd turned the gun around and was staring down its oily, smoking barrel.

He saw the front door shut before he pulled the trigger.

If anyone in the neighborhood heard the gunfire, they mistook it for the storm.

CHAPTER FOUR

Orville spotted the cop car.

"We won't get past them," he whined.

"They're already dead," Eunice stated.

Griffin looked flabbergasted. "How do you know?"

"Because Mr. Friendlyman wants us in The Home. It's where he's at his strongest. If there was anything that would stop us from walking into his mouth, he'll take care of it."

"Oh God," Griffin said. "Is that blood on the—"

Orville squeezed into the space between the driver and the passenger. His face flushed red when he saw the spiderweb cracks on the driver's side window and the red soup dribbling down the door.

"We're driving right into Hell, aren't we?" Griffin asked, clutching the steering wheel so tightly his fingers looked like frozen shrimp. He turned into the driveway. "Do we even know who was living here?" He put the car in park. The headlights bore down on the closed garage door. Orville saw that the front door was wide open. A long spear of light fell out of The Home and landed on the ground. In the rain, the light should have been broken, but it was as strong as concrete.

"They were the Pertwee family," Orville said. "That's what they said on the news. They showed a picture of them . . . but it was pretty blurry."

"They won't—They won't still be in there, will they?" Griffin asked, his breath shaking.

"No!" Eunice said. "But . . ."

"But what?"

"It will be bloody." She spoke in a whisper, as if she could downplay it.

Orville shuddered. He could only imagine the mess Mr. Friendlyman had made of the poor Pertwee family. Blood splashed on the walls, limbs clogging the pipes, and heads rolling away from smears on the carpet—like Catherine.

We can't do this.

We're old and frail and scared . . . and we can't do this!

We need to call professionals.

Professional whats? Professional ghost eaters? Ha! Good luck finding them in the phone book!

Gazing at Eunice, Orville was still struggling to believe that any of this was happening. He especially couldn't fathom that she somehow had a plan that would put a stop to this madness.

She devoted her whole life to it. She said so herself: this is what drove her husband away from her.

He wished he knew more about the woman Eunice had become. When he thought of her, he still pictured only a teenager. The girl he'd spent a few shaky weeks with, battling his trauma with her friendship.

Why didn't the three of us live our lives together? After what happened to us . . . we should have.

"Oh, God." Griffin put his hands together and bowed his head.

"Are you praying?" Eunice asked.

"Yeah. Didn't really think too hard 'bout believing until today . . . but I guess I do. I believe in God, the Devil, and everything in between, Lord, help me."

"I agree," Orville said. "I think we should all pray."

Eunice glowered. "Have at it."

"You don't think God can help us?"

"I think God lives in that place." Eunice pointed toward The Home.

"You can't be serious."

"I think whatever Mr. Friendlyman is . . . No . . . I *know* that he's more than just a monster."

"How do you know that? Is it in that strange book?" Orville asked.

"No. It's what I saw when I went into the lighthouse."

"I thought you couldn't remember—"

"I don't remember all of it, but I remember pieces. I can't describe them. You can't describe something like *that*."

A chill passed through the car.

"Eunice . . ." Orville started.

"What?"

"What else aren't you telling us?"

"I've told you everything."

"No . . . you haven't." Orville swallowed a lump. He remembered when Eunice had randomly told him to meet her in the woods behind his house. There, she'd spread out a picnic blanket, and she lay waiting, naked, for him. It had been the one and only time he'd ever made love with anyone, and he'd been frightened every second of it. Frightened because although she held him carefully and moaned in his ear, she said nothing. And when he'd filled her, she didn't even flinch. After he came, she stood and walked over to her folded clothes. He lay on his back, watching her, fearing her silence, enraptured by her movements. And then, the next day, she told him and Griffin together that her parents were moving her away from Starch.

She never once brought up what she and Orville had done, and he was too nervous to bring it up himself. Now, it hung over him like a cloud.

Everything she's done has been with purpose.

Was that act even a part of this? Somehow?

Was that how the ritual began?

Eunice turned her head and smiled softly at Orville.

"I'm sorry. I can't tell you everything. It won't work if I do."

"Please, just tell us . . . w*hat* is he?"

"I don't know. Even with everything he told me . . . I still don't know."

"What's his real name?" Griffin asked. "You know it, don't you?"

Eunice nodded. "It's unpronounceable. He's not just *one* thing either, remember? He's every ghost he's ever eaten."

"Make it make sense, Eunice," Griffin pleaded. "Before we charge in, we have to know what we're up against."

"But you won't," Eunice said. "You never will. It's beyond comprehension."

"That's a cop-out," Griffin growled.

"It's the truth. What I saw inside the lighthouse was . . ." Her voice trailed off. "It was a man once. But before that, it was a worm. A parasite that chewed on the corpse of an ancient god. The man was hired by the founders of Starch to purify the land. He didn't know what he was eating when he picked up the ghost of the parasite and consumed it . . ."

Orville saw that she was shaking.

"I can't explain it. You'd just have to see it yourself. Hell, you just might!"

Another cloud of silence passed through the car. Orville wrung his hands and chomped on his tongue.

"Oh," —Orville pointed— "do you see that?"

They followed his gaze. Griffin gawked at the sight.

Imprinted in one of the windows was the slender silhouette of a man. Even without seeing his features, they all recognized the figure.

"It's him, isn't it? Robbie?" Griffin asked.

"It has to be," Eunice said.

Orville swallowed loudly. "I can't believe it. We

saw him die." Again, the memory played through his rattled brain. His thoughts were interrupted by a loud thump from behind him. He spun, expecting to see a monstrous face pressed against the rear window of the vehicle. But alas, the air behind their car was filled only with rain. The thump rose again, and this time, Orville knew where it originated from.

The blood rushed out of him.

"Th-there's noises," he stuttered.

"What is that?" Griffin asked.

"They're moving in the trunk!" Orville exclaimed.

Griffin turned toward Eunice. "Did you know *that* would happen?"

The thumping in the trunk became percussive and constant like hail hitting a roof.

"Something must have been trapped in the body bag with one of them. A rat or something," Orville rationalized.

"No. It's my siblings," Eunice said placidly. "They've woken up."

Burning with confusion and panic, Orville looked out of the car and toward The Home. Still, Robbie stood by the window. Only now, he was waving a slow and slender hand, and Orville swore he could see a glowing, lime-green smile in the center of his shadowed face.

CHAPTER FIVE

The neighbors on either side of The Home had left for the week. In the Rankin house, it was decided that Phil Rankin needed a vacation anyway. Their two children, Donna and Charlene, were too young to understand what had happened next door, and Sally Rankin didn't want any nosy neighbor kids telling them about it during playtime.

So the Rankins packed up and left early that morning, and they were now resting at Sally's parents' house, which was the closest of Donna and Charlene's grandparents.

Over beers, Phil spoke to his father-in-law. He was very lucky that his wife's dad liked him. When they'd been courting, Quinton Parker had acted like a hard-ass. He was the sort of dad who sat on the front porch and cleaned his guns on prom night. But Phil had taken the relationship seriously and hadn't gotten Sally pregnant until after they were married. So now, after ten years, the old guy had warmed up to his daughter's scrawny husband. While Phil and Quinton may not have seen eye to eye on all things—and they purposefully avoided discussing politics—they got along as well as they could, which meant that after dinner, they sat on Quinton's porch and drank Blue Moon together.

It was on this porch, after Donna was born, that Quinton Parker told Phil Rankin, "You can call me Dad, sport. Yer part of the family." Phil hid it well, but he'd been elated. Stiffly, he shook Quinton's hand while the old man laughed. "Welcome to parenthood, son! Get ready! It don't get any easier!"

Phil had brought an extra six-pack to make up for the visit on such short notice, and they had already drank their way through half of it.

"Don't understand it," Quinton said, more to himself than to Phil. He scratched his chin with his long fingernails and shook his head.

"Don't understand what?" Phil asked, adjusting his glasses. His vision was starting to get blurry, so he needed to slow down. His girls still expected their kiss good night, even when he was toasted.

"Why people gotta be so bad to each other," Quinton mused.

Phil flinched. He'd almost forgotten why they'd run away from home today.

"Those screams wake up the girls?" Quinton asked.

"No. Thank God. It woke Sally up . . . then me . . . but the girls slept through it. By the time Sally and I realized what was going on over there, someone else had called the cops."

"Miserable." Quinton shook his head. "Miserable business. Hell, I remember when the Zodiac Killer was active . . . back . . . When was that, the late sixties?"

"I think so." Phil shivered. He'd never been a true crime junkie; that was Sally's bag. And she never thought she would live next door to an actual murder case. Not for the first time, Phil wondered if they could sell the house if need be. They weren't in debt yet, but they were getting awfully close to it.

"I didn't think a man could get much worse than that. But I was watching the TV before y'all rolled in . . . You even know what this bastard did to your neighbors?"

Phil nodded. He'd talked to his buddy Rodney Hoh, who was a cop and had been first on the scene. Hoh told him the bodies hadn't just been killed . . . they'd been destroyed. Phil could picture it, even though he didn't want to.

"Not sure I wanna talk about this stuff, Dad," Phil said, trying to politely draw a line. "Especially after such a good meal."

"Yeah. Ruth can cook, can't she?" Quinton grinned, happy to be talking about his doting wife.

"I feel like Thanksgiving came early."

"How long you reckon on staying?"

"I called in to work. Had some sick days lined up. Probably head home by Wednesday. Hopefully, everything will be cleared up by then."

"Yer welcome to stay longer if you can."

"Sally and the kids might, but I'll need to work."

"We'd be happy to have them."

Phil nodded, hoping things would work out. He didn't want to sleep in his house alone, next to that . . . slaughterhouse.

Phil took a long drink. The glass bottles were still cool, thanks to the stormy breeze that rocked through the hills and bent the trees. The last thing Phil wanted at that moment was a warm beer.

"Pass me another 'un, son," Quinton said.

Phil obliged. He listened to the bottle cap hiss as it was cracked off with the wedge affixed to his father-in-law's key chain. The keys clanged like a cat's bell as Quinton pocketed them.

"It's a beautiful night, isn't it?" Phil asked, inspecting his bottle. It was nearly empty.

"Yes. Beautiful. God's blessed us, at least."

"Yessir."

"You all can stay as long as you like," Quinton reiterated.

"Thanks, Dad."

"Long as you like," Quinton intoned.

"Thank you," Phil repeated.

"Long as you like."

Phil screwed his brows together and turned his head. His father-in-law was smiling, but it wasn't his usual sly smirk. This was a big, clownish grin. One that almost broke his face in half.

Quinton turned his head jauntily, beaming despite the tears rolling down his face.

"It got your daughters, Phil. Got them a long time ago. Snuck in while they were sleeping and . . . got them. You didn't even notice the changes, did you?"

"Dad?" Phil felt something crawl through his guts.

"And then they brought it here . . . and Ruth and I . . . Hell, we're too old to fight it off."

"Mister Parker?"

"Charlene was *born* there. Born right in the kitchen of your house. And Mr. Friendlyman . . . he's been livin' with her ever since she came gushing out of your wife's bleeding cunt!"

"What's the matter with you?" He crossed from angry to concerned. Obviously, his father-in-law was having some sort of episode and he needed medical attention. Quinton would *never* use such foul language. It was against his Christian nature. And especially to talk about his own daughter that way.

Phil took Quinton by the shoulders and jostled him. "You in there, Dad?" he asked. "Can you hear—"

Quinton swung his bottle. It thunked against Phil's skull—not breaking like they did in the movies, he realized. Phil stumbled back, sliding down the porch steps and landing on his rump in the grass. He grabbed at his cranium, whining at the bruise that was already pressing against his shaky fingers.

From inside the house, he heard a scream. Long, shrill, and girlish. Forgetting his injury, he took to his feet and charged toward the front door, but Quinton stepped in his way, holding his arms out, clutching the bottle by the neck.

"Get out of my way!" Phil shouted.

He heard Ruth cry out. Then there was a loud *pop*.

A gunshot!

He grabbed Quinton and shoved the old man aside. Stumbling on his rickety feet, Quinton spilled onto the ground. He rolled weakly like a baby on a blanket.

Phil burst into the house. He didn't realize he was praying aloud when he swept through the living room and made his way to the kitchen.

"Oh, hi, Daddy!" Donna said with a wave. Only seven years old, the gun looked like a cannon in her pudgy hand. "I'm jus' feedin' Mr. Friendlyman! Wanna help?"

The little girl beamed.

Ruth lay on the floor, a red cave between her eyes.

In the corner, Sally had already been devoured. The thing that clutched her body was shapeless. A blob with multiple arms, legs, and faces. Each mouth was stuffed with stringy gore. The ground was painted bloodred. Sally's body had been reduced to mulch, and all that was left were her twitching legs and a few chunks of disorganized flesh scattered like dead jellyfish throughout the kitchen.

"Do you wanna feed him too?" Donna asked.

Phil covered his mouth with his hands, too frightened even to scream.

The mass of monster parts in the corner began to congeal into a single shape. In seconds, it looked just like his daughter again . . . just like four-year-old Charlene. Except, of course, for the mouth full of razor blades and the eyes which shone like burning headlights.

***

The house on the other side of The Home had been occupied by a single man. His name was Rupert

235

Anderson, and he'd been keeping a secret from his friends and neighbors. One he worried had gotten loose when he'd woken up the previous night to find the neighborhood aswirl with cops. But, alas, he hadn't been their target, and no one approached him with a warrant, so his basement—and its secrets—were safe.

But still, he wanted to get out of town after being so spooked by the commotion, so he'd gone ahead and killed the kid—poor brat—and buried him with the others. Afterward, he packed his bag, told his boss about the murder next door, and took a quick vacation for "mental health reasons." Thankfully, his boss didn't put up any fuss aside from a "We really could use you tomorrow."

Fuck you, Rupert thought. *Get someone else to clean yer floors.*

He'd gone to the airport and bought a ticket to Texas, where his friend Brock lived. Brock was the only person on Earth who knew about Rupert's proclivities, since he had a few of his own. Brock was no longer a killer; now, he simply took kids for a "joy ride" in his ice cream truck.

"You gotta kill 'em," Rupert had once told him. "Otherwise, they'll blab."

Brock waved him off. "No one's gonna say nuthin' about me. Besides, I'm the ice cream man! Everyone loves the ice cream man!"

Brock was waiting on his porch when Rupert's Uber dropped him off. In the driveway sat Brock's ice cream truck, with its smiling, anthropomorphic cartoon cones painted on both sides and a giant plastic clown head bobbing on a rusty spring on the truck's roof. The truck looked cheery and happy from a distance, but the closer you got . . . the more *off* it seemed. The cartoons looked lumpy and mutated, and their smiles were more like frozen screams. The clown itself looked like it was glaring, even when it nodded.

Brock was skinny, so clean-shaven he looked like he'd only just been born, and his eyes were the size of tennis balls. He smiled and waved, happy to see his pal.

Rupert walked up to the house, lugging his backpack. "Heya, Brock!"

"Hello, yerself, stranger." Brock sneered. His mouth was thin and sharp, like a blade. "You get . . . scared?"

Rupert sat next to him. "Honestly, a little bit. I worried you'd gotten caught and tolt 'em 'bout me."

"Even if I do get caught, and I won't, I wouldn't tell," Brock said. "Why would I wanna spoil someone else's happy-happy good times?"

Rupert sighed with relief. He and Brock had grown up together and killed their first kid together when they were teenagers in Starch in the nineties. Neither of them could explain *why* they liked killing children. It just sprang to mind one boring summer day that that was what they most wanted to do. Brock seemed to think it was because they lived on either side of The Home—that creepy house at the end of Sycamore Lane, which was supposed to be haunted. Rupert didn't give much credence to this theory until, of course, now.

What if that place somehow . . . influenced us?

Rupert didn't reflect on this long. If it had, so what? Doing what he did . . . Hey, it felt good. There was nothing like stalking and capturing a child, tormenting them for days, then putting them through the worst death he could conjure.

Brock had been into it until he moved. Now, all he wanted was his little games—his fun.

According to Brock, killing didn't feel the same outside of Starch. "I tried it a few times . . . but I was just chasing the dragon."

Rupert rubbed his skull. Like Brock, he was totally bald from tip to tail. Unlike Brock, Rupert was a beefcake with arms like tree trunks and legs as thick as barrels. His black T-shirt was tight around his chest, and his shorts showed off his bulging package.

"Shame I had to kill the runt." Rupert sighed. "He'd lasted about two weeks. Another three and he woulda beat the record."

"You get to kill him good?" Brock asked.

"Nah. Just cut his skinny li'l neck."

"Shame."

"Who was the last one you got?"

"She was walkin' by herself at night, crying. I pulled up and told her she could pick any flavor she wanted." Brock smirked. "Poor little angel. Whatever she was cryin' about before, I bet it don't seem quite so bad after I was through with her!"

Brock laughed. Rupert joined him.

Later that night—around the time Orville, Griffin, and Eunice were driving up to The Home—Brock proposed that they go for a late-night ride and see if there was anyone worth picking up. In the cab of the ice cream truck, they laughed over old memories. Rupert recalled, with glee, their first kill: some little shrimp of a boy they'd taken into the woods together. They had tied him up, forced sticks beneath his fingernails, set his hair on fire, then finished the job with a rock to his burned skull. They had to beat him until he was mushy before he stopped moving. They discussed this memory like it was Christmas past.

"Those were good times," Brock said.

"Yes. Can't be beat!" Rupert agreed.

"Hey, you know how many folks died in that house next ta yers?"

Rupert shrugged. "I know there was a family livin' there, but I never spoke to 'em."

"Three. A teenage girl and her folks."

"Nice. Wish I knew who done it. Maybe he could

join the team!"

Brock guffawed. "I'm surprised you aren't more . . . territorial."

"Nah. There's plenty of folks worth killin' in Starch! Ain't no way *I* can kill 'em all!"

"I am."

"What?"

"Territorial." Brock's eyes glazed over.

"So what's that mean . . . you beat up on other pedophiles?"

"*No.*" Brock shook his head. "*No. No. No. No. No!*"

Rupert shook his head. There was something weird about Brock's voice. In seconds, it had changed. Almost as if it was being processed through a machine.

"Brock, what are you talkin' about?"

"*I've been hoping you'd bring yer little* victims *into* my *house.*" Brock smiled, showing all of his immaculately white teeth. He stomped on the gas. The ice cream truck rocketed forward. Rupert braced himself, surprised by the lurching speed. "*But you kept killing them . . . out of my reach.*"

"Brock, slow down!" Rupert whined.

"*I would be* so strong . . . *if you'd killed them in The Home!*" Brock turned his head owlishly. His teeth were clenched together, and yet the voice still oozed clearly from his mouth. "*Since I couldn't take their ghosts, Rupert . . . I'll take yours!*"

"What are you talking about?" Rupert repeated.

Brock spoke in multiple voices: "*I laid . . . claim to . . . your soul. To both of your stupid souls. Now . . . Mr. Friendlyman's come to collect!*"

The ice cream truck slammed into a brick wall. Brock smashed his face against the steering wheel, seeming to swallow it into his brow. Rupert flew ahead, scraping the flesh from his skull as he was driven through the windshield.

Then his soul went screaming into the night's sky . . . into the heavens . . . and then back down . . .

He was dragged through the soil until he was returned to Missouri.

He saw other souls joining him. People who'd been infected by Mr. Friendlyman—the thing in The Home. Rupert dug his ghost hands into the dirt and tried to hold on, but he was vacuumed into the vortex that had become Mr. Friendlyman's hungry mouth.

***

In the neighborhood where The Home sat, the populace was beginning to go insane.

It happened first in the Culver house when ten-year-old Ray Culver walked into his parents' room and woke them by flicking on the light.

Trudy Culver was the first to wake, since her husband could "sleep through World War III if they let him." It was a joke she said often, and Ray never understood it. Even though he was ten, he was quite ignorant of the world. His parents kept him sheltered—"infantilized" was the word most of their acquaintances used. He was homeschooled, but unlike many homeschoolers, his parents didn't socialize him He spent each and every day of his little life in his house, which was located right across the street from The Home.

The Home, of course, was not haunted to Ray Culver. It was just like any other house in his neighborhood, and he thought the family that lived there was awfully handsome. Especially their daughter. His mother would kill him if she knew he'd been watching The Home closely from his bedroom window, using his bird binoculars he'd gotten for Christmas to peer into the Pertwee family's life. He'd been hoping to see Ocean naked someday, but she always shut her curtains whenever she was getting dressed.

But the night she died . . . he'd been watching.

Had seen it all.

And, as most children would do, he blocked the memory of it the moment after it happened. He went to the bathroom, threw up, then went back to bed and closed his eyes tight. He tried all night to ignore the police sirens, the shouts, and the commotion. The next day, when his mother woke him, he played ignorant and acted as if he hadn't even noticed what was going on at the end of Sycamore Lane.

And predictably, his parents didn't tell him. Instead, Trudy Culver said, "There was some commotion over there. We just hoped it didn't wake you." And she left it at that.

All the while, Ray worried that whatever had killed Ocean would slink over to his house. He imagined waking at night and seeing a flurry of monstrous shapes floating over his bed, reaching down with long, curved talons, smiling from a thousand different mouths.

Night fell, and then it started raining. The rain was like a heavy blanket that coddled Ray into uneasy sleep. Just before his eyes were too stiff to hold open, he thought, *I hope I don't dream.*

But he did.

It happened instantly.

Ray dreamed he was walking toward The Home—which he now knew was what it was called. He was barefoot and shivering, and the rain lashed him, reminding him painfully of the whips that battered Jesus Christ before he was crucified. The Bible had been filled with horror stories to him, and he blamed many of his nightmares on it. And yet his parents insisted that he turn to it for comfort and security, despite all the beheadings, the torture, and the monsters the book held within it.

Uncomfortably, he made his way across the yard and toward the front door, which hung open. Sharp beams of light poured out of The Home, and when he stepped into them, they poked him like blood-crusted spears.

Swallowing a clump of spit, he pushed his way through the pain because he knew—somehow, he knew—that he needed to be *inside* The Home.

A voice crawled out of The Home. It was slithery and wet, like the sort of sound Ray expected to hear in a swamp.

"Mr. Friendlyman wants everyone to come in! Everyone*! Even the little children! Even* you*!"*

The light parted like a curtain, and then Ray saw what was inside The Home.

He woke up screaming. Then he rushed down the hall and charged into his parents' room. When he turned on the light, his mother sat upright and his father turned over.

"Ray, what's the matter?" Trudy asked, instantly awake and sober.

"Mama!" Ray cried before bounding into her arms. "I had the worst dream of my entire life!"

"Oh, sweetie! Hold on, hold on," she cooed.

Trudy picked Ray up and carted him downstairs. There, she turned on all the lights and made him a glass of warm milk, which he guzzled like a drunk. By the time he'd stopped crying, Arthur was walking down the stairs, yawning and cinching his bathrobe closed.

"What's the matter?" he asked.

"Nothing, hon. Poor Ray had a bad dream. I'll take care of this." She kissed his cheek and sent him back upstairs with a pat on his heavy rump. Then she returned to Ray's side. "You can tell me what happened, dear."

Ray shook his head. "I don't know. It was just a really bad dream."

"It shook you up."

Judith Sonnet

"Yeah."

"You know, you used to have terrible night terrors when you were a kid."

"Night terrors?"

"Like nightmares . . . but worse. Maybe you caught one again."

"I hope not."

"Well, you're all good now. You're awake, and safe, and you don't have to worry about it anymore, right?"

"I guess."

"If you don't want to talk about it . . . that's okay too."

Ray nodded slowly, looking down at his scrawny fingers. "I saw . . . you and Dad. You both were in The Home. The . . . Home . . ." Ray muttered. "That's what it's called. The place where all those people died."

Trudy looked like she was about to cry. "You . . . you know about that poor family that died last night?"

"Not just them," Ray said. "Everyone that died there. All the ghosts."

Trudy's expression changed, turning cross. "No, Ray. There's no such thing as ghosts. You know that, right?" She squeezed both his hands. "Ghosts are demons trying to trick us."

"It wasn't real. It was just a dream," Ray said, surprised that the tables had so suddenly turned. "I'm just telling you what I saw."

"I know. Sorry. We just have to guard ourselves, you know? Spiritually. Otherwise, the Devil finds a way in."

Wow. Thanks for the comforting thought, Mom, Ray thought sardonically. Then, as always, he felt guilty for even *thinking back* to his mom. If he'd actually ever *talked back* to her, he thought God would smite him on the spot.

"Can I ask you . . . do any other kids ever talk to you

243

about . . . that house?" Trudy asked.

What other kids? Ray thought glumly. He had no friends. The other kids in the neighborhood thought he was weird because he talked to them about God all the time, and he didn't even get along with the kids at church, who were more social and outgoing than he was.

"No, Mama. Why?"

She shook her head. "Just never mind. It was a bad dream, and that's that. Now, let's get you back to bed where you belong, okay?"

"Okay, Mom."

He walked into his room, thankful that he hadn't wet the bed, even though the nightmare had truly been that bad. Slowly, he sank under his covers and let his mom tuck him in.

She planted a kiss on his forehead, then frowned. "You're burning up, sport. That must be why you're having such a rough night!"

"I'm sick?"

"Feels like it. How about this? We can stay home tomorrow."

"Really?"

"Well, don't look *too* giddy about it. Skipping church is a serious thing."

"Sorry. I just meant it'd be good to rest after having such a bad dream."

Trudy smiled pleasantly. "Okay. I believe you. Anyways, hope you sleep better, okay?"

"Hey, Mom?"

"Yeah?"

"What's Dad doing?"

"Dad?"

"Yeah. He's right behind you."

She turned—

—just as Arthur Culver pulled the trigger.

The back of Trudy Culver's head seemed to jump away from her, splattering all over the wall and coating her son's face in red. Ray, shocked and terrified, sat up and held his blankets in tight fists.

His mother slumped over, then wilted to the ground in a tangled heap. Ray watched her fall in slow motion, enraptured by the sight of the massive hole that had replaced the firm back of her skull.

He looked up at his dad, who stared mutedly at the smoking pistol. Arthur Culver didn't look scared or angry at all. He seemed confused. Steadily, he lifted his head and glowered at Ray.

"You think I wanted to do that, don't you?"

"N-no!" Ray mewled, hoping to appease the madman who had replaced his loving father.

"I didn't want to . . . Mr. Friendlyman did." He put the gun in his mouth and pulled the trigger.

Ray remained in his bed, realizing with shock that his parents looked white as snow now that they were running out of blood, and that had been how they'd looked in his nightmare. That had been what had scared him so.

Because his parents looked like ghosts.
***

In every house on Sycamore Lane, the residents began to kill each other and themselves.
***

Lloyd Wilkers took his seventy-year-old wife, Andrea, to the backyard and strangled her with the garden hose. She didn't even beg for her life because she'd been in a trancelike state ever since the lights turned back on in The Home. After she'd died, he shoved the garden hose down his throat and turned the faucet on. He died while his belly expanded, inflated with garden slug and grime infused water.
***

Eighteen-year-old Vickie Holmes went from room to room until all four of her siblings were dead. She used a kitchen knife to cut their throats. When she came into her parents' room, she was disappointed to see her mother already dead. Her father had forced her jaw so far open that her head was split in two like a Pez dispenser. Smiling at Vickie, her father said, "Cut my throat and I'll cut yours."

They cut each other open simultaneously, her using the kitchen knife and him going downstairs first to retrieve one of his own.

***

Pete Ballinger had lived by his lonesome ever since his husband died in a car accident in 2010. At fifty-five, he was sure that killing himself was the right idea. The method, he only realized too late, was the problem. After all, no one he knew had ever killed themselves by dragging their lawnmower into the living room, turning it over, starting it, then leaning face-first into the rotating blades.

***

Tammy Thompson poisoned her husband. She gave him a late-night glass of tea laced with rat poison. He drank it gladly. After he was done, Tammy broke the bathroom mirror and began to swallow the shards like they were potato chips. By the time she died, her throat was cut to ribbons.

***

Up and down the street, people died . . . and their ghosts were consumed by The Home.

CHAPTER SIX

The lights in The Home began to flash and flicker, making it look as if there was a rave going on inside. In the flashes, Orville could see silhouetted figures, just like Robbie Miller's. Some were adult-sized; others were children. There were animals too, as well as lumpy alien shapes. Creatures from this universe and the ones that surrounded it—or, he figured, coexisted invisibly with us. The Home was beginning to rumble. He could see the glass panes shaking before they all spiderwebbed, cracked, and then imploded loudly.

"He's awake too," Eunice said, pointing out the obvious.

"The neighbors are gonna call the cops," Griffin observed. "We need to hurry up if we're gonna do this thing."

"There's no hurry," Eunice assured. "I'm sure that by now, everyone on Sycamore Lane is dead."

"What do you mean?" Orville asked.

"I told you . . . Mr. Friendlyman won't let anyone stop us from coming into The Home. He *wants* us too badly for that to happen."

Wishing he knew more, but accepting that he didn't, Orville hauled himself out of the car and went to the back. The rain pelted him, flattening his beard to his face and chilling his sagging skin. He felt a sneeze building up behind his nose.

Great . . . on top of going insane, I'll probably end up with the sniffles when this is all said and done!

He opened the trunk. The smell of grave rot rose up to meet him like fumes from a hot spring. Coughing, Orville reached into the darkness and took hold of the first body bag he came upon. He jerked it out, hoping Griffin would come around and help him.

The body shook in his hands. Yelping, he dropped it helplessly. The bag hung half-in and half-out of the trunk, writhing around like it was filled with irate rattlesnakes.

Griffin hobbled over.

"Eunice says we don't need to carry them!"

Orville frowned. "What do you mean?"

"She says they'll go in on their own!" Panting, he squatted down and heaved the rest of the body bag out of the trunk. "All we gotta do, she said, is open the bags for them!"

"Oh," Orville said. His blood ran cold.

Slowly, gently, Griffin took the zipper and drew it around the writhing figure. The grave smell grew somehow more pungent, clogging Orville's nostrils and blurring his already soaked vision.

The rain was coming down in stinging torrents. It was as if God had forgotten his promise and was prepared to flood the world all over again.

The tab chewed through the zipper, and then Griffin lurched away, turning just before a string of bile left his crumpled mouth.

Orville watched in shock as the zipper blew open and . . . human crumbs began to pour out of the bag. He could not tell whether the debris belonged to Ed or Catherine, but they were human all the same. Shards of bone and gristle crawled and flew through the air toward The Home like a sweaty hive of bees. Soundlessly, the body parts passed through the beam of light and vanished into the yawning door.

"That was Ed!" Eunice cried, standing at the front of

the car and watching on. "I could hear his voice! Could you?"

All Orville could hear was his heartbeat in his ears.

"I believe her." Griffin gulped, his voice raspy from dry heaving. "God. That means that the next one is Catherine."

"I'll open this one," Orville volunteered, even though he wished Griffin and Eunice would handle everything from here on out. "Just . . . help me get it out of the trunk, okay?"

"Okay," Griffin agreed. "I'll help you, buddy. C'mon . . . let's get this shit over with."

Together, they opened Catherine Lee's body bag.

Unlike Ed, the pieces and parts had more form here. With grueling terror, Orville watched as her skull rolled away from them like a loose bowling ball. It bobbed up the steps and toward the door, then vanished into the light.

"Oh, how I missed that voice!" Eunice chuckled. "Can't you hear it? She's singing 'The Itsy Bitsy Spider!' She used to sing it all the time when we were home alone. She could never explain why . . . it just got stuck in her head!"

"I'm glad someone's happy about all this," Griffin mumbled.

"Do you think she means it?" Orville asked, looking around at the houses that surrounded them. "Do you think everyone in the neighborhood is . . . dead?"

"He killed those cops. He's capable of doing whatever he wants here, I think." Griffin scratched his head. "Christ, Orville, we're in the shit now, aren't we?"

"Oh, crap! Look, there she goes!"

Abandoning her walker, Eunice was walking toward The Home. She wobbled on her legs, unsteady in the blustery rain and on the uneven ground.

Everything began to shake. The closer Eunice got,

the more The Home *rattled.* The lights began to swirl around, flashing like strobes, spinning like they were attached to the top of an ambulance. Then, much to Orville's unrelenting surprise, they began to change color. Green, red, yellow, orange, then bright white. It was as if The Home had been replaced with the most elaborate disco ball on the planet.

A tree in the yard toppled, cracking down the middle like it had been struck by invisible lightning.

Orville could hear noises coming from The Home. Long screams. Happy laughs. Dark songs.

He barreled ahead, catching up to Eunice, who was pushing through the rain like it was pushing back.

Yes, Orville . . . come back . . . come back, like I wanted!

The voices in his head became a flurry. A snowstorm of words assaulted him, splitting his brain into fractured pieces. One part was consumed with terror, while another was doused in sorrow. A third was surprised to feel, of all things, nostalgia. Because the voices brought with them happy memories.

Memories from the early '60s, when Orville North had been a teenager. Before he'd ever published a book, and when he thought that he and Eunice and Griffin would be friends forever, even though their time together was only fleeting.

He remembered going to movies with them, laughing at how cheesy the horror flicks seemed now that they'd lived through the real deal. He recalled lying on the picnic blanket with Eunice, working himself between her splayed legs and finally believing, if only for a few moments, that there was a God—because how could there not be a God to create such a beautiful woman?

He remembered giving Fincher back the keys to his car after another late night of cruising with Griffin and Eunice. The old man had inspected the keys in his gnarled hand, then tossed them back at Orville, who caught them like a fastball.

"Keep it, son. After what you went through . . . you've earned it."

"But, Finch, what about you? How are you gonna get anywhere without it?"

He patted his pack of cigarettes in his breast pocket. "Believe me, kid, I've got it covered."

Fincher died of lung cancer a month later. It had been advanced already, but he'd refused to show it until his time had all but run out. Even now, Orville wished he'd gone to visit Fincher in the hospital. The old man had shown him a fatherly sort of kindness, which Orville hadn't realized he'd missed.

He remembered the musty smell of that car and the ordeal of cleaning it out shortly after Eunice had left town.

Griffin had joined him, and the two worked stoically, getting rid of all the garbage they'd added to it. When every piece of trash was removed and they'd tried their best with the stains, Griffin and Orville sat in the front seats and listened to the radio.

"You loved her, didn't you?" Griffin asked suddenly.

"Yes," Orville answered.

"I thought I did when I first met her. I don't know. I guess I love her in a different way."

"Think we'll ever see her again?" Orville wondered, nervous that Eunice hadn't kept her promise to write him.

"Yeah. No. I don't know." Griffin turned up the radio.

Orville looked out the foggy windshield. "This car is a real fixer-upper, I can tell."

After he left Starch, he gave the car to his mom, who got it properly repaired. It was the same car she'd eventually die in when she drove through a red light and wound up T-boned at a four-way intersection.

Ghosts.

My life is made of ghosts.

Orville stepped up onto the porch. He was to Eunice's left, and Griffin was on her right. They held both of her arms, like gentlemen, and walked her up the steps toward the open door, then into The Home. The lights were moving faster now . . . faster still . . . and the voices were all screaming.

***

Orville opened his eyes.

Just like last time, he'd fallen unconscious the second he went through the door.

And just like last time, he was tied to the floor.

He saw that the order was exactly the same. Griffin was across from him, and Ed and Catherine were where they'd lain when Robbie Miller/Mr. Friendlyman had butchered them. They were still corpses, but after entering The Home, they'd been gifted some substance. Pale, shimmering, and stiff, they lay on the ground like the silvery sheen Orville saw ahead of him when he was driving on hot days—that illusion that looked like melted metal or pools of floating water.

"Hey!" Orville whispered. "Eunice, wake up! Wake up! We're here!"

She slept on, her head flat against the carpet.

It was nice to see that the inside of The Home had been remodeled. Last time he'd been here, the walls and floors were bare, save for the bloodstains. Now, it looked like an average house. Over the fireplace, on the mantel, was a family portrait. The Pertwees were smiling and happy, unaware of what was dwelling in the house with them.

Orville shook his head. He hated visualizing the Pertwee family because that drew his mind to the crime scene footage Mr. Friendlyman had shown him on the TV.

252

And it's not just them. Eunice thinks the rest of the neighborhood is dying too. All those innocent families. Maybe if we had gotten here sooner, we could've stopped it. No. That would have expedited things. He would've killed them if we'd come here at noon, the same as he did when we came in after midnight.

He looked back toward the corpses of Catherine and Ed. They looked so peaceful and placid, resting on the floor like they'd only just gotten back from a long hour of play.

"I'm sorry," he found himself saying. "I'm sorry we . . . couldn't let you rest."

Catherine lifted her head. The movement was jarring, as if she was in a flip-book instead of reality. Orville squeaked at the sight of her open eyes. They were reflective, as though her eyeballs had been replaced with mirrored orbs. She smiled, and her teeth were reflective too. A lance of light bounced off her smile and nearly blinded Orville, causing him to squint and his vision to blur.

"You fool . . . you old . . . fool . . ." Catherine's voice was muddy.

Orville blinked. She was lying on her back again, and her eyes were closed.

Did I actually see that, or was it one of Mr. Friendlyman's tricks? Like the things he showed me on the TV.

"Eunice, please wake up!" Orville pleaded.

"She's awake. She just can't hear you," a snarky voice chirped.

Orville turned his head and spotted the speaker. The figure was standing in the corner, his back to the tangled knot of victims.

His mouth went dry when the speaker stepped backward, then spun on his thin heels. Exposing himself to the light, Robbie Miller smiled happily. Naked and covered in tattoos, he hadn't aged a day. The only difference now was the ragged hole in his throat.

"Hey, kiddo!" Robbie brayed. *"Good to finally see you again. Pick up where we left off, right?"*

Orville felt his heart racing. Soaked with rainwater, he shook deeply. Something sour stained his tongue.

"You . . ."

"Me! Li'l ol' me! Hey! You like the light show?" Robbie sneered. *"I enjoyed it. That wasn't me, though. That was all* him. *Not* me *him, but* him *him."*

Orville couldn't believe that jumbled sentence made sense to him. Robbie Miller was giving credit to his master, the creature he'd merged with when he died.

"There's not much worth doing in the Netherworld . . . all the action is up here! So when we come here, we gotta put on a show!" He squatted down ahead of Orville. *"You're lucky, kid. I hope you recognize that. Lucky to be alive. But you've been away for so long—oh, so long! You've gotten old. And weak. And believe it or not . . . in all this time . . . guess who got stronger?"*

Robbie held up a slender hand. It changed shape, morphing from fingers to spinning, glinting blades.

"You . . ." Orville stated.

"Me . . . You're right. I'm here. I'm part of it!" Robbie cackled madly. *"You wanna see me change?"*

Robbie's face distorted as if it had been smashed inward by an invisible sledgehammer. Then the pieces began to rotate and turn. Huge shards of bone broke through slippery flesh, flaying it wide and red. Blood hosed from the distortions, then curled under his chin like a liquid beard. Soon, a red mat hung out of the place where Robbie's face had been. A sticky wad of congealed gore, which gleamed and flexed like a living organ.

Orville bit into his tongue, wishing Griffin and Eunice would wake up so he didn't have to suffer alone.

They are awake. They're probably having their own

conversations with Robbie.

He's basically a god now. He can do what he pleases.

What's the damn ritual? Why didn't Eunice tell me what to do?

Robbie drove his spinning blades into his own gut. There was an automatic slurry of flying blood and a quick, wrenching tangle of guts. He doubled over, gasping through the gore.

"W*e wanted you here, Orville . . . We always wanted you here . . .*" A stream of voices crawled out of the mushy mess that had once been Robbie Miller. "W*e wanted to show you . . . what we are!*"

Then, in a flash, another monster replaced him. A giant face with a wide-open cave for a mouth. It consumed the entire field of Orville's vision, its mouth fuming with noxious, rotten odors. Inside it, Orville saw a storm of ghosts. Shadowy figures of varying sizes infested the creature's gut like botflies. They wormed around in the murky darkness, crying for freedom and finding none.

I'll be swallowed up too . . . just like these poor bastards . . . unless I do something.

Why didn't Eunice tell me what the ritual was?

Or . . . is this it?

Is not knowing a part of it?

The giant mouth enveloped him. It happened quickly but not noiselessly. The moment the mouth descended, it was as if Orville had stepped in front of a jet engine. He felt his skin blast away from his skeleton, and his spirit went falling . . . falling . . . falling . . .

He saw stars all around him, and then the stars expanded and grew until they were touching each other. The stars became walls of fog, which wavered like curtains around Orville's soul.

He knew where he was.

Knew that ahead of him stood the lighthouse.

This is what happened the first time.

We didn't just close our eyes and find ourselves in the Netherworld.

No!

Mr. Friendlyman brought *us here!*

"*No!*" Robbie Miller's voice broke through the hazy atmosphere. "*No! You promised me! You promised I'd kill them! No!*"

Orville heard someone breathe harshly behind him. He turned over and saw Griffin . . . then Eunice.

They'd come to join him.

And then—

Robbie Miller was there.

He'd changed once again. Still naked, but instead of tattoos, there were actual eyeballs growing out of his skin like olive-sized tumors. His face had thinned as well, so the skin looked like a slimy liquid that rested upon his cadaverous skull. His eyes, Orville observed with slow horror, were on fire. The orange flames curled out of his sockets and crawled up his skull, turning his red hair into a brilliant, sparking bonfire. He stood ahead of the threesome, his arms held out to his sides, his hands changing shape rapidly. One second, he was holding a gun, then a knife, then an ax, then—The weapons shifted so fast they were simply a continuous blur of sharp edges.

Robbie's lips pulled back, exposing his teeth. They'd been replaced with corkscrews, which had been roughly shoved into the gums. Blood dribbled down the spiraling metal and danced off the sharpened tip of each tooth.

Eunice groaned and lifted her head. Blinking slowly, she roused herself.

Griffin lay still, like he was being displayed in a coffin.

Robbie spoke, even though his mouth didn't move.

It hung open stupidly, and the words simply fell out, along with strands of knotted, sizzling blood.

"He's . . . feeding . . ." Robbie took a jaunty step forward. *"He's older . . . than . . . God . . . and . . . he's . . . always . . .* hungry!"

Orville scrambled over to Eunice, hooked his hands under her arms, and began to drag her away from Robbie. Each step the monster took was longer than the last. His legs seemed to stretch like taffy, raising his height as well. He towered over the old people, looking like a falling tree.

"I've . . . got . . . special . . . ghosts . . . for you . . ." Robbie said, his words leaving him like gas. He stumbled on his stilt-like feet, then reached down and held his stomach again. The hole he'd bored into himself with his bladelike fingers was still present, only it was absent of gore. The tear was like a rip in a dark blanket. Behind it lay shadows.

He inserted his fingers into either side of the hole . . . then pulled it open. The wider the gap became, the darker his insides seemed. It was no longer simply that Robbie Miller was filled with shadows. His belly was the deepest, most secretive pit in Hell.

"Get up, Eunice!" Orville cried. "Please!"

Griffin had lurched into a sitting position. He watched as Robbie approached them, enraptured by the impossibility of all he was witnessing.

"Shake out of it!" Orville shouted. "Both of you!"

Eunice reached over and clasped Orville's wrist. "Stand me up!"

Orville heard a strange noise coming from the darkness inside Robbie Miller. It chimed and dinged, moving slowly at first before picking up speed. It was, he recognized, a clanky rendition of "Turkey in the Straw."

The ice cream truck song, he thought, befuddled.

"Ghosts . . . for . . . you . . ." Robbie began to laugh. It was a sickly sound that clashed with the ice cream jingle.

Two beams of light broke through the darkness.

Orville jerked Eunice to her feet. She wobbled, then leaned against him.

"Come on, Griffin!" Orville roared.

He was working his way to standing, but it was slow going. Orville could hear his bones creaking. Griffin released a small whimper, then began to tilt over to his side.

He's gonna fall!

Griffin righted himself and struggled to his feet. Orville had become so entrenched in his memories, he'd forgotten just how old and weary the three of them were. Back in the '60s, they'd been children. The mere act of standing was no big deal then. But now, it was a battle unto itself.

The front of a broken ice cream truck appeared inside the hole. It pushed against the edges of Robbie's form, sliding out of him like pus from a pimple. The windshield was shattered, and the grill smoked. On top of the truck sat a bouncy clown face, which glared down at the trio.

Orville spotted two ghosts in the front seats. One was muscular, and the other was reed-thin. Both were bald. The skinny one looked as if its face had been punched into his skull, while the beefy ghost looked as if the skin had been flayed from his bones, exposing his grinning chompers.

"Oh Christ!" Griffin declared.

The truck lunged out of Robbie, then hit the ground with a metallic clatter. Inside the engine, something whistled, then popped. More steam rose up from the grill, obscuring the ghoulish figures inside.

Griffin backpedaled, holding his arms out to his

sides so he didn't spill onto the ground. Orville and Eunice shuffled together, trying to put as much distance between themselves and the ice cream truck as they could.

The truck was half in and half out of Robbie's figure. The wheels spun madly, desperate for traction. The passenger ghoul—the one whose face had been shaved away from his skull—leaned leeringly toward the broken window, drool and blood unspooling from his ragged mouth.

All of a sudden, the apparitions vanished. A cool darkness overtook the cab, then crawled around the front of the truck and began to reel it back into Robbie's body.

"No!" Robbie screamed. "No! *They have to die! Let me go!*"

Confused—but grateful—Orville continued to drag Eunice away from the scene, with Griffin in tow behind them.

"What's happening?" Griffin cried.

"Mr. Friendlyman wants us to himself. He and Robbie . . . are disagreeing!" Eunice clarified.

Robbie whirled around in a circle, desperate to push the ice cream truck out of his Goliath-sized body. His flickering, fiery eyes were snuffed, replaced with dark caves. His scalp was acrawl with weeds and lichen, making him look like an animated tombstone.

"*Stop! You promised! You promised!*" Robbie whined, sounding less like a monster and more like an ill-tempered child.

The foggy walls that surrounded them flexed. The rippling motion was oddly organic, as though the fog was covering a thick layer of muscular skin.

Orville saw a skull appear inside the fog beside him. He shrieked and pulled Eunice away as a gory skeleton came clattering out of the haze. The bones splashed across the ground, chiming like bells. The skull rolled over and stared up at Orville, its mouth agape.

On the other side of the trio, another skeleton appeared, being pushed out of the fog like sick from a dog. This skeleton was fresher, with red and yellow musculature twined around its bones, holding it together even as it hit the floor.

"*No!*" Robbie brayed. "*You promised!*"

More bodies began to appear. Orville couldn't help but think of this as an unearthly and unholy form of digestion.

These are the people he just ate. The neighbors.

He's processed them . . . and now he's ridding himself of the parts he doesn't like.

Or, he's ridding Robbie Miller of his abilities to summon them the way he did the ice cream truck!

Orville turned and looked down the long landscape ahead of them. In the distance, he saw the twinkle of the lighthouse rotating slowly. Each time the beam passed overhead, he wondered if he was going to learn something else from it.

"Robbie is defying him," Eunice muttered, her voice slurred with agitation and tiredness.

"What's happening to him?" Griffin asked.

"He's going to be expelled," Eunice stated.

Expelled from Mr. Friendlyman? What happens to a ghost when its powers are stripped from it? When its connection to a stronger ghost is severed?

I'm about to find out.

Robbie stood upright, holding his head in his clawed hands. His mouth was a deep, dark vortex, and jeweled tears fell from his hollow eyes. Then, like a wad of paper, he *crumpled*. It happened suddenly and shockingly. One second, he was as tall as a building, and the next, he'd folded inward, then sideways, then inward again. His flesh tore, and out of it poured black blood, which rained down on the corpses that were still being pushed—one at a time—out of the foggy walls that confined them.

The ball of Robbie's flesh hovered . . . then split. All the blood had been squeezed out of him when he collapsed, so nothing was produced from the fissures. Instead, the tears were neat—again, like paper.

The pieces and parts were reabsorbed into the walls, which seemed to suck them in like spaghetti.

All movement ceased. The skeletons stopped falling from the fog. The blood froze on the ground. Even the trio of old people felt their breath go silent in their ragged throats.

Slowly, one last corpse was excreted from the wall nearest Orville.

Naked, tattooed, and with a massive cut across his throat, it was Robbie Miller. His wet and sticky body flopped out of the wall and landed on the ground with a squishy *splat*.

"Lord! Lord God Almighty!" Griffin mused, stepping toward the body and leaning over it. "He's . . . he's just like he was when he died!"

Robbie's bloodshot eyes burst open.

"Griffin, watch out!" Orville shouted.

It was too late. Robbie lunged up and grabbed Griffin by the neck, digging his thumbs into the space beneath his Adam's apple. Griffin *hrked* loudly and tried to step away from Robbie, but the fiend was towing him down to his knees.

"*I . . . won't . . . be . . . left . . . behind!*" Robbie wailed.

Orville jumped to action. He released Eunice and pounced upon the boy. Without thinking, he drove a fist into the tattered hole in Robbie's neck. The killer released Griffin and turned his attention to Orville. He grabbed the old man by the ears, rocked his head around, then raked his nails down his face.

Griffin landed on his butt, wheezing for breath. Meanwhile, Eunice stood nearby, wanting to help but physically unable. She cried Orville's name as if it was a spell that would grant him strength.

Ignoring the pain in his face and ears, Orville pushed his fist deeper into Robbie's neck. Instead of wet blood, he felt something icy and cold surround his hand. The farther he put himself inside Robbie, the colder it got.

Despite the obstruction in his throat, Robbie spoke clearly: "*You . . . don't . . . understand . . . what . . . he . . . wants!*"

"I don't *care!*" Orville shouted.

He forced all of his weight into his arm and pushed ahead. Underneath him, Robbie slid across the bloodstained flood. He grappled with Orville as he went, sliding like a hockey puck on ice.

"*I'll kill you! Kill you! Kill all of you! I don't care what he wants, I'll kill every last fucking one of you the way I did—*"

Orville pushed Robbie's head toward the fog.

"*I'm a god! I'm a GOD!*" Robbie laughed as his thumb punctured Orville's eye and dug in deep.

The pain couldn't be ignored, but it wouldn't deter him. Despite the screaming agony and the wet fluids that dribbled down his cheek, Orville raged on.

"*I'm* The Eater of Ghosts! *Not him! Me! Me! He was mistaken when he chose Eunice! It's ME! ME!*" Robbie cried.

Baring his teeth, Orville pushed again, harder this time, and propelled the top portion of Robbie Miller's head into the fog, which did exactly what he'd hoped it would do.

It burned the way it had Orville's finger.

Robbie thrashed madly on the ground, his arms and legs swirling around like tree limbs caught in a thunderstorm. He screamed . . . and screamed . . . and screamed . . . but the noise was muffled by the fog.

Then it was completely destroyed. There was a startling sound like timber breaking, and Robbie's arms and legs fell dramatically still.

Orville grabbed hold of the ragged edge of Robbie's mortal wound . . . then pulled the heavy body up into a sitting position.

Nothing remained of Robbie's head. It was cut cleanly in half, exposing his waggling tongue and his bottom teeth. Everything above that was simply blood-misted air.

"That was for Ed . . . and Catherine . . ." Orville rasped before he let go of the body. It flopped onto the ground, dead at last.

CHAPTER SEVEN

"Griffin, are you okay?" Orville asked.

"Me? What about you?"

"Huh?"

"Your eye!" Griffin's face went white.

Orville nodded and put his hand over his left eye. It smarted as though a hot poker had become lodged in the socket. Even speaking around the pain was difficult.

Wonder if they've got a first aid kit somewhere in the Netherworld. Ha!

"Orville, oh." Eunice waddled over to him, took his hands, and helped him to his feet. "You . . . killed him."

"Good thing too. It looked like he wanted us dead no matter what!" Griffin said.

Orville looked sternly at Eunice. "What did he mean?"

"About what?" Eunice asked, looking furtive.

"About Mr. Friendlyman choosing you."

Silence fell upon the three.

"I don't know, Orville. It was . . . crazy talk. He's been a part of Mr. Friendlyman all these years; and it must have made him . . . even crazier than he—"

"Oh, bullshit, Eunice!" Orville stepped away from her, wincing as another spark of pain went through his dislodged eye. He felt hungover with agony and wished to God he could go home and rest, but there was more work to be done. He needed answers.

He needed to understand what Eunice was doing.

Griffin stood on slow feet. "Yeah, Eunice . . . what

did he mean?"

Eunice looked from one man to the next, her jaw crumpled and her eyes watery.

"This is what I know so far," Orville said. "We went through hell back in sixty-one. Then life evened out. Sometimes, I was even able to forget about this shit. Then, I started having visions . . . and right when Mr. Friendlyman reached out to me . . . so did you."

Eunice shook her head. "I want to stop him, Orville."

"Then what did he *choose* you for?" Orville took a step toward her, hoping to intimidate her into spilling the beans.

"You went into the lighthouse. We didn't," Griffin said. "What did you see, Eunice? Don't lie. Tell us!"

Eunice frowned. "We need to finish the ritual."

"This doesn't feel like a ritual!" Orville snapped. "In fact, it feels like you're keeping us as blind as humanly possible!"

"Oh God," Griffin said. "I figured it out."

Eunice's eyes widened.

"Bringing Ed and Catherine here was part of it because . . . we aren't performing a new ritual," Griffin stated.

"Griffin—" Eunice started.

"We're finishing the old one!"

Orville's jaw fell open. "No. That can't be it."

"We were positioned the same way we were back in sixty-one when we first met Mr. Friendlyman. And now we're here . . . and we can't leave until . . . until what, Eunice? What are you doing to us?"

Eunice shook her head. "I didn't want to explain it to you . . . because it would have been better had you *seen* it."

"Jesus! What the hell are we doing, Eunice? Are we *helping* this thing?" Orville barked.

"No!" Eunice cried. "No . . . not unless we choose

to."

"What the fuck do you mean? Tell us!" Orville stomped closer until they shared one breath. "Tell us!"

The walls flexed again, cracking like thunder.

Eunice turned and started walking, leading the way down the hall. "We haven't much time. He'll lose patience if we don't come to him."

"Eunice!" Griffin cried. "Eunice, come back! Just talk to us!"

Orville pinched his right eye shut. It was getting hard seeing with only one eyeball. He furrowed his brow and breathed huskily.

"What do we do?" Griffin asked.

"What else? Follow her."

"I'm right, aren't I? We're just finishing what Mr. Friendlyman started, aren't we?"

"I hope not," Orville said. "Christ . . . But it looks that way."

Every inconsistency in Eunice's story played through his mind again, and Orville wished he had all the answers. Slowly, on trepidatious feet, he followed the old woman closely.

The pain in his head couldn't be dulled or ignored. It stung greatly, causing his skull to thump like the taut skin of a bongo drum. Orville pushed through it, noting each step he'd taken, hoping the simple act of counting would help distract him. It didn't, but he tried anyway.

"What's the plan, Eunice?" Griffin shouted. "Going back to the lighthouse to finish what he started?" He jerked a thumb over his shoulder, indicating Robbie's corpse.

"You'll understand when we get there," Eunice answered. She was walking at a pitiful pace. It was easy—even for two bruised, scraped, and battered old men—to catch up to her.

"This ritual isn't even going to make us into ghost

eaters, is it?" Griffin asked.

"It will. That's the whole point."

"You've been lying too much, Eunice. You have tells."

"No, I don't!" she insisted in a childlike manner.

"Guys, please," Orville muttered, holding a hand over his oozing socket. The blood was becoming sticky between his fingers, like a crimson webbing. "Stop fighting. There's nothing we can do about it now. Eunice won't tell us the truth . . . so we'll just have to follow her anyways. Otherwise, where else are we going? Back to hang out with the skeletons?"

Griffin shook his head. "It's not right, what she's done."

"No. It's not."

This seemed to hurt Eunice. She lowered her shoulders and dipped her head. "You'll understand," she repeated. "Soon, you'll understand."

"I'd *like* to 'get it' now. Clue me in, Eunice."

"It's just not what you think. Trust me on that."

Orville felt a surge of warmth run over him. Again, he remembered the picnic blanket in the woods. The way they'd held each other, the way she'd divided herself for him. Were these thoughts distracting him from the present? Had he missed a piece of the puzzle because of those happy memories? He couldn't tell or know, so he did the only thing he could. He walked beside Eunice, hoping and praying she would tell them the truth.

CHAPTER EIGHT

They spotted the lighthouse. It had changed over the years since they'd last seen it. It was now overgrown with ripe barnacles, which looked like broken flutes and spongy pipes. The rocks around it had somehow turned a darker shade, like dried magma. Orville noticed an array of skeletons squeezed between the stones, one of which was a lizard-like creature with dried-out bat wings on its spindly back.

The light swirled around, big, bright, and beautiful. It was a long, white lance that swooped and whooshed right over their heads. Every time it passed, Orville heard a deep voice whisper in his ear, speaking in a language he did not recognize. Something old. Primitive, even.

The door stood ajar, and behind it was a cloak of darkness so deep it looked like spilled ink.

Eunice stepped onto the stones. Slowly, she turned.

"You don't trust me now, I know . . . but you must do what I say, or the ritual won't work."

"What happens if it does work?" Griffin asked. "Will the world end? Will Mr. Friendlyman kill all our friends and family? What does the ritual *do*, Eunice?"

"I told you already . . . we're going to kill Mr. Friendlyman. We're going to become ghost eaters . . . and we're going to eat him."

"But why? Why would he want us to do this? Why did he stop Robbie? Why? Tell us!"

Eunice shook her head again, a motion she repeated

rhythmically. "You just have to trust me. I'm going in first, like last time. This time . . . you two must follow me."

"Eunice—" Orville started.

"It will be scary. I won't lie. But you *must* do it. If you don't,"—she pointed down at the skeleton of the lizard-like creature—"things that stay here have a tendency to starve."

"So . . . you walked us right into this, knowing we'd have no choice in the matter. Knowing we couldn't turn around once we got this far?" Griffin scowled. "Eunice, I thought we were friends."

"We are. What I'm about to give you . . . Griffin, it's the greatest gift the universe has to offer." Her eyes were wet and pleading. She clenched her wrinkled paws together.

"Are you on Mr. Friendlyman's side? Or ours?" Griffin asked.

Eunice began to sob. "To kill him . . . to put a stop to him . . . I *have* to be on his side."

"What the hell, Eunice? I mean it! What the hell?"

The beam crossed over them. The voice in Orville's head spoke in choppy English, using multiple overlapped tones at once.

Come . . . to . . . me . . .

See . . . what . . . I . . . see . . .

The pain in Orville's skull flared as if a firework had been directed toward his face. He stumbled and swayed, catching his balance before he ended up on his butt.

"Griffin, the night you picked me up . . . that was the night I found my purpose. The night I discovered what I was destined for. For that, and so much more, I owe you my life."

"What are you talking about?"

She turned toward Orville, who was in the middle

of wincing. Tears faded the vision in his right eye. He had squatted down and put both hands over the ragged wound on his bloodstained face.

"Orville, you're so important to me. All these years we spent apart, it never should have been. If I'd been brave enough . . . Well, let's just say things would have been different."

"Eunice, I need a hospital," Orville whimpered.

"I want you to know, our son died painlessly."

"Eunice, I—"

"When I brought him here, he was so calm. Even with all the noise. It's like he knew what he was becoming a part of."

"Eunice—" Orville tipped back, sitting down with his legs spread. He held his hand away from his face, squinting hard to see it. The hand was so matted with blood, it looked like he was wearing a scarlet glove.

Slowly, he began to pick up on the awful things Eunice had said.

"What do you mean . . . 'our son'?"

Eunice smiled sympathetically. "I'm sorry. I couldn't tell you, so I fibbed a little."

"Jesus, Eunice, what the fuck are you talking about?" Griffin asked, stepping toward the madwoman. "What the *fuck* are you talking about?"

Eunice began to walk backward, navigating over the stones just like she'd practiced.

"You'll need to follow me," she said. "Both of you. One at a time. Orville is losing a lot of blood. He should go next."

"Eunice!" Griffin started to chase after her. "What do you mean? You and Orville had a *son*? Tell us—"

But she was gone. She backed into the open door and was consumed by the darkness within. She vanished soundlessly. Griffin went after her, shouting Eunice's name, ignoring her directive that Orville go next. The second his foot crossed the threshold, he, too, dissipated into the nothingness. Even his shout was cut silent, as if someone had pressed MUTE on an obnoxious television.

Orville sat on the ground, only feet away from the stones. He kept his eyes shut, and he rocked back and forth, whimpering to himself. The silence around him was cloying until the beam passed overhead.

Come . . . to . . . me . . .

See . . . what . . . I . . . see . . .

Come . . . see what Eunice sees . . . what Griffin sees . . . what Robbie Miller saw before he defied me . . .

Come, Orville . . . come into the lighthouse.

Orville crept like a baby. His hands scrabbled over the stones. They were so sharp it seemed like he was crawling on razor blades. The stones shredded his palms and knees, cutting deep and causing more blood to flow. With his eyes closed, he couldn't see the trail of red he left behind him. He also couldn't see the darkness reaching out to him from the doorway, its hands as big as bear claws, each digit tipped with streaming plumes of wafting smoke.

She killed my son. Our son. She said it herself. Somehow, we had a son . . . and she brought him here and fed it to this horrible thing. *Painless, she said. Our son became a part of . . . of Mr. Friendlyman. Who isn't a man at all and certainly isn't friendly.*

I'll be friendly to you, Orville. I'll be your best friend. I want you here.

Stop it! Stop thinking my thoughts for me! Get out of my head!

Orville pressed onward, unaware now that Ed and Catherine were walking by his sides. Ed was smiling just like he was on the one and only night Orville had known him.

I know a surefire way to summon ghosts.

Catherine had her hands clasped together like she was saying a prayer, her eyes milk-white and her teeth reflective, shining brightly, as though she was holding a lightbulb in her mouth.

As Orville crawled, the two children led him as though they were sharing the task of walking an old, injured dog around their yard.

He neared the door, now in so much pain that he couldn't even feel the new cuts on his hands and knees. Blood drooled out of his socket, pooling up on the stones. Around him, the foggy walls shuddered and shook, vibrating as if they were solid and a train was passing behind them. The ground, too, began to quake, making Orville fall to his elbows and giving him glistening new wounds.

So close, the voice said. It sounded like Eunice.

The darkness felt warm and comforting. Orville nudged himself through the doorway and then he was falling falling falling falling falling falling—

CHAPTER NINE

Eunice had been changed when she first went through the doorway the night her siblings died, the night Robbie Miller killed himself, the night she met Griffin and Orville. Orville saw now what had happened. In flashes, he had visions of Eunice returning to The Home late at night while her parents were sleeping. She slipped out through the window and came back as the moon shone like a spotlight over her head, while all of Starch believed that monsters weren't real—and if they were, they were only human.

What had been a fraction of a second outside the lighthouse was a year inside. Time moved sluggishly, just like the air around him. Orville pushed through the darkness, hoping to see some light at its end. He trudged slowly, his injuries miraculously healed, both eyes working but neither having a thing to see.

It's because I'm no longer in my body. I'm a spirit now. That's what The Home does: separates flesh from soul.

And this is The Home . . . The lighthouse is! Not the house on Sycamore, that's simply a door. The place where Mr. Friendlyman lives is here. Here in the shadows.

He saw Eunice. She was walking through the streets of Starch at night, following the chiming call of Mr. Friendlyman, who wanted to see her again. He called to her from shadows and from beams of light which danced beautifully on the street, glittering like spilled star-blood. She followed the trail, knowing as it snaked through Starch that she was going back to that place.

And when she arrived, she was comforted by the shining lights in the windows and the figure that stood in the doorway. Not Robbie Miller, no. He was being put aside for a while to rest and recoup before Mr. Friendlyman would need him again. The person standing at the door, who Orville saw through Eunice's young eyes, was Mr. Friendlyman himself. Not an illusion, or a ghost he'd consumed, or a shape-shifting storm, but the actual creature. And looking upon him framed perfectly in the doorway, Orville understood her comfort.

He was neither monstrous nor bloody-mouthed, and his eyes weren't lit fires. Instead, he was an old man with wispy strands of white hair struggling to hold on to his dry scalp. His nose was crooked, and his eyes were bright blue jewels. He beckoned her the way a grandfather does before giving his grandchild the kindest hug they've ever experienced.

He was dressed in an old-fashioned outfit of dark clothes and buckles and a tall hat. He looked like a pilgrim.

Eunice walked toward him.

Toward the man who had consumed the worm from ancient Earth. The man who had consumed the ghosts of Cthulhu, Yog-Sothoth, and Shub-Niggurath, which in turn transformed him from a human being into an amalgamation of cruel, cold, and hungry entities. The Old Ones, they were called.

"*We persist*," the old man said in multiple voices. "*When we die, we do not go to Heaven. We do not go to Hell. We simply* move."

Eunice knelt down on the lawn just ahead of the old man. She raised her hands up and tilted her head to the side.

"I see what you see," Eunice said. Her voice was a whisper, but the moment she spoke, all sound was deafened around her. Crickets no longer chirped. Birds no longer sang. Bats refused to flutter. Even the dripping of dew from the grass was as silent as a breath.

In the stillness, the man stepped off the porch and toward Eunice. He held his arms out to his sides as if expecting her to embrace him. From his chest, long, dark tentacles grew. They did not break through the flesh or his clothing. They simply extended out of him like steam from a marsh. They wafted through the air, curling and uncurling like inventive fingers as he approached Eunice.

Eunice stood and ran, leaving the man behind. Dashing down the street with tears in her eyes, she cried out for God to help her, believing she was being pursued. It wasn't until she had returned home and tossed the covers over her head that she realized Mr. Friendlyman wasn't at her heels.

The next day, Eunice reread the book she'd received in the mail. It told her many things—things she would keep secret from Orville and Griffin. One of which was that Mr. Friendlyman was a parasitic entity and he needed a host body to survive. Without a willing host, his spirits would become fractured. The amalgamation of ghosts would dissolve, and he'd lose strength until he was no more than a cold chill in an otherwise normal house.

There *was* indeed a way to stop Mr. Friendlyman . . . and it was much simpler than the ritual Eunice had forced upon them. It simply required that he be denied his next host. Without a host, he'd shrivel up like a dried sponge and—

But according to the book, Robbie was expected to be Mr. Friendlyman's next host. After serving the dark entity until he was an old man, he'd be required to give himself to the beast. It would invade his body, overtake it, change its shape. And that was what Robbie had attempted to do after his ghost was consumed. He became a parasite to a parasite. But he served his purpose despite his ultimate defiance in the end. Robbie had killed for Mr. Friendlyman, giving him the strength to complete the transformation. To overtake the body he had chosen—

Eunice.

Who had been worshipping him ever since.

She returned to The Home the very next night. She spoke to the old man who stood at the door, surrounded by shifting shadows.

"What are you?" she asked.

"I'm . . ."—the spirit smiled, showing reflective teeth— "tired. And hungry."

"You want to eat me, don't you?"

"No. I want to eat *with* you," the spirit stated.

"Don't listen to him!" Orville shouted, knowing she couldn't hear him, knowing he couldn't change the past.

"Your followers sent me this," Eunice said, holding out the book.

"It's a rough draft. I know who's going to write the full version," the Old One said.

"I can't stop thinking about it. About everything you showed me inside the lighthouse."

"Beautiful, wasn't it?"

"And . . . terrible." Eunice shivered.

"It doesn't have to be. It can be beautiful all the time, Eunice." The smoky tentacles began to grow out of his chest once more.

She left again, backing slowly away from the tentacles as they drifted toward her.

"Come back, Eunice. Anytime. Come back, and I'll show you the most beautiful things your eyes will ever behold."

And then Orville was jumping through time. Her

parents wanted to leave town, and she was terrified. Eunice knew the beautiful dreams would stop the farther away from Mr. Friendlyman she got, but her parents could not be persuaded. Starch was, they said, filled with bad memories. But not for Eunice, no. Because she saw what was inside The Home, and she could talk to Catherine and Ed there anytime she liked. Their voices came out of Mr. Friendlyman's mouth, sure, but it was as if they were alive all the same to her. In fact, as much as she pretended, Eunice didn't miss them at all. Not even a little bit.

So, she went back and asked Mr. Friendlyman for advice.

"I don't want to lose you," she said, weeping. She was inside the house, kneeling on the ratty floorboards. Mr. Friendlyman stood in the corner. Robbie had been trying to break through, and he was struggling to keep the murderer at bay, fearing that he'd strike out at Eunice, blaming her for his own death. Mr. Friendlyman was turned around, so all Eunice could see was his rigid back.

"I'll need a connection to you," Mr. Friendlyman said. "If I have one, I can reach you even when you're a million miles away."

"What kind of connection?" she asked.

"Blood and spirit. Not of kin but of offspring."

"What does that mean?" Eunice wanted to know.

Orville shook his head, suddenly and horrifically understanding the answer to a mystery that had plagued him since his reunion with Eunice.

What happened to her son?

Orville squeezed his eyes shut. When he opened them, Eunice was back in the room, only she was wearing different clothes and it was the middle of the day.

"Mr. Friendlyman?" she asked meekly. "Where are

you?"

"I'm here. I'm very weak," he said in a whisper. "I can't take shape."

"I'm sorry," Eunice said.

"I'm sorry . . . I wanted to see you once again before you left. But you'll be back, Eunice. You and Orville and Griffin . . . you'll all be back. With purpose."

"I did what you said," Eunice stated, putting her hands on her belly. "I hope it worked. We did it a few days ago, right before I told them I'm moving."

No, Eunice, Orville thought. *Not like this. You couldn't have—*

If it was an unwanted pregnancy, he would have been more forgiving. But she'd purposefully gotten pregnant with the intent of sacrificing their unborn child to this . . . demon. It was a hideous, disturbing, and painful thought. Orville felt his heart and soul flare up with rage. His spirit burned all over, hot with sorrow and anger.

"You're pregnant," Mr. Friendlyman said. "I can feel it. I see its absence in the Chamber of Guf. You are with child."

Eunice nodded, considering things.

"Don't, Eunice!" Orville cried. "Please!"

"Then take it," she said. "And we'll be together forever."

He saw darkness. It crawled up from the floorboards and inched up Eunice's legs. Her eyes furtive, she stood still despite the heat of the tentacles.

They didn't have to invade her body to steal the child from her womb. Instead, they simply rested on her and thrummed with mystic force. Soon, they slipped away, and as easily as that, Orville and Eunice's son was gone. Devoured by Mr. Friendlyman.

"The ultimate sacrifice," Mr. Friendlyman cooed. "How do you feel?"

"Empty," Eunice said.

"Now, I'll never leave you. All you need to do, Eunice, is close your eyes and call my name. I'll guide you. No matter what."

And he had.

It had been his idea to kill her parents.

She did so only a few months after moving, and she did so with no qualms. They had, after all, been the reason she was separated from The Home and from the physical version of Mr. Friendlyman in the first place. So, much like Robbie Miller, she slaughtered them late at night.

Even that was a lie, Orville said, remembering how detailed she'd been when he asked what had become of her mom and dad. If she'd told him the truth—

"I slipped into their room while they were sleeping. Killed Mom first, Orville, by cutting her throat wide. She made this awful coughing, spluttering noise. I couldn't stand it. So I shot Dad. Got his handgun out from beneath his pillow and put it against his temple. He died without a peep. Oh, and that husband storyline? Total bullshit. Sorry, buddy."

He didn't want to believe it, but he was seeing it. In fact, it was being shown to him like it was playing on an IMAX screen. He saw the bodies, both smeared in blood and frozen in pain. Smoke poured out of the hole in her father's dome, and he was convinced for a moment that it was one of Mr. Friendlyman's dark tendrils.

He saw that she ran after killing her parents, only to find a home with a group of followers who claimed to be the Brides of The Ghost Eater.

Another lie. She told us they all committed group suicide after mailing her a copy of their book.

The police mistakenly assumed someone had kidnapped her after killing her parents. They searched for Eunice high and low until eventually, after some decades in hiding, the young girl whose siblings and folks had perished had been forgotten. And by then, no one in Starch, apart from Griffin Chalks and Orville North, even remembered her name. She was as much a ghost story as Mr. Friendlyman.

While she was being searched for, the Brides kept her well guarded and hidden, exalting her as their Chosen One. The true bride. The one who would, at the right time, not only become a part of Mr. Friendlyman but would in fact become host to him. She was treated like royalty in their compound, wanting for nothing. Around campfires, they allowed her to speak, relaying messages from Mr. Friendlyman. He used her as a mouthpiece, preaching directly to his flock through her.

Years stretched into decades, and Eunice became old. It was becoming doubtful that she'd be capable of making the journey back to Starch. But Mr. Friendlyman insisted that they finish what they had started.

So he'd initiated things.

He sent visions to Orville and Griffin, making them susceptible to whatever Eunice suggested. He even used the strength he gained from Ocean Pertwee's death to erase from their minds the rumors they had heard so many years ago of Eunice's disappearance. So when she showed up at the nursing home to retrieve Orville, he followed her.

Against his better judgment and fear . . . he followed her.

Just like that.

Now, the ritual was nearing completion.

Orville rolled through the darkness, tumbling head over heels, seeing flashes of memory, which gave him pangs of nostalgia and starts of fear.

And then . . . he was on solid ground. It happened so

suddenly that he collapsed as if he'd fallen off a ladder. The air whooshed out of him, and he felt a drilling pain in his skull where his eye had been dug out of its socket.

He was relieved by the pain.

It meant he was back in his body.

He strained to see through his right eye, hoping to be back in the living room, untied and able to run. He didn't care about leaving Griffin and Eunice behind. As far as he was concerned—

He felt something shake underneath him.

Struggling, his vision came to him. He was lying on a dirt floor in the middle of a circular building. It was the lighthouse, he realized, only the interior was entirely hollow. There was no spiral staircase leading up to the top, simply dirt and dark walls circling him like a vulture.

Was he alone?

No.

He sat upright and looked toward the corner.

Eunice was hovering over Griffin.

His skull had been broken open.

Her mouth was full of blood.

"No . . ." Orville started.

Eunice looked up at him jarringly. Long strands of gore hung from her jowls and slipped down her breasts. She was embracing Griffin from behind, both arms lashed around his frail chest. His eyes had gone white, and his mouth hung agape.

"No!" Orville wailed.

Eunice smiled. There were black chunks between each tooth.

"No! No! No!" Orville got to his feet and backed away. He was alarmed when he turned and saw there was no door behind him. In fact, there was no door at all.

You may enter, but you may not leave.

Eunice dropped Griffin to the side. His head smacked the ground with a meaty *squelch*. Orville saw a sloppy stew of brain matter slip out of the gorge in his skull. The gore sizzled on the dirt floor.

"No! Eunice!" Orville screamed. "How could you?"

Eunice stood. She'd gained height. Now, she towered over Orville, a full three feet overhead. He saw that her fingers had been stretched as well. They were long, white, and quadruple-jointed. Each one ended in a curved talon that sparkled with gold flakes. She started toward Orville on unsteady feet.

He wailed with fright, "Eunice, please! I know you're in there, please!"

"I am in here," Eunice said in her own voice. Then she spoke in the voices of others.

"*I'm here as well.*" Robbie Miller.

"*So am I.*" Ed Lee.

"*Me too.*" Catherine Lee.

"*I'm in here, Orville,*" Griffin said through Eunice's mouth.

"No!" Orville repeated, hugging himself and weeping.

"The ritual worked," Eunice stated. "I consumed Mr. Friendlyman . . . and every ghost he has ever eaten . . . and every ghost that the worm fed on as well. I am all of them, Orville. All and more. I'm Cthulhu and Yog-Sothoth and Shub-Niggurath. The Old Ones live through me, by me, with me. I am *them* and *they* are me!"

Her hands shot over her head. She leaned backward and opened her mouth as wide as it could go. Suddenly, a dark tentacle burst through her maw and whipped through the air. It turned and corkscrewed like a tornado. It bulged her throat and broke her cheeks, slickening itself with blood as it bloomed, pulsed, and *expanded*. Soon, her head had cracked apart and all that sat between her shoulders was the black tentacle.

In every single voice at his disposal, the dark god declared his name to Orville North. "*I . . . am . . . Nyarlathotep . . . THE WALKING PLAGUE.*"

Orville screamed as his remaining eye turned ruby red and his ears began to bleed.

CHAPTER TEN

The congregation grew outside The Home. None of the people gathered were residents of Starch. They were strangers who had each traveled many miles to witness what was promised to them by their high priestess, Eunice Lee. She'd been speaking for many years on what would happen in Starch and how the ending of one ritual would be the beginning of another.

Unlike most religions, the followers of Eunice Lee knew they did not need mere blind faith to be converts. No, because in no time at all, their god would show them proof of his existence. Eunice would be the vessel that brought him to the earth, and then he would begin his walk. One that would spread sickness and chaos to every corner of the earth, sparing only those who walked ahead of and behind him.

This had been centuries in the making, and now it was coming to fruition.

The cultists wore white robes and clay masks of their own design, which would allow them to peek at Nyarlathotep's image, but only just that. A full look at him would drive even God insane, Eunice had assured them.

Much to their delight, the door swung open.

It was the scribe who exited The Home first. His remaining eye was so red it looked painted. He'd been stripped of his clothing, and his naked body was covered in tattoos of glaring eyeballs. In his shaking hands, he held a leather tome, which he presented to the growing crowd.

"Is that The Word?" someone whispered.

"It is." Another cultist stepped forward and held out his steady hands.

Orville North handed the book to him. The moment it was taken, he felt as if a stone was being extracted from his chest. He swayed and stumbled.

Two cultists caught him and dragged him away from The Home. He jabbered to himself as he went, but the cultists weren't interested in what he had to say. They were only compelled by what he had written in their new Bible.

They set him on the ground a ways away from The Home, leaning him up against the sign indicating that this neighborhood had once been called Sycamore Lane.

"Think he'll follow us?" a cultist asked.

"He won't. His journey ends here," another replied.

They left him there, forgotten on the ground. He curled into a fetal ball and stuffed his thumb into his mouth, feeling smaller and sadder than he ever had in his entire life. In his head, all he could see was the creature that Eunice Lee had become: the amalgamation of ghosts and spirits that had finally found the missing piece of its own puzzle. Eunice had united them all into one being, one entity . . . one god.

And then it had made him write The Word. Its Testament.

Orville cried, knowing what he had done would bring about the end of all things.

And I had no clue. Not until it was too late.

I didn't even know after we'd first been to the Netherworld that Eunice had been so distorted by it.

The ground shook beneath him.

Orville looked toward The Home. His vision was tinted red, and his eye was swollen with pain, but through the haze, he could see what was happening.

The lighthouse had broken through the middle of The Home like a weed breaking through concrete. It rose up and pointed toward the heavens, looking less like a lighthouse and more like what Orville envisioned when he'd first heard of the Tower of Babel.

The crowd erupted into applause.

Nyarlathotep stepped out of The Home.

As one, the cultists bowed.

The creature was stick-thin, nine feet tall, and reptilian. Its fingers ended in golden hooks, and its feet were cloven hooves. Instead of a head, a giant black tentacle wavered in the air between its shoulders. On its chest was a circlet of jeweled eyes, which did not blink or move. The eyes stayed fixed ahead on the path that Nyarlathotep would walk.

The earth will rot beneath each footstep.

All who see him will fall.

All who hear his voice will weep and wail.

He is the manifestation of destruction, death, and the end of all things on Earth.

All of us will be forgotten. All our accomplishments. All the ways we lived. Soon, we'll be fossils buried too deep for his kind to care to discover.

The creature walked down the steps of the porch, standing tall the second it cleared the roof. Then it began to walk through its crowd of worshippers. They sang loudly to it, praising it as it passed by them, thanking it for its mercy and its power.

Orville turned away, not wanting to see any more.

He shut his eye, but he couldn't block out the earthshaking sound of its mighty footsteps, nor the wailing in Heaven and the celebrations of Hell below.

Overhead, a long beam of light began to spin.

WHO IS JUDITH SONNET?

Judith Sonnet (she/her) is a horror and splatter author from Missouri, although she currently resides in Utah... where she spends every day reading, writing, watching Italian horror movies, and listening to loud music. She's a trans woman, an abuse survivor, and is thankful to be involved in the horror community. Noteworthy publications include No One Rides For Free, The Clown Hunt, and Summer Never Ends

MORE BOOKS FROM
JUDITH SONNET

Low Blasphemy

No One Rides for Free

Magick

Hell: A Splatter Novel

Pysch Ward Blues

Beast of Burden

Tapewyrmin'

Repugnant

Carnage on 84th Street

Toreture the Sinners!